Gregory Thomas Jeffers

Stones in the Garden

A Novel

Shady Grove Press, LLC

Stones in the Garden

© 2019 Gregory Thomas Jeffers

Issued in print and electronic formats.

Fiction – General

Shady Grove Press, LLC
Deerfield Beach, FL

www.gregorytjeffers.com

ISBN-13: 978-0-9990292-3-7

Gregory Thomas Jeffers is a philosopher,
student of American History, farmer, and former Wall Street
financier.

He is the author of:

"Prosperous Homesteading" - ClubOrlov Press

"Duress and Desire" - Shady Grove Press, LLC

"Seven Years of Famine" – Shady Grove Press, LLC

*"In a room where
people unanimously maintain
a conspiracy of silence,
one word of truth
sounds like a pistol shot."*
— *Czeslaw Milosz*

Prologue

A winter garden is a glorious thing; the demands upon the gardener are not so rigorous as they are in a summer garden: or perhaps the work is just different. A winter garden's vegetables lack the sweetness and indulgence of the summer, but they are packed with nutrients if not sugars and starches.

A solitary figure, an old woman, labored in her garden in the mid-autumn sunshine. In a spring and summer garden, the battle is with the weeds. But every year, in addition to the delightful bounty of fresh fruit and vegetables that her garden produced, arose a crop of stones brought forth from the depths of the earth by the torturous freezing and thawing and flooding that beset the fertile ground. And there was some weeding to do too.

Annie reached for an emerging stone, but she could not pick it up. Even kicking at it, she could not move the rock. She fetched a prybar from her toolshed and spent the next half-hour digging and wrenching the lump of uncooperative and hardened earth from its place. Finally, Annie loosened the grip that the lifeless slab had on her garden. It took another half an hour for Annie, with the help of her prybar, to move the block to the pile of rocks she was accumulating.

"What would possess a merciful G-d in heaven to put *Stones in the Garden*?" Annie asked herself. "He could have made things so much easier if He stacked them to the side where they wouldn't cause so much mischief."

Winded and warmed by the exertion, Annie returned to her garden to do battle with its weeds and stones.

Perhaps fifty or sixty miles north of Annie's garden along the Kentucky and Tennessee border, a cooperative and interdependent community was taking shape—piecemeal—in the aftermath of the unimaginable tragedy that left a famine of biblical proportions across North America right at the onset of winter. Twenty-five farming families—eleven Amish and fourteen typical American families who barely knew each other "Before"—thrown together by circumstance, banded together to survive. New additions to the Sulphur Springs community, as they called themselves, arrived here and there throughout the brutal winter.

Jason Thomas, a transplant to the Tennessee and Kentucky border region from New York City, lived with his family on a cattle farm in Sulphur Springs. Hours "After," Jason's son, Roone and his girlfriend, Pilar, left their college in Atlanta and walked three-hundred miles to Jason's farm. Jason's brother, Walter Thomas and his family, and his friend, Martin Weiss, and his family left New York's Hudson Valley by sailboat the day "After," landed in North Carolina and walked to central Kentucky over the Cumberland pass to Jason's farm. The evacuees from New York were thin, bordering on starved and quite frail, but alive. Together, the Thomas clan were a powerful influence in the community. The deacon of the Amish settlement at Sulphur Springs and an experienced subsistence farmer, Abraham, feared another *Seven Years of Famine*. The survival of the people of Sulphur Springs depended on the results of the next spring growing and fall harvest seasons, and so Abraham led his people to throw their lot in with the Thomas clan.

A little over a month into the crisis and in the grip of winter, McCoy O'Neil and his son, Trevor, arrived at Jason's farm with eight starving teenaged girls they had rescued from certain death but who would not have survived the final leg of their journey. The Thomas clan took them in and fed and bathed and nursed the girls back to health, and then sent them on to the O'Neil farm when they looked strong enough to make the trip; their story was one of many tales of survival in that winter season of starvation and death. Some people, through extreme good fortune or bold action, survived the winter. Most did not. Every new arrival at the Sulphur Springs community had survived an improbable journey. What follows is the story of one of those journeys.

Chapter 1

An obnoxious car horn sounded off and on just outside Philip Troyer's workshop. *What the heck?!* He looked out his window and down to the small parking area outside his harness and tack shop in the Old Order Mennonite settlement in Shady Grove, Kentucky. Now 60 years of age, Philip was sure he would never understand the English and their urgencies. The man in the pick-up truck, his neighbor Ed Campbell, continued to honk his horn but did not get out of his vehicle.

Philip got out of his chair and headed down the creaking wooden staircase and onto the cement and cinderblock stoop outside of the workshop's front door. His wife and the three oldest daughters still living at home were hurrying down the walkway from the house, and his youngest son was leaning out of the front door of the stock barn to see what the commotion was. No one had ever stood in their gravel driveway and honked their car horn like this. It must be something important. The look on Philip's face changed from a sense of irritation with this interruption of the peace to bewilderment. Ed had been their neighbor for thirty years and had never turned up in their driveway like this.

Philip reached the driver's side door at the same time his wife and daughters did. Philip spoke first.

"Ed! Why are honking your horn like that? Look! You've got everyone upset!"

"There's been a nuclear war in the Middle East. The moment I heard I ran to my car and drove out of downtown Nashville, but it still took me four hours to drive the 60 miles to here. The stores are mobbed, and there is not a thing left on the shelves, so I drove through your community to tell them what happened. I thought that because you don't have phones in your homes, they might not have heard. Most didn't, but some did. Bad news must travel fast."

"Well, I am truly sorry to hear about this, Ed. But I am not sure what it has to do with my family and me."

As their faith requires, The Mennonite community of Shady Grove made every effort to live apart from the society at large.

Ed Campbell understood his old friend and neighbor. Though they lived in different worlds, the two men would often visit over coffee in Philip's leatherworking shop.

"Philip, the radio in my car is not working. My cell phone is not working. And the electricity is off, or at least most of the traffic lights are not working, and the stores look dark. I haven't been home yet."

"Well," said Philip, still a bit unraveled from this exchange. "I think you should get home and check on your wife."

"My wife and daughter are up in Louisville at my daughter's bridal shower. They were supposed to stay overnight in a downtown hotel. My cell phone doesn't have a signal. I can't reach her."

Chapter 2

Dr. Roger W. Little, Ph.D., a tenured professor at Vanderbilt University, with advanced degrees in psychology and sociology, pulled into the entrance to the "Garden of Eden" commune, a three-hour drive northeast of Nashville outside of the small town of Napoleon, TN. In the vehicle with him were three grad-students. Another car following behind him held one grad-student and three undergrads. The party from Vanderbilt came to interview the residents of the "off-grid rainbow coalition community dedicated to living without money or social class and in harmony with the Earth." Dr. Little had focused his studies on alternative living arrangements but had never encountered an LGBT commune before. Tiny houses, off-gridding, collectives, cooperatives, Anabaptist communities, secular organizations—anything that didn't conform to the suburban living arrangement—these he had studied extensively. He had planned to move onto greener pastures—nothing he had seen so far seemed to have much to recommend it, except for the Amish and Mennonite communities. And that was saying something, considering how bleak the suburban living arrangement appeared to him. But his students were still idealistic and were looking forward to spending a couple of days at GED—an acronym the students took to calling the Garden of Eden commune.

The drivers of the two vehicles from Vanderbilt parked their cars in the grass-covered open area adjacent to the untended farm stand. With its colorful, hand-painted signs, cedar posts and barn-lumber awning the stand had serious hipster street credibility. Upon closer inspection, the limited produce on offer did not. The party from Vanderbilt exited their vehicles and looked around for a welcome party.

There was none to be found.

"Hello!" Dr. Little called out. There was no answer.

Without signaling his intentions to the students, Dr. Little took off at a brisk walk towards the three derelict school bus residences stranded there on the south side of the property. When he got close enough to be heard clearly, he called out again, "Hello!"

There was no response.

Roger turned on his heels and headed back towards the place where they had parked their cars. There was no sign of life to the north, so he proceeded downhill to the east. He came upon a makeshift chicken coop made from cedar posts like those on the farm-stand but taller and with chicken wire stretched around them to contain the poultry. On the south side of the coop was a tool shed, its doors open and filled with every imaginable garden hand-tool. His practiced eyes swept the ground around him. To his right, he saw a weed-choked vegetable garden. Past the garden, a stand of unpruned fruit trees grew in a riot of foliage and little fruit. Someone came into view coming up the hill from the east.

"Hello!" Roger called out in a firm voice.

"Hello," the man replied in a meek voice.

"I am Dr. Roger Little from Vanderbilt University. We've come to spend a little time with you to learn how you do things."

"Hi," the man said quietly. "Everybody is down in the kitchen." There was no commitment or invitation—just a statement of fact.

"Should we go down there now? I believe we are expected."

A shirtless man wearing shorts and sandals was striding purposefully towards them. It was a hot day for mid-autumn, even for Tennessee.

"I'm Evan. Come on," the bare-chested man said as he turned around and waved for them to follow him.

Dr. Little and his party followed the man down the hill towards a wooded area. As they came closer, they could see the kitchen and dining hall that was hidden from view from the parking area by the slope of the ground. There was a small, weed-filled garden in front of the kitchen and dining area with three small solar panels facing away from the kitchen towards the west. At least Roger thought that was west. Perhaps his sense of direction was off. Fixed solar panels should face south. He let that thought go as he took in the structure before him: more cedar posts with a metal roof and barn timber walls on this side that did not reach all the way to the sloping metal roof.

For shade, Roger said to himself. *I must have gotten turned around. I am looking mostly north.*

In truth, Roger had a terrible sense of direction that he worked hard on but never got good at. Still, he was fascinated by the passive arrangement of buildings and trees to help make life without automated climate control systems more comfortable. He and his party were invited to sit at the long dining room table. On either side of the table were long benches. Both the benches and the table were secured to the earth with more cedar posts. Sanded and varnished boards provided the surface area of the benches and table, and the floor was fine silt from dry clay with slate rocks without mortar embedded in the earth covering half of the floor space in the dining hall. Two more shirtless men and one overweight shirted man sat at the table, while two scantily clad women worked in the kitchen. Evan and the other man who had not introduced himself sat on one side of the table and signaled for Dr. Little and his party to be seated on the other. All eyes of the residents of GED focused on Dr. Little.

"Thank you for having us! My name is Roger Little. We are excited to learn more about your community and your methodology. We don't have any preconceptions. I hope you will feel free to share with us anything you want us to know about you."

"We want to live without money, fossil fuels, and depending on corporations for jobs," Evan replied as soon as Roger stopped talking. "And we want to live in harmony with the earth. We practice permaculture and no-till sustainable gardening techniques."

"Thank you for opening the discussion," replied Roger. "How long has GED, that's our shorthand for 'Garden of Eden,' been here?"

None of the "Gardeners" seemed to know how long. Karl, the first person they had met upon arriving, had lived there off and on for three years. Roger did his best to reserve judgment, but he had seen this movie before.

These were the "true believers." A well-worn book on "Permaculture" sat prominently on the dining table—that meant that they had planted some fruit trees that none of them would ever care for or eat from—an expressed desire to live without money, but where every single one of the residents was receiving food stamps—a form of currency. They hated "Big Oil"—but most of them owned a car. They planted a massive garden—and then never bothered to weed or water it. They were running around half-naked because it was still hot even though it was mid-autumn, but as soon as the cold weather shows up most of them will decamp for points South. On the blackboard on the wall in front of Roger was a sign enumerating "projects to do," and a list of things they needed from town: coffee, rice, jelly, peanut butter, flour, oatmeal, walnuts, milk—in that order. The property could have supported ten milk cows; and yet they needed milk from town—purchased with their food stamps, now called SNAP cards.

So much for self-sufficiency. Still, Roger had his students to think about. They would have to come to their own conclusions about the sort of self-delusion practiced here.

"I see a list of things you need from town. How often do you run into town to provision yourselves?"

"We do a lot of dumpster diving," said Evan.

"Dumpster diving?"

"Yea, we make a run down to Nashville at least once a month and go through the dumpsters of grocery stores and restaurants. In between trips to Nashville we will head over to Cookeville, Tennessee and hit the dumpsters of the restaurants along I40. We get lots of food that way. We try to do it on Sunday's in the spring and summer. That way, we can go to the farmer's market just before it closes for the week on Sunday evening. The sellers are happy to give away what they couldn't sell. They don't want to have to bring anything home."

Roger was impressed with this level of honesty. There was no falseness here. The residents of the Garden of Eden were forthright and practical. Roger saw it all perfectly well. The gardens they planted were nothing more than photo-ops for their social media page. Food stamps and dumpster diving sustained

11

them as they indulged their fantasies of self-sufficiency by looking at propaganda photos in permaculture books. He didn't have to look around at the faces of the students to know that they were crestfallen—this was not what they were expecting.

Roger looked down at his cell phone. There was no reception signal. He changed the subject.

"Is there any cell phone reception service anywhere on GED?" Roger asked.

"No," replied Evan. "No cell phone service, no land phone service, and no internet service. No electric service and no municipal water service. We are completely off the grid."

Evan was bursting with pride as he said this.

It occurred to Roger that Evan was a serial virtue-signaler and wondered what part of his past he was hiding—or hiding from. Roger reached for the camera he brought along and took off the lens cap.

"Do you mind if I take some photos?" he said just to be polite as he snapped away. He noticed that as soon as the camera came out that the two shirtless young men at the end of the table looked down and away. Roger immediately concluded that they were fugitives from the law.

"Oh, great," Roger muttered under his breath.

Evan turned to Roger and said, "Excuse me?"

"Great stuff!" Roger replied without skipping a beat.

After a complete tour of the Garden of Eden property the team from Vanderbilt were directed to bring their backpacks and sleeping bags to a circular structure the residents called "the schoolhouse." Roger didn't see any children and guessed that the schoolhouse might be meant to be used in some form of right or ritual. LGBT people didn't tend to have a lot of children in his experience. The building had a dirt floor and a center pole holding up the roof with support beams that had been nailed at a 30-degree angle into the center pole and ran up to intersect with the rafters. Roger felt that a strong wind could bring the roof down upon them and kill them all.

"We brought tents," Roger said to Evan. "Given the warm temperatures, I think we will sleep better outside."

"Suit yourself," said Evan. "I sleep in a tent. It's just too damn hot to sleep on the bus." Evan was referring to one of the stranded school buses some of the people at GED used as housing. "Some of us were planning to make a trip down to Cookeville to work the dumpsters. If any of you would like to come along, you are welcome to."

Roger looked over at his students. The students looked at each other and Mark, the lead grad student, said, "We're in!"

Three cars left the Garden of Eden commune grounds early that afternoon headed for Cookeville, TN, about an hour's drive south. The Vanderbilt team crowded into Roger's SUV, driven by the senior grad student, Mark, and the two others crammed into cars driven by the GED residents. Roger saw them off at the driveway and headed back to where he left his bags to pitch his tent. He was an old hand at this, and the tent was up, and his sleeping bag unrolled in a matter of minutes. The sleeping bag called to him, and Roger sprawled out on top of it and fell asleep. He awoke two hours later, right in the middle of a dream, and felt unrested. It took another 30 minutes before Roger could gain enough motivation to stand, but finally, his full bladder forced him out of the tent. After relieving himself, he took a walk about the GED grounds.

The place was a pig sty.

He peered inside of the school bus housing. It looked and felt like a typical abandoned inner-city house occupied by squatters. There were three of them, and each one had a small wood heat stove but no insulation—sitting out in the sun they must be unbearable in the summer heat and deathtraps in the cold of winter. Roger concluded that the buses were used for storage more than living, and shelter during heavy rain and wind. He walked along the edge of the orchard with its fruitless trees to the kitchen and dining hall where he met two young women, one he guessed to be in her early thirties, the other just out of her teens— if that—cooking tomatoes down in a large pot on a metal grill over an open wood fire. After speaking with them for a short while, Roger remembered the old LGBT joke: *What does a lesbian bring to a second date? A U-Haul! What does a gay man bring to a second date?* **What** *second date?* He concluded that the younger woman, as the old joke went, had brought the proverbial U-Haul to their second date and had been coupled with the other woman since that time.

Roger Little accepted people as they were. But he was an intellectual, not an ideologue. He couldn't help but feel a pang of sorrow for this young woman and the difficult life ahead of her.

Ah, well. She is not my daughter.

"May I ask what you are preparing?" asked Roger.

"Salsa," the older of the two replied. "Would you like to try some?" She pointed down to a cutting board that had some flatbread and a bowl filled with a red sauce.

"Thank you." Roger helped himself. "My name is Roger Little. May I ask your names?"

"I'm Flo, short for Florence. This is Mel, short for Melissa," replied the older woman without looking up from carving out the inside of a vegetable Roger didn't recognize and dropping its contents into the pot with the tomatoes.

Roger, amused by the situation, smiled and replied, "Hello, Flo and Mel." He felt like he was just introduced to this generation's "Rosie the Riveter" and a friend.

The two women studiously avoided eye contact and did not reply as they carved and sliced the vegetables.

"Do you mind if I take some pictures of the kitchen?" asked Roger, his camera already out and raised to his eye. Roger understood that cameras have a fantastic effect on people: Still-cameras make people smile; video-cameras make them nervous. And rightly so—a video-camera was rarely your friend.

To get them talking Roger peppered them with nonintrusive questions.

"Do all of the vegetables in these boxes come from your gardens?"

"No. Most we get from a Mennonite farmer who stops by with a truck and driver."

"How did you come across these old cast iron pans?"

"I don't know. They were here when I got here."

"Do you have refrigeration?"

"No. Sometimes we have ice for the coolers; most times we don't."

Flo and Melissa were still avoiding eye contact and were not very friendly, but at least they were not overtly hostile. Roger kept it in mind that both of these women were holding a very sharp kitchen knife in their hands. It had been his clinical experience that such women had challenging interpretations of their past and powerful emotional responses to men. People with statistically significant issues with anger and poor impulse control holding knives in their hands, innocuous circumstances or not, must be handled delicately. Roger remembered that his height and heft—he was nearly 6', 6" tall and was heavily muscled for a 44-year-old man—often made people uncomfortable. He decided to sit down on the end of the bench on the dining area, perhaps six feet off the kitchen. In his seated position and with the dining room a step down from the kitchen Roger was now a head shorter than the women. Having signaled his nonaggression, he waited for one of the women to speak. Flo stepped right up.

"So, you're from Vanderbilt?"

"Well, I was born and raised in Atlanta. I work for Vanderbilt as a professor of Sociology. Where are you from?"

Roger always volunteered something personal about himself as an offering, and never mentioned his training and experience as a clinical psychologist. He didn't want people to think he was analyzing them; and told himself that he did that for their comfort and not his purposes.

"I'm from all over." Flo didn't seem to be interested in volunteering anything about her past, and Melissa remained silent as she worked the knife on the cutting board. Roger retreated.

"I see that you have some solar panels outside the kitchen. Are they to power the lights in here?" Roger backtracked a bit.

"Yea," was all that Flo would manage.

Roger looked up and counted six LED light bulbs strung the length of the structure with two over the dining area and four in the kitchen. It must be bleak in here after dark.

"Are you planning on staying here this winter?"

"No!" Flo laughed. "I never stay here for more than a few months. I would go crazy! As soon as it gets cold, we are heading down to Panama City. Or maybe Charleston."

"Panama City? What's there?"

"A beach and warm weather. Well, mostly warm weather. North Florida can get cold in winter, but not like here."

"Will you come back here next year?" asked Roger.

"Maybe. Probably. As long as it is still here. It might get sold."

"Who owns the property?"

"Felix. He's up at a pipeline protest in the Dakotas. Most of our people went up there with him."

"The Dakotas?" replied Roger. "Winter is closing in up there this time of year."

"Yea," said Flo with a laugh. "That's why we didn't go. I don't like to wear a lot of clothes."

Roger took in Flo's outfit. Bare feet and legs, short shorts with a peculiar faux-fur fashion accessory slung around her hips. Her belly was exposed, and though she was not a big woman she was flabby around the middle. He doubted that she had ever borne children; she must be older than he initially thought. 35ish? An earth colored bikini top completed the ensemble. Florence wore her wavy hair up, adorned with what appeared to be either a bone or a tooth—Ivory perhaps? No. Ivory would offend her environmentalist sensibilities.

Flo contrasted strongly with Melissa, who was very pretty, young, and fit and dressed in short-short jeans, sandals, and a black cut-off t-shirt that exposed her toned belly. Melissa looked like any athletic college woman on campus this fall. Roger wanted to ask if Melissa would be traveling to Panama City too but decided to backtrack.

"Why would you go crazy if you stayed here?"

"I like to travel around from here to there. Sometimes I get on the road and follow a music band I like around. When that gets old, I crash here and a few other places."

"Do you own a car?"

"Of course!"

"And you sleep in your car when you are on the road?"

"Sometimes. Sometimes people let us stay with them. We couch surf a lot."

"How do you meet the people who own the couch?"

"On social media. Plus, it's a small community."

"What community is that?"

"The queer women community."

"Oh."

"We are very active politically. So, we make friends at protests and marches, and they let us stay with them. We have contacts from New England to Texas and out west too."

"Do you enjoy traveling like that?"

"Sometimes. But it can get old too. That's why we are here now. But soon this will get old, and we will get back on the road."

Roger looked down at the table in front of him and frowned—this was a fairly typical story. There were thousands upon thousands of people in America who were migrant non-workers. Far more than the thousands of migrant farm workers. They attended protests and slept in their cars and couch surfed. They eat by dumpster diving and with food stamps. They will work if necessary, but only enough so that they know they have enough money for a fast food meal. Roger theorized that the complexity and demands of modern society were just too much for some people. The act of renting an apartment and signing a lease and hooking up a phone or internet or other utilities was just too much for them. They did seem to be able to keep their cell phone bill paid, and they usually owned an automobile, but that was about it. They saw themselves as victims, and they were, but they were also perpetrators. Roger recalled the New Testament reflection on society: *The poor you will always have with you.*

A car horn blared in the distance, cutting through the silence of the countryside, and whoever it was, was sitting on their horn and getting closer. Flo and Melissa put their utensils down and rinsed their hands with water from a five-gallon plastic jar—the water flowed through a spigot at the bottom of the bottle and designed for the purpose—and walked out of the kitchen with

Roger right behind them. The three walked the 150-yards uphill to the road entrance just as three vehicles, two of the three packed cars that had left on the dumpster diving mission to Cookeville and another car carrying two women, the drivers still working their horns, were pulling in. The car with the two women pulled to a stop in the driveway forcing the other two to drive around them to park near the farm-stand. The women were wild-eyed and put their car's transmission into park before they had come to a full stop, locking up the wheels in the grass in the process and jerking them forward and then back against their seats.

Roger looked to the other cars carrying his students. They were wild-eyed too.

The driver of the first vehicle opened her door and with some difficulty due to her heavy build got out of the car and screamed at Flo and Melissa.

"Israel started World War Three! They just nuked Iran!"

"What??!!" Flo shrieked in response.

The GED residents and the Vanderbilt students in the other cars were now standing next to the women from the third car. Mark, the graduate assistant, made eye contact with Roger.

"Apparently, there was a nuclear exchange in the Middle East," Mark said to Roger over the chatter and handing over the keys to Roger's vehicle.

Roger left the hysterical residents of GED and walked to his SUV with Mark in pursuit. Roger hopped in and turned the key to power the radio—nothing. He changed channels up and down the FM radio band and then switched to AM—nothing. Roger looked up at Mark who was now seated in the passenger seat of Roger's SUV.

"We lost reception as we came up the hill from the river," said Mark.

"They don't have cell reception here. Maybe they don't have radio reception either."

Roger turned the ignition over and put the car in drive without asking Mark if he wanted to come and turned right out of the driveway towards the town of Napoleon, Tennessee. It was late afternoon, and the sun was in their eyes as they drove, the glare on the windshield so strong that Roger had to slow to half the speed-limit as Mark worked the radio. But there was no reception.

They arrived at the outskirts of Napoleon and pulled into one of the ubiquitous dollar stores operating in this part of the country. The building was dark. Roger pulled back onto the two-lane country highway in the same direction. After a mile, they arrived at a gas station with a large convenience store and a fried chicken franchise. The power was off here too, but there was an orderly line of people paying cash for the food and drinks from the store.

"Should we try to buy water?" asked Mark.

"No," said Roger. "They have a well at GED that is powered by a solar panel, not to mention the river at the bottom of the hill. Water is the least of our problems."

Roger turned the car around and headed back to GED. Mark seemed frantic as he searched for a channel on the radio.

"Easy, Mark. I don't think you are going to find any reception," said Roger.

Chapter 3

A half-hour after Ed Campbell started honking his horn in
their driveway, Philip Troyer was driving his horse and buggy
into the loading area of the community feed mill. No cars or
trucks were waiting for their turn at the empty loading dock. Four
members of his church, the owner of the mill, Daniel Hoover, his
two young-adult sons, and another young man were standing on
the interior loading dock waiting to see who it was that was
driving a buggy with steel-rimmed wheels up their gravel drive.
Philip tied his horse and walked to them.

"I imagine you have already heard, Daniel," Philip called out.

"Well, we heard something," said Daniel. "There was a car in
here and several pickup trucks waiting their turn to get loaded
when all of a sudden, they all left. The fellow in the car just
closed his trunk and said he had to get home. That there was a
nuclear war in the Middle East—that was the last we saw of
anyone."

"Ed Campbell showed up in my driveway a half-hour ago
honking his horn and sounding very emotional. He said he drove
up from Nashville and that it took him over four hours to drive 50
miles. He said there is nothing left in the grocery stores and that
the electricity is out. I came to ask you to shut your loading
operation down. Our community might need the livestock feed
you have in inventory. We might even need the shelled corn for
people."

"We just thought that ourselves," Daniel replied.

"I am heading over to the Bishop's house. Would you like to
go with me?" Philip directed this request to Daniel, but Daniel
was already in motion towards Philip's buggy. Then he stopped
and called back to his sons.

"Please close everything up, curry down the horses in the
turnstile, and put a wagon across our drive down by the road."

His sons, Zeke and Jed, and the other young man, Felti Fisher,
sprang into action.

"Jed," Daniel called to his younger son. "You best go home and tell your mother what is going on so that your sisters can send word to everyone."

Chapter 4

When Roger and Mark arrived back at the GED compound, the Vanderbilt students were waiting for them in the driveway. Roger parked the car, and the two got out of the vehicle. The students surrounded Roger.

"Hold on," Roger said. "We might as well do this together. Come on."

Roger took off at a brisk walk for the kitchen and dining area. As the group from Vanderbilt approached, they could hear one of the GED residents, a woman, squealing at the top of her lungs.

"Those fucking Zionist occupiers have finally done it! They nuked Iran, Saudi Arabia, and Pakistan!"

Just as she finished saying this, Roger and the students stepped into the area between the kitchen and the long dining area table. The woman stopped her howling for a moment and took in the strangers with wide eyes.

"Who the hell are you?" she demanded, addressing her question to Roger.

"I am Dr. Roger Little from Vanderbilt University. We arrived this morning." Roger said this matter-of-factly as if that should explain everything and would be all that this woman would need to know.

The woman stared at Roger blankly, as if she had not understood any of it. She rudely turned her back on Roger and faced the GED residents gathered around the dining room table.

"Who the fuck are these people?" she asked as she hooked a thumb at Roger & Company. Roger felt that she was on the verge of hysteria.

"Easy, Sandy," said Karl. "They were expected. World War Three wasn't. But they were."

The woman, Sandy, turned and looked at Roger. The expression on her face was wild and incomprehensible. She was an enormous woman of average height, short thick legs and a long tubular body, no neck and a short hairstyle that was 70 percent pepper and 30 percent salt. Next to her sat an even bigger though considerably younger woman with a similar haircut, her face red and her eyes nearly swollen shut from weeping as she rocked back and forth on the end of the bench in the dining room.

"How do you know Israel started it?" asked Mark. Mark was of Jewish extraction, though not a believer. "I listened to the entire broadcast. No one said Israel started it. They said that Iran, Israel, Pakistan, and Saudi Arabia all experienced a 'nuclear event.' The broadcaster used those exact words. 'Nuclear event.' And then the radio signal stopped. We just went to town and back to see if we could pick up a signal, but we got nothing. The electric power was off, and people were lined up at the gas station to buy the last of the food and drinks."

"How do I know?" Sandy screamed at Mark. "Because those Zionist bastards have been murdering Palestinian women and children for decades!"

"You don't know what you are talking about: you are just repeating some protest slogan you heard someplace."

"Oh, yea?!" Sandy wanted to add something but stumbled over her words.

"Professor, I'm out of here. I am not spending another second with this depraved individual."

And with that Mark and the rest of the Vanderbilt students walked out of the kitchen. Roger remained behind. An embarrassed silence fell over the other GED residents while the two women who arrived back at GED at the same time as the Cookeville dumpster-diving party, Sandy and her partner Mindy, fumed and wept.

"So, when you drove to town there was no radio signal and no power?" Karl asked Roger. It seemed to Roger that Karl was the voice of reason among the GED residents.

"Yes, indeed. There was no cell phone signal in town either."

"Those fucking Zionist scum! Oppressive mother-fuckers!" Sandy screamed at the top of her lungs.

"Sandy," said Karl, visibly losing patience. "That is not going to help us right now. We've got problems. Let's go sort out the booty from the dumpsters. We had a pretty good haul, and the cars are full to the brim with stuff."

The rest of the GED residents murmured their ascent and followed Karl up to the parking area. When they got there, Mark and the other students gathered around Roger's SUV, the vehicle they had taken to Cookeville. The cargo area was piled high with the proceeds of their dumpster expedition. Roger went to his students, and the GED residents followed Karl to his car.

"Professor," said Mark. "We want to head back to Nashville."

"Yes, I thought you might want to."

Roger made no effort to convince the students one way or another.

"Are you coming with us?"

"I am not going anywhere tonight. I've got a tent and a sleeping bag and some food and water. My car still has a quarter of a tank. I think I am just going to hang out here in the country until I know more."

Roger did not invite any of the students to stay. His voice had a far-away quality to it that Mark, who had studied in the department for two years, had never heard before.

"You should take the food out of my car and get going."

Just then Sandy and Mindy walked up to the students.

"Can you unlock your car?" Sandy directed her question to Mark. "We need to unload the food."

After their first interaction, Mark was not disposed to cooperate with Sandy. "Well, it is his car," replied Mark as he nodded to Roger. "And it is our food. We gathered it ourselves from the dumpsters."

"Yea? Look, our people took you there to watch and learn. Not to take our food."

Mark looked for direction from Roger. Roger just shook his head and rolled his eyes. Mark took that to mean that he should handle this as he saw fit.

"Look. We are leaving now," Mark said to Sandy. "For your safety, my safety, and the safety of everyone here don't get in my face, okay? Don't try to intimidate me. Don't make me think that you are a danger to us in any way. If you do, I will knock your teeth right down your throat. Do you understand?"

Sandy turned red with rage.

"I would listen to him," Roger said to Sandy. "Believe me; you can't bully him. Also, you can't call 911, the hospitals might not have power, and he has a black belt in Tai Kwon Do. I don't think you are in any position to make demands. Just let us leave peacefully."

Mark stared unblinkingly into Sandy's eyes. She took in his physicality. Well over six feet tall, athletic, fifteen years younger and a foot taller than she was. He didn't appear to be bluffing. She stormed off with Mindy following close behind.

Roger took Mark's elbow and led him away so that they could speak privately. Once out of earshot of everyone they stopped.

"So, you're coming with us?" Mark asked Roger.

"No. I am staying here tonight. We will see about tomorrow. I just said that to present a united front. She seemed on the verge of something rash."

"Doctor Little," said Mark, sounding exasperated. "You have to be kidding me. These people are fucking crazy. Please! Please, tell me you see that?"

Roger chuckled softly. "They are a bit off, but I don't think they are particularly violent, as you have just proven. Her bark is pretty bad, and she might nip, but I don't think she has much of a bite. And anyway, I don't expect to have much contact with her. If she gives me any trouble, I will park down by the river and pitch my tent there."

"Why don't you just come home with us?"

"Well, I don't wish to influence your decision here in any way. Each of us must make our own choices and accept the consequences."

"Let's just go back to the school and find out what exactly is going on," Mark pleaded with Roger.

"Mark, I am in no hurry to find out what's going on, but I respect the fact that you *are* in a hurry. It won't make any difference if I find out what happened in a few days or tonight. I bet that with a nuclear war in the Middle East classes will be canceled and nobody will be looking for me. So, I am going to take a few days off."

Mark considered that and regarded his academic mentor with some amusement. "Well, I can't argue with that."

"No, you can't," said Roger as he took Mark by the arm and led him back to the parking area where the other students stood waiting with their bags that they had retrieved from the schoolhouse.

"Alright! Pile in," said Mark. "We're out of here."

"Hold on, Mark. Don't go without the food. Leave me one-seventh and take the rest with you."

Mark stopped dead in his tracks.

"What are you saying?" asked Mark.

There was a brief pause, and Roger did not answer. Mark answered his own question.

"You're saying that we need to bring the dumpster food because there won't be any food in the grocery stores."

Roger pressed his lips together, frowned, and looked down.

"Then I have to get back to school right away. Jill is alone." Mark was talking to himself as much as to Roger. "Okay!" Mark said to motivate everyone. "Let's pack some of the dumpster pickings in my car and leave some for Dr. Little."

Chapter 5

Roger woke up in his sleeping bag in the small, one-room cabin—really a shack—where he slept for the past three weeks. Autumn weather arrived with a vengeance a few days "after," and while his sleeping bag kept him warm, he was afraid that the wind and rain that accompanied the cold would shred his tent, so he decamped to the cabin. Roger was stiff, cold, and hungry— and he had enough. He packed his backpack, sleeping bag, and clothes. Today he was going to leave for the Mennonite settlement at Shady Grove. Several years ago, he spent a growing season living in that community studying their socio-economic system and befriended the local harness-maker there and visited with them often over the years. It was an odd friendship, but Roger felt that they might be willing to feed him in exchange for labor.

The GED commune ran out of dumpster booty and their garden pickings and meager supplies within a week. Since that time, they drove three miles to a cornfield and helped themselves to ears of field corn every few days. The corn kernels were as hard as little rocks and were inedible as they were. First, they tried boiling them—this yielded a disgusting, bland, and mushy foodstuff that bore little resemblance to canned sweet corn. Roger retrieved several flat rocks from the river bottom and proceeded to crack the corn into a coarse texture more than a step or two away from flour, which could be cooked like flatbread or pancake into something barely edible and seemed to be almost one-part stone flakes or sand for every three-parts corn.

They took turns driving into town to conserve fuel, but none of the stores or restaurants reopened since the day of the bombings. Now, three weeks later, and having only corn cakes and quack grass roots to eat, they were cold, hungry, and desperate with their vehicles running on fumes. And winter hadn't arrived yet. Roger decided it was now or never. He walked down to the kitchen to say good-bye. Many of the residents had already departed, most sneaking off in the night without saying anything to the others, and one of the cars driven by the GED residents on the Cookeville dumpster-diving-run never even returned.

"So much for their idea of community," Roger snickered to himself.

When Roger entered the kitchen and dining area, he saw Flo, Melissa, Sandy, and Mindy working the stones to grind some corn for breakfast. Evan and Karl sat bundled in layers of clothing and wrapped in blankets.

"I wanted to tell you that I am leaving and to say good-bye," said Roger, getting right down to business.

"Where are you going?" asked Melissa.

"I am going to hike up to Shady Grove, over the Kentucky border. There is an Old Order Mennonite community there, and I am friendly with one of the families."

"Why?" asked Florence. "Do you think they will take you in?"

"Well, I don't know about taking me in. But I think my friends might be willing to feed me if I can work and bring something to the table."

Melissa stopped grinding the corn and moved away from Florence and in front of Roger. "I want to come with you," said Melissa.

Roger noticed that Melissa did not say anything about "we." From the look on Florence's face, she saw it too. But she was a bright person and did the mental calculations.

"I want to come with you too," said Florence.

There was perfect silence in the kitchen and dining area as everything came to a complete stop. Mindy looked at Sandy with a pleading look on her face, but before either of them could speak, Roger spoke.

"Well, you can do as you see fit. But I must tell you. You will not be welcome there. The Shady Grove Mennonites take a literal interpretation of the Bible. They will turn their backs on you."

"Why are you going there then?" asked Florence.

"Because I have friends there. And they have cows, sheep, goats, horses, and woodstoves and woodsheds, and insulated houses—and I am sick of freezing here and eating stone-ground field corn breakfast, lunch, and dinner."

"So, you are just going to leave us here?"

"I didn't bring you here, Florence! And I have not taken anything from you. If I didn't show you that you could harvest the corn and cook it, you would already be dead. So, don't give me that shit."

Roger was in no mood for guilt.

"I want to come with you," Melissa said again. "I won't cause any trouble. I can't stay here."

Melissa didn't look well to Roger. She was a hard-bodied young woman, not overweight like Florence and morbidly obese like Sandy and Mindy. The older women had lost a lot of weight over the past three weeks, but Melissa didn't have anything to lose. The way she spoke to him along with the hungry look on her face caused pain in Roger's chest. She was very young. Roger felt a pang of guilt.

"Pack what you think you will need and want and meet me at the farm stand in 30 minutes," Roger said to Melissa. "It will take us at least four or five days to get there."

After he finished speaking Roger walked out of the kitchen and dining area of the Garden of Eden commune and up to his SUV parked in the grass area adjacent to the farm stand. When he turned the ignition over the fuel "idiot light" glared at him from the dashboard. He had consumed fuel for trips to town in the first days after the bombings and later to bring grinding stones up from the river and bags of corn back from the field. Still, he felt that he shouldn't have gone through a quarter-tank of gasoline given the limited usage of the vehicle and was sure that someone had siphoned fuel from his tank while Roger slept, though he never heard or saw anyone. Roger turned the ignition back to the off position and waited.

Twenty minutes later Roger was surprised to see Florence, Melissa Sandy, and Mindy walking toward the farm stand dressed for travel and wearing backpacks. He got out of his SUV.

"Whoa. Whoa. Whoa. I can't bring all of you with me."

"Why not?" asked Florence.

"Because it is one thing for me to show up there alone. It is another thing altogether to show up with five mouths to feed."

"Please," Florence pleaded. "Let us come with you! If they don't feed us, we will move on. But we can't stay here. We will starve and freeze."

It was at this moment that Roger realized why no one came to say goodbye when they left GED over the past several weeks. Perhaps he should have gone without saying goodbye too. Oh, well. Too late now.

"Alright. Get in."

"I thought you said you were walking?" asked Florence.

"We will be," answered Roger. "I doubt we will get ten miles before we run out of gas. But that will be ten miles less we will have to walk."

"But then your car will be left on the side of the road somewhere. Don't you think you'd be better off leaving it here where it will be safe?"

Roger paused for a moment and looked down. There was a melancholy look on his face when he finally raised his face and looked up at them.

"I don't think it will matter much where I leave it. Now get in."

That night it rained: Hard. Roger and his traveling companions took refuge in an old tobacco barn along the road. He chose that barn because there were no houses nearby. The doors of the barn would not close, and the wind swept through the center aisle uninterrupted. There were tie stalls arranged along the walls with partitions separating the livestock that were fed by twos here when the barn was not drying tobacco, though Roger doubted that this barn had been used in many years. The roof leaked but there were dry spots. Even so, the party pitched three tents inside the barn.

Roger's SUV ran out of fuel just after they passed through Napoleon, Tennessee, three miles from GED. After a thorough search of the interior for anything useful, he left the vehicle on the side of the road without ceremony.

As they started, Sandy asked, "Do you know the way without a map?"

"Sort of," replied Roger.

"What does that mean?"

"It means, you're right. We don't have a map. I have a general idea of where Shady Grove is. Eventually, if we keep heading west, we will run into state road 41E. Maybe we will see a road sign along the way that will allow us to take a shorter route."

"Does this road lead to 41E?" Sandy asked.

"That I don't know. But I do know which way west is, and 41E runs north and south. Once we get to 41E, I know the way cold."

"Yea. But if something happens to you, we will have no idea where we are."

That was 8 hours ago. Now they were laying in their tents wet as a fish as they were unable to make a fire in these conditions. There were several pieces of dry barn lumber in the barn, but Roger was afraid of setting the barn on fire, and it was impossible to start a fire out in the rain. Their flashlights were dead, and their butane lighters were low on fuel. It was depressing—besides being wet and cold, they were hungry and couldn't see a thing. Roger heard at least two of the women get up in the middle of the night and relieve themselves in the corner of the barn.

Driven from their tents at first light by unimaginable hunger, the party struck their tents and packed their sleeping bags and headed west, walking directly into the wind and light rain on the two-lane country road. About a mile from the barn where they spent the night, they saw a car on the side of the road, a late model sedan, with one of the doors on the right side open. They stopped and looked behind them, and listened as well, none of them moving a muscle. They didn't know where they were. They only knew that they were on a deserted stretch of road somewhere between Napoleon and Shady Grove. There just wasn't much in the way of civilization here. A car parked in the westbound lane of the highway warranted careful consideration. After a few minutes, Roger determined that nothing seemed out of the ordinary and he walked ahead and approached the vehicle on the driver's side, ready to spring into action or run for his life.

Neither would prove necessary.

There was a corpse in the front seat. A body with shoulder length blonde hair, wearing a white blouse, and on closer inspection, a string of pearls around its neck. The skin had turned dark. The woman had been dead for several days. Roger wondered—sarcastically—how a preppy Nashville housewife got this lost. He circled back around the rear of the car. The vehicle had Tennessee plates. Roger shrugged to himself and said, "Anything's possible," under his breath. But as he got to the passenger side, Roger saw that it was the back door that was open, and as he pulled up even with the door where he could look inside, Roger felt like his heart seized up in his chest and that someone punched him just below the front breastbone of his ribcage. What he saw there froze the blood in his veins.

There in the back seat was a child's empty car-seat.

Roger called out to his fellow travelers, "There is a kid's car seat in the back. The door was open, so the kid must have left his dead mother to look for help."

"We didn't see anything the way we came," said Sandy. "So, the kid's gotta be up ahead or in the woods."

"Good grief, in this miserable weather?!" said Roger.

Mindy and Sandy took to the south side of the road, and Melissa and Florence took to the north side, Roger strode ahead in the middle, and all of them calling out, "Hello?!" and "Can you hear me?!"

For the next hour there was no sign of the child, but at the crest of a small hill, Roger saw scavenging birds about a quarter of a mile ahead in the middle of the road. His heart sank. Then he took off at a run for the vultures. The scavengers stopped what they were doing long enough to get a fix on Roger and estimate when he would arrive, and then went back to work on the meal before them in the road. Roger wasn't a young man anymore, but he was able to run there without stopping. Still, it did take him nearly two minutes to cover the distance, and the vultures waited until he was almost upon them before flying off.

Roger stopped 50 feet from whatever it was lying dead in the road. The carcass was unrecognizable from where he stood, and he dared not move closer for fear of seeing something he would never be able to un-see: something that would haunt him in the closing moments of wakefulness when sleep is within reach but the mind races in the frightening places and spaces in between.

Soon, the women caught up with Roger, but they could hear him sobbing and weeping long before they got to where he was standing. After a few minutes, Sandy spoke.

"Shouldn't we bury it?" The word "it" stung them all.

"We don't know if that is the remains of a child or an animal," said Florence.

"Okay," said Roger, screwing up his courage. "I'll go up and look."

Florence grabbed him by the forearm. "Don't," she said. "Don't look. We don't have any digging tools, and we can't wash our hands. If we get sick, the vultures and the coyotes will be gnawing on our bones next. So, don't look. Walk past, and don't look."

Roger met her eyes as she said this, then he looked down and nodded his head, over and over again as he sobbed. Melissa took his other hand and led him and Florence around the carcass, and the other women followed. All averted their eyes. When they got to the other side of the grisly scene, Melissa stopped and let go of Roger's hand and collapsed on the ground.

Chapter 6

The gears of the Old Order Mennonite community of Shady Grove that typically turned so very slowly went into overdrive after the impromptu meeting of the Bishop, Eli Borntragger, and the deacons, Philip Troyer and Daniel Hoover, in the immediate aftermath of the bombings and blackout. Kerosene for their lamps might be hard to come by, so they arranged a tallow candle-making operation in the cannery which stood empty at this time of the year. The men slaughtered hogs, cattle, and horses nearing the end of their useful lives—they could not afford to feed them through the winter—and rendered the fat and bones for tallow and grease, the processed bones smashed and ground for fertilizer and calcium supplement for chicken feed, and the offal for hog, chicken, and pet feed. The women filled every available canning jar with the meat or fat for candle "wax." The children took scythes and sickles and loaded their wagons with cut browse for the goats and sheep. The objective was to get as much done as possible before the harsh cold of winter settled in and to keep their people busy while creating a store of tradeable goods.

The leaders feared their non-Mennonite neighbors and other outsiders. They thought they would be overrun by people marching across the countryside looking for food. In the end, their fears proved unfounded. Few people sought them out, and this created another problem. There were 150 families in the community, and all of them farmed and raised livestock. They had far more livestock than their community could consume or otherwise put to profitable use—but these animals still needed to eat. The problem was that the community could not continue to feed the livestock for the winter which in other times would have already gone to market. But if they just turned them loose, these animals would have no natural predators. And next year, there wouldn't be a vegetable garden or field crop left standing.

The animals would have to be destroyed.

Eli wondered if the other farming communities in the region considered this and how they handled it. This scene was playing itself out across rural America east of the Mississippi. Kentucky was not the vast range of the American West. The livestock here were confined in pastures and paddocks. They could graze in these spaces in spring and summer, but grass and clover didn't grow in fall and winter. The cattle herd's hay and feed must be brought to them, or they will graze the pastures down to the dirt and then starve anyway—but not before destroying next year's cattle forage. There was no trucking transportation operating to get the animals to market or to bring in the feed necessary to sustain them.

These circumstances weighed on the mind of Bishop Eli Borntragger as he sat on the bench swing on his front porch. If waste was a sin, why was G-d visiting this upon them? What would people eat? Eli knew from personal experience that without animals for food people who work hard with their bodies cannot maintain their health and strength. And now they were going to destroy thousands of head of livestock? Millions of people must be starving only a hundred miles away. But what could be done? Was he going to organize a cattle drive to a city filled with desperate people who don't know how to slaughter and butcher an animal? People who don't know how to cook and don't have the utensils and tools and fuel to cook even if they did know how? Then what? And who would provide for *his* people while the men were away driving the cattle to the city?

Eli stood up from the bench swing and walked down his long gravel driveway. He could see his third son's youngest children playing in the front yard of their house across the street from his farm. They laughed and ran without a care in the world, and Eli found himself smiling at the sight of it. He was about to walk up there and say hello to his grandchildren when another thought came to him, stopping him in his tracks and then forcing him to retrace his steps.

It is impossible to know the mind of G-d.

Chapter 7

A well-tended farm with four large farmhouses arranged around a square and more than a few barns and outbuildings came into view as Roger, and the four women from the Garden of Eden commune turned a bend in the two-lane highway. Pale blue-grey smoke issued from the chimney, a color Roger was familiar with from his many visits to the Shady Grove Mennonite community. It was the unique color of smoke that a wood cooking stove produces when burning seasoned hardwood with the airflow dampened to maintain a consistent temperature for baking or roasting. The houses were sheathed in the uniform white vinyl-siding favored by the Anabaptist—Amish, and Mennonite—communities in the region. But Roger didn't see any similar houses along the way, so they must be entering into an Anabaptist community, and this farm must be the furthest outpost of this particular church group. And not a moment too soon.

It was noon on the fourth day of their trek, and although Melissa was the youngest in their party, she was nearing the limits of her endurance. Roger was amazed at the transformation in the physiques of the other women since he met them nearly four weeks ago. Florence was now as slim and trim as a school girl, and Sandy and Mindy—while still stout—were no longer obese, and their clothes were now baggy and ill-fitting. But Melissa's gaunt and haggard appearance was cause for alarm. She needed help.

A man stepped out of the first house on the left. There were two houses on the right side of the driveway and two on the left facing each other in pairs. Roger could hear the playful sounds of children, lots of children, coming from the other side of the houses but he couldn't see them. The man stopped when he saw Roger and his companions and then walked briskly into the house across the drive. In a moment he was back outside standing on the porch and looking at Roger. Another man came out of the house on the right and then turned around and went back into the house. The first man headed down the driveway towards Roger but stopped in the driveway about 50 or 60 feet away. Roger spoke first.

"We are on our way to the Old Order Mennonite community in Shady Grove. But we've got a sick woman here, and she is not going to make it."

"You say you're going to the Shady Grove?"

"That's right."

"What's your business there?"

"I have a friend there," Roger replied. "I hope to apply to him for assistance."

"What's his name?"

"Philip Troyer. He is the harness maker for the community."

"We know Philip well. We buy all of our tack and harness from him. You say you got a sick woman? Are any of you armed?"

"I've got a kitchen knife and a hatchet in my bag."

"I mean firearms."

"No. No firearms."

"OK, bring her and follow me to the first house on the left. Do not approach the house on the right. We don't know you, and you might get shot. Do you understand?"

Roger only nodded and waved his hand and arm in ascent and followed the man up the driveway and onto the front porch of the house on the left.

"Have a seat. I have to explain the situation to my wives."

Roger and Florence helped Melissa to the wooden chair next to the ubiquitous bench swing that seemed to occupy a prominent place on every Amish and Mennonite front porch. The man stepped into the house and closed the door. Five minutes later the man, three women, and a dozen adolescents and teenagers poured out of the house. The women and girls instinctively zeroed in on Melissa and helped her into the house, while the boys stood on the porch in wide-eyed wonderment at their visitors. Another wave of women stepped out of the house and ushered Florence, Sandy, and Mindy inside.

Another large group of people, two adult women, and another dozen teens and adolescents came out of the house that was on the same side of the driveway, and they stood in the front lawn staring at Roger without saying anything. Coming down the path from the area behind the houses Roger saw what looked like the contents of an entire elementary school. There must have been forty children in the group following a middle-aged woman.

Roger didn't know what to make of them. While modestly dressed, they were not clothed in the German peasant garb of the Anabaptists. Neither were they the typical residents of rural America—their eyes were clear, their teeth bright white, and they were in excellent physical condition. They were not practicing any form of birth control. If anything, given the ages of the women of childbearing age that he could see, they must have been making great efforts toward conception.

The man who met them at the road stepped out of the house and onto the porch. He approached Roger and extended his hand.

"My name is Enoch Cluff. I am sorry if I appeared gruff. It all happened so fast."

As soon as Enoch said his name, Roger put it all together and understood what he saw here—this was not an Anabaptist settlement at all. These were Mormons.

"Not at all. I am grateful. My name is Roger Little."

"Is she your wife?"

"No. I don't know these women very well. I met them under unusual circumstances the day the power went out. They wanted to come with me to Shady Grove."

Just then a young girl came out of the house with a peanut butter and jelly sandwich on a plate and a mason jar filled with milk and offered them to Roger.

"Oh, my word!" Thank you!" said Roger.

"Please, sit down and eat," said Enoch. "We can talk later."

After Roger, Sandy, Mindy, and Florence finished their sandwiches, Enoch led them to an outbuilding just past the houses but before the large livestock barn. As he opened the door, he said, "We put your friend in a bed in the house to recover. You can bunk in here and rest. Feel free to light a fire in the stove if you are cold. There are several outhouses on the other side of the barn and corn husks in a crib directly across from them. I will come back and get you for supper."

They entered the large one-room building: woodworking, tool, and repair shop with a set of sliding barn doors large enough to let equipment in need of repair to pass through on the side closest to the houses and a walk-in doorway in the middle of the building off of the gravel drive. An old-style cast-iron woodstove sat directly in the center of the floor with a long chimney pipe reaching up to a pass-through cut into the roof—stacks of lumber in different stages of finishing lined the wall opposite the walk-in door. Roger collected some kindling and stove billets from the woodshed on the other side of the drive and a couple of handfuls of hay from the floor of the barn for tinder and used a match from the box on the table nearest the stove. Soon they were arranged on the floor with their sleeping bags around the warm stove.

Sandy spoke first. "What the hell is this place—some kind of religious retreat? I offered to shake that man's hand, and he just waved at me and took off."

"Many faiths prohibit or discourage physical contact between men and women. I would think that you would support that practice."

"I 'discourage' the unwanted sexual advances that men inflict on women and sexual relationships where a power imbalance exists. Not hand-shaking."

"In these small tribal religious sects, the leaders want to protect the men as much as the women. They don't want to have to punish their young men for their natural inclinations, or they will lose them—families would turn on each other. And without those men and their families, their community would collapse and disintegrate."

"Men are dogs," Sandy said. "Nothing more. They want to mark their territory and hump anything that moves."

"He's got Melissa alone in that house," added Florence.

"Try not to offend these people, eh?" Roger said to them both. "They have been gracious and kind. If we had not found them, we would have been burying Melissa by the side of the road by tomorrow at the latest. And maybe one of us soon after."

Roger then spoke to Florence. "And he doesn't have Melissa 'alone in that house.' There must be fifteen or twenty people in that house."

"Yea, and what's up with that?" asked Sandy. "They don't look Amish. That man has that spooky bible salesman quality to him. I find it completely disgusting."

"Yes, well,' Roger replied with a snicker. "Funny that *you* should mention 'disgust.' I can only imagine the welcome a sick and starving heterosexual man would receive if he showed up at your commune. Somehow, I don't think you would take him into your home, care for him, feed him, and nurse him back to health."

Sandy's eyes narrowed, and her face was pure venom.

"They are not doing this out of the goodness of their hearts. They want something."

"Everybody 'wants something,'" Sandy. "But maybe what these people 'want' brings life and results in a future for humanity."

Sandy and Florence looked at each other in equal parts astonishment and rage. Then Sandy responded to Roger.

"What the hell is that supposed to mean?"

"I think you know what it means. You saw all of those kids. Where are your children?"

Florence and Sandy glared at Roger. Mindy declined to engage. It occurred to Roger that Mindy always declined to engage.

"It means that if the situation was reversed," Roger continued. "And Enoch appeared at the Garden of Eden in search of food and care; you wouldn't have lifted a finger, never mind nursing him back to health, because the very essence of what and who he is disgusts you. And that disgust response is elemental and fundamental to your very existence."

Sandy declined to address that.

"I doubt Enoch is nursing Melissa," replied Sandy. "I'm sure the women are doing all of the nursing. Same as it ever was."

"Is that what is on your mind? Unfairness in labor distribution? Who do you think built these buildings?" Roger asked Sandy. "You see all of that woodwork in varying stages of production? That is furniture in the making. Who do you think did that? How do you think the windmill in the center of the driveway got there? That's where their water comes from, and people can't live without water. Who do you think drilled or dug that well? Who do you think does the heavy work around this farm? Their men did all of that and plenty more. And the women have their jobs to do."

"Sexist bullshit. Gender Stereotyping. All I see is that the Patriarchy is alive and well here."

"No, Sandy. Life is alive and well here. You can insist out loud that there is no such thing as gender, human nature, or objective reality. But in your heart-of-hearts, you don't believe that. Just put your hand on that hot stove. Then tell me there is no objective reality."

"That wouldn't prove a damn thing," replied Sandy.

"Wouldn't it?" asked Roger. "Well, the lesson's over. We can talk about this later if you like. Right now, I need some sleep. And when I wake, I hope it is when they call me to supper. My bet is these people are not starving like the people of the Garden of Eden commune."

As Roger expected, one of the children was sent to call them to the evening meal. As Roger followed the child to the house where Melissa was recuperating, he noticed dozens of children spying on them from the windows, and chimney smoke bellowed from the stovepipes on all four houses. All of the homes had real front porches with a roof, 12-feet deep and spanning the length of the structure—this was typical of the Anabaptist homes he had visited and was a feature in most American houses before the widespread use of air conditioning. In the heat of summer, people spent their evenings visiting with families, friends, and neighbors on the front porch—not watching TV in modern air-conditioned brick-faced bunkers.

Of course, it wasn't evening yet. Roger estimated that there was at least another hour of daylight left, and maybe two. But as soon as they stepped into the house, he understood why they ate their supper so early. Cooking and cleaning up by candlelight would be impossible for a large family.

There was a mob assembled and standing in the house. Melissa was seated at the table with two adolescent girls sitting on either side of her, and she looked infinitely better than she did this morning. She smiled to Roger as he and Flo, Sandy, and Mindy stepped into the house, and he smiled back instinctively, quickly realizing that she did not seek to greet her partner, Florence, first. Roger thought he could feel the tension but kept his eyes away from both women.

The bottom floor of the house had an open floor plan with a massive kitchen and dining area on the right and a family room of the same size on the left with a partition wall hiding a staircase at the back. The open floor plan was big enough to seat a church group—which is what it was designed for. The kitchen had two wood cooking stoves, and three women and at least a half-dozen teenaged girls were bustling back and forth between the stoves and the countertop that ran the length of the wall on the right, though that wall had a door leading to what appeared to be an enclosed summer kitchen right in the middle. There was also an electric range and a large refrigerator/freezer on the left in the back of the kitchen. There were light switches on the walls and light fixtures on the ceiling, though there was no electric power to the house. Two large rectangular tables, Roger estimated them to be 12-feet in length, were arranged in the kitchen area, and two smaller round tables occupied the family room.

Enoch, the man they had met in the driveway that morning, stepped through the assembled children and teenagers with three women following him.

"I apologize for the rude welcome this morning. I hope you will understand and forgive us. Let us start anew. My name is Enoch Cluff, and this is my wife, Sariah, my wife, Jenedy, and my wife, Eliza. And these are our children."

When Enoch finished speaking, he smiled kindly at the unkept travelers. The contrast between their disheveled and hungry appearance and that of the healthy and well-kept family standing before them was striking, but nothing compared to the expressions on the faces of Florence, Sandy, and Mindy. Roger had to suppress a laugh by speaking up.

"Well, I think I can speak for all of us when I say that we never found you rude, and we thank you for caring for Melissa. It is a sincere pleasure to be introduced to your wives and children. My name is Roger Little."

Here, Roger turned to allow the women he was traveling with to introduce themselves, but after an uncomfortable but short silence, Roger continued.

"And this is Sandy, Florence, and Mindy. I see you have already made Melissa's acquaintance."

Enoch and his wives seemed to be just as pleased as they could be to have company.

"G-d is always trying to teach us something, and is always testing us," Enoch said. "Please, join us for our evening meal. Have a seat anywhere you like."

The guests took their seats on the bench immediately to the left of Melissa. All eyes were upon them. Then Enoch and his wives sat down at the table with their company while the older girls brought several large pots to the tables. When they were seated, Enoch looked around and spoke.

"Can the Cluff family please come to order so that we may give thanks before the meal?"

And with that the house was silent.

"Dear Lord, we thank you for another day together in our warm home. We thank you for the love of our family, the blessings of the food on our table, and the company of your wandering children that you have brought here to break bread with us this evening. May we honor your wishes with this simple meal, in the name of Jesus Christ, Amen."

"Amen," replied the wives and children of Enoch Cluff.

"Amen," replied Roger and Melissa.

With the meal of sheep stew, potatoes, bitter broadleaf plantain greens—Roger recognized the plantain leaves immediately from his travels along the road to the Cluff's but didn't know they were edible—and buttery cornbread finished, the guests expressed their gratitude. Melissa and some of the younger children colonized the floor in the family room while the older Cluff girls cleared the table and cleaned the dishes. Enoch and his wives sat quietly with Enoch looking down and his wives looking at him. After a couple of minutes, Enoch spoke, and he got right to the point.

"We were on a job site at a fast food restaurant along I40 in Lebanon, TN, when we heard the news that a nuclear war took place in the Middle East." When he finished speaking, he looked up at Roger, and his wives did too. Roger said nothing. "The job was about an hour and a half away," Enoch continued. "As soon as we heard, we packed up and drove off for home. When we got here, the power was still on, but our cell phones stopped working almost immediately after the news broke. My wives said the internet worked for a while before pages wouldn't load. We listened to the radio on the way here, but that is the last we have heard of anything."

"Have you traveled out and about since then?" asked Roger.

"No. At first, we were scared. So, we piled up some logs to block the driveway with our skid steer. Cars were still passing by for the first few days, but after about, I don't know, ten days we stopped seeing or hearing cars out on the road. So, we cleared the logs out of the way, and my brother and I drove one of the trucks over to Shady Grove's downtown and then over to Napoleon's downtown. Well, Napoleon doesn't really have a downtown, but over to that big gas station there. We talked to a few people, but there just weren't that many people around. The power was out, the stores and restaurants were dark, and it was cold and raining. So, we came home. You're the first people we've seen out on the road since the power went down."

Roger sat quietly to see if Enoch had anything more to say. When he didn't, Roger figured Enoch was expecting him to share his circumstances.

"I was traveling researching for Vanderbilt University when I heard what happened. I met these women at a campsite, and we camped there until four days ago. We got cold and ran out of food. I don't know anyone up this way other than Philip Troyer and a few other families in the Shady Grove Mennonite community. So, I told my friends here that I was leaving, and they wanted to come with me. So here we are. Today was our fourth day on the road."

Roger would let his traveling companions speak for themselves and share what they will.

"You couldn't have picked a worse time to go for a 100-mile walk," Enoch said.

"I didn't know exactly how far it was, or I might have left sooner. The weather would have been better a few weeks ago."

"How do you know Philip Troyer?"

"Oh, I guess it's over ten years now. I spent a growing season at the Troyer homestead studying the socio-economic strategies of their community. I came to admire him, his family, and their community and their way of life. I stayed in touch with Philip and bought livestock for freezer meat and vegetables from them every year. Sometimes I would volunteer at his farm during hay season just to make myself useful. They used to let me drive a team hitched to a hay mower. I think that was my favorite job ever."

Enoch laughed through his nose, "Hmm!" and nodded knowingly. "Yea, I understand! I like to work hay with horses too."

"But you had electricity here. And you use vehicles. You mentioned a skid steer, and I see a tractor parked under the barn eve."

"Well, as I am sure you have figured out, we are not Anabaptists. We are fundamentalist Mormons. We moved here just a couple of years ago and bought this place from two Amish families. Two of the houses were here, and we built the other two. We bought their workhorses, forty Jersey milk cows, and their farming equipment and learned how to work horses from Philip's son, Timothy."

"May I ask how you came to Kentucky?"

"Well, we are in Tennessee here. The Kentucky border is just a couple miles north. We were in Utah, but the state passed a law making it a crime for me to declare that Jenedy and Eliza are my wives publicly. I could call them mistresses, girlfriends, or lovers—but not 'wife.' Many of us feared persecution, so my brother and his family and two other men and their families came east to Tennessee. And now this. Somehow, I don't think this is a test or a lesson. I believe G-d is punishing Man for his wickedness."

"Well, it seems that G-d is not punishing you. Your people prepare for this sort of thing."

"So, you are familiar with Mormon practice?"

"I wouldn't say that. But I understand that you are called to prepare for calamity. Well, it seems that calamity is here."

Sariah put her hand on Enoch's hand. He turned to look at her, and they shared a sad smile. Then he turned and did the same with Jenedy and Eliza, and they reached their hands to his other hand in a touching display of solidarity and empathy that melted Roger's heart—and froze the hearts of Sandy and Florence. Mindy didn't notice. She had other things on her mind.

"Well, we can talk some more tomorrow. I expect you people are exhausted. One of the kids will get a candle for you and lead you back to the shop."

As if on cue, a girl of about ten appeared holding a kerosene railroad lamp in one hand and a candle and holder in the other. Roger, Sandy, Mindy, and Florence said their goodbyes— Melissa was already asleep on the floor—and the child led them back to the workshop and set and lit the candle in its holder on a workbench. As soon as she left, Florence padded to the door to watch her form, shadowed around the lamplight, retreat into the darkness. Then she spun around.

"We've got to get the hell out of here!" Florence spat out. "This is a cult!"

Roger chuckled.

"What?!" Florence shrieked.

"Oh, boy, if that isn't the pot calling the kettle black! What the hell is the difference between these Mormons and the LGBT Garden of Eden commune?"

"What the fuck do you mean? Do you see these crazy fuckers?! 'Bible salesman' is too kind. They are a bunch of fucking zombies!"

"I agree," said Sandy. "This guy has got himself a fucking Jesus approved harem, all pregnant and barefoot. He should be in jail in Utah! I am out of here."

"Me too," said Florence.

"Well, you two can do anything you want," said Roger. "I didn't ask you to come with me. It would probably be better if you left now. No need for a confrontation with these good people in front of their children. Just pack your things and hit the road."

That line of reasoning caught Florence and Sandy up short.

"What about Melissa?" asked Florence.

"Yea, what about Melissa?" Roger replied sharply. "In this weather, she was a day or two from death. You couldn't feed her. You couldn't clothe her. And you can't shelter and provide for her. But Enoch can."

Florence's eyes bulged, and her mouth hung open as if she just got the wind knocked out of her.

"What's the matter? Don't you have a smart-mouthed slogan response? Isn't this where you tell me that you are a strong and independent woman? And that you don't need a man or men, right? Well, then you really should pack your stuff and go make your way."

Florence's mouth worked, but nothing came out.

"We don't have any food," Sandy croaked.

"Yes, well, that's my point. And it is not just food. You don't have anything. You don't have skills; you don't have tools or equipment, you don't have a family or a community with resources and a reason to share those resources with you. What you do have are a self-destructive political belief system and arrogance. You have arrogance in spades."

Florence was standing with her back to the entrance door to the workshop. Now she leaned back and slid down letting her butt hit the floor, and her feet slide out from under her. Roger could hear Mindy sobbing quietly in the shadow caused by the workbench. Sandy stood motionless, still facing Florence but looking down at the floor.

"Look, the world has changed," said Roger, softening his tone. "You don't get to bully people around anymore. There is no authority for you to call on to point their guns at your ideological enemies in exchange for your political support. You are going to have to stand up to your own hypocrisies—and then face them down."

"What do you mean by that?" Mindy asked from the shadows, her voice as meek as a little girl's—this was the first time Mindy spoke directly to Roger.

"There was a nuclear war in the Middle East, and there is no electrical power here in the U.S. for 25 days now. People are cold and hungry, and there is no food. And what is it that concerns you? That these women welcome a man into their bed and the children that result into their hearts? A man who then spends the majority of the time of his life working to provide shelter, clothing, and nourishment for his women and children? You, who fought for the rights of homosexuals to love and have sex with whom they wish?"

"LGBT," said Sandy.

"VQRST, etc.," replied Roger. "I was baiting you. What you really should have said is *people. Individuals.* That human beings have the right to "marry" who they wish and to define marriage in any way that they see fit. A man and a woman. Two men. Three women. Whatever. But you didn't do that. No, you let your in-group preferences become out-of-group bigotry. And you prevented everyone from challenging you with practical censorship and grievance politics by labeling any narrative you didn't approve of as 'hate speech.' But that's over. Right now, we, you and me, need friends, and to make friends we have to make ourselves useful and valuable members of a group or community. Not piss people off."

When Roger finished speaking, he sat on the floor and rolled his jacket into a tight bundle to use as a pillow. After a while, Florence broke the silence in a sad voice as she sat on the floor against the door.

"Yea, but I don't think that this is the community for me."

"I wouldn't worry about that," Roger scoffed. "I don't think we are going to be welcome here for much longer. The best thing you can do is not leave a bad taste in their mouths before you go."

"What do you mean?" Florence asked.

"I mean I don't think they are interested in having a man my age as a son-in-law. And I can't picture any of you as the third or fourth wife in a Mormon household. Ergo, they are going to show us the door very soon. I have no doubt they will be nice about it, but we will get the hint."

"I was married before," Mindy interjected out of the shadows—and from left field.

"Let's not get into that," Sandy said sternly.

Mindy shuffled out of the shadows and into the candlelight.

"To a man," Mindy continued, looking at Roger and ignoring Sandy's exhortation.

"Yea? And how'd that turn out?" Sandy hissed.

Roger held up his hands' palm out between Sandy and Mindy.

"Alright," Roger said, breathless. "I can see that a couple of decent meals has reenergized you. The point is that you are free to go and do, as you wish. It is my opinion that none of us will be asked to stay. You are going to have to sort things out for yourselves."

"So, what about you?" asked Sandy.

"I am headed for my friend's farm in the Old Order Mennonite community in Shady Grove, Kentucky. I don't think you are going to approve of their way of life any more than you approve of the way these Mormons live. And I don't think they will accept you. I don't even know that I will be welcome there, but it's the only thing I can think of to do. I am not going to walk back to Nashville. I can't even imagine what it is like there right now."

"How far is it to Shady Grove?" asked Florence.

"I think it is two days from here. Maybe three."

"I want to come with you. I want to get Melissa out of here."

"What if Melissa wants to stay?" Roger asked.

Florence broke down in sobs.

"Look, I'm sorry. I am not trying to upset you. Okay? I think that's enough for tonight. Maybe these good people will feed us for another day in exchange for some work. Or maybe they are going to ask us to leave first thing in the morning. Either way, we need to get some sleep."

The morning came, and Roger, Sandy, Mindy, and Flo were again invited to a meal at Enoch Cluff's house. But this time, there was no one in the kitchen except the four guests and Sariah, Enoch's first and oldest wife. Roger reckoned her to be in her mid-40's. Melissa was not there, and Roger could feel the intense concern Flo radiated, as did Sandy and Mindy. Sariah was polite, but not chatty. She served them a breakfast of biscuits and gravy, grits, and milk. When they finished their meal the four guests rose to take their dishes to the sink, but Sariah intercepted Roger and took his plate and directed him to sit down, and then sent the women to the sink and told them to leave the washed dishes and utensils in the large wooden rack on the counter. When they finished, Sariah spoke to Roger.

"The men are working stone. You will see them off in the field if you walk behind the barn."

Then Sariah turned to the women and said, "I should think the boys have shoveled the barn and the cows are waiting to be fed and milked. Please, follow me."

That afternoon the guests from the Garden of Eden commune were given a bucket of warm water each to wash and a wheelbarrow to deposit their soiled clothes in. One of the Cluff girls brought them a basket of food for their dinner and a bucket of drinking water. They only had one change of clothes, and these were nearly as soiled as the clothes they wore while working around the Mormon homestead that day. When the guests were finished with their ablutions and reassembled in the workshop, Roger got right to the point.

"Well, I had a long talk with Enoch today. It seems that he and his wives believe that G-d has brought Melissa to them to expand their family, and Enoch plans to ask her if he can court her for marriage."

Florence screamed and shrieked. "I fucking knew it!"

"I told you they wanted something!" Sandy shouted.

"Look. I am just telling you what is on Enoch's mind. He is not forcing Melissa to do anything. He wants to ask her if he can spend time with her to see if she wants to join his family as his wife."

"You mean to join his fucking harem!" said Florence. She was red with rage, and the tears came in torrents.

"What do mean you don't think he is going to use force?" asked Sandy. "Look at the power imbalance between Enoch and Melissa. He is a grown man. If she does not say yes, he is going to kick her out and cut her off. That is force. Consent is not an option—this is rape!"

"Asking her if he can spend time with her to see if she would like to join the family is rape?"

"He has three wives already!" shouted Florence. "Tell him to leave her the fuck alone!"

"Whoa. I am not telling Enoch anything. From my perspective, Melissa is free to leave. Enoch is free to ask her if she is willing to consent to become his wife. It will be between the two of them to outline and define the responsibilities they would have to each other in any such marriage. I don't see any improper coercion in any of this."

"He's a fucking rapist," Sandy said flatly.

"Look, I am just filling you in on my conversation with Enoch today. I don't have any skin in this game. I will be departing first thing tomorrow morning for Shady Grove."

"What about us?" sobbed Mindy.

Roger forgot all about Mindy. Again. She had only just started to engage with Roger, but he sensed that she was a very different creature than Florence and Sandy. Those two seemed to share a broad suite of personality traits.

"Mindy..." and here Roger paused for a few moments after saying her name. "I get the sense that the other men here would be willing to take on another wife. I think all of you would be well served to consider all of your options and alternatives."

"Oh my God!" Sandy exclaimed. "Are you out of your fucking mind? I am not going to be subjugated to a man and his dick. That's just disgusting."

"Yes, well, I thought you might feel that way. Still, I felt I had an ethical duty to inform you of your options."

"That's not an option, Roger," replied Sandy.

Roger only shrugged.

"I am not leaving Mel here," cried Florence.

"What does that mean exactly, Florence?" asked Roger. "What are you going to do if she wants to stay? Drag her out—caveman style—by her hair? Kill Enoch? Melissa does not belong to you. She is not your slave. And you don't have any control over Enoch. He's a free man. And a good man. He saved Melissa's life. You get that, right?"

Florence collapsed to the floor and curled up in a ball and stayed perfectly still. Sandy and Mindy stood in silence. After a while, Roger spoke.

"Look. You people are scaring me. I am leaving first thing in the morning, and I suggest all of you do the same before something terrible happens here. I will tell the Cluff's that we are leaving. But I am not inviting you anywhere, and I am not accepting any responsibility for you. You are going to have to learn to provide for yourselves."

Roger woke before first light and packed his things. The clothes they wore the day before were washed and delivered back to the workshop after supper along with a wooden drying rack, which when set by the woodstove worked like a charm. The four guests exited their sleeping quarters and were surprised to see all four households standing in the driveway gathered around the windmill. As they walked from the workshop to the windmill, the Mormon families parted leaving Melissa standing alone. She was dressed and had her backpack. Roger walked toward Enoch and Enoch extended his hand with a warm smile on his face.

"We made you some breakfast sandwiches and packed some food for your hike," Enoch said to Roger as he took Roger's hand. "You might not recognize pemmican, but we wanted you to have it in case something happens, and the hike takes longer than expected. Mormons learned to make it from native Americans. It's high in calories, and it will keep indefinitely. My wives also packed you some comfort food."

Enoch's wives and older daughters were holding long sticks with little packages tied hobo style made of cut up livestock feed bags. Enoch took one and handed it to Roger. His wives handed one each to Sandy, Mindy, and Florence, and Enoch's daughters

52

gave one to Melissa. Melissa and the teenaged daughters appeared to be in tears.

"Will the community please come to order so that we may pray for the safe travels of our friends?"

Silence descended.

"Dear Lord, we thank you for bringing your children to our home and for the warmth of their friendship. If it is your will, Lord, I will ask before my family and community, that Melissa might one day soon be inspired to return to join our family as my wife. We ask that you hold them in your hands and bring them safely to the destination of their journey, Amen."

The entire community responded in unison, "Amen."

Chapter 8

American lore has it that vast numbers of unemployed men
stole onto railroad freight cars to travel the country during the
Great Depression of the 1930's. It would be more accurate to say
that many men took to the rails as walkways and paths to avoid
coming into contact with unfriendly locals and police and that
some of these men occasionally jumped a freight car. The terms
"bum," "tramp," and "hobo" evolved to describe the nuances
some people claimed to find within this itinerant population. The
image of a hobo walking with a stick on his shoulder and piece of
canvas or cloth tied in a bundle at the end of the stick holding all
of his worldly possessions is as inaccurate as it is universal. In
reality, the stick was a hoe for weeding crop fields and these hoe
boys—hobos—were looking for work. Tramps were not
interested in working, but perhaps they picked up on the utility of
carrying their possessions with a stick and a cloth. Bums were not
interested in working or traveling.

The homeless party from the LGBT Garden of Eden commune
that departed that morning from the fundamentalist Mormon
compound and bound for the Old Order Mennonite settlement in
Shady Grove, Kentucky, certainly looked like hobos. Of course,
they were walking down the middle of a two-lane highway and
not stealing through the shadows of a railroad right-of-way. And
they lacked the requisite hoes. But they were, after a fashion,
looking for work, so strictly speaking they couldn't be classified
as tramps.

Roger walked ahead of the women to avoid the tension. Not a
word passed between them during two, five-mile treks and the
15-minute rest in between. But now they were hungry and tired,
and they stopped to sit and rest on an exposed granite out-
cropping on the side of the road and see what the Cluff family
packed in their hobo bundles. Inside of each pack, they found two
peanut-butter and jelly sandwiches, a half-dozen hard-boiled
eggs, a wedge of hard cheese, a small loaf of butter-fried
cornbread, and several large oatmeal cookies. And a block of the

pemmican that Enoch spoke of wrapped in another piece of fabric cut from a feed sack. Roger had never seen pemmican before.

Melissa burst into tears.

Florence shot to her feet, ran out into the road, and spun around and shouted at Melissa.

"You wanna go back to your boyfriend and his three wives?! Fucking go then!"

When Melissa raised her head to look at Florence, Florence started to run towards Melissa, but Roger stood up and between them.

"Whoa! Whoa! Whoa!" he shouted at Florence. "What the hell do you think you are doing? I don't know what's going on with you, but I think that Melissa is overwhelmed by the kindness and generosity the Cluff family packed into these bags. I know I am."

Mindy was sobbing right along with Melissa, and Roger looked over to her.

"I guess Mindy is too," added Roger.

"Kindness and generosity?" Florence asked. "I guess he can afford to be generous! He's running a fucking plantation there with his wives and his children as nothing but slaves!"

"Is that what you learned from our experience back there?"

"What the fuck else would you draw from it?! He's a fucking polygamist! We used to hang those bastards! I'd strangle him here and now!"

"Enoch opened his home to us and saved Melissa's life. And you would kill him because he loves more than one woman?"

"Would you shut up!" said Sandy. "I can't take it anymore! Shut up!"

Roger turned to respond, but Sandy wasn't speaking to him or Florence. She was talking to Mindy who was now balling out loud.

Incredulous, Roger watched as Melissa and Mindy tried to compose themselves. He wondered what would have happened if he had not been here. Apparently, angry outbursts and threats of physical violence were a regular part of their relationships.

"Do you realize that if you were men and you conducted yourselves like this just four weeks ago, you would be arrested and charged with domestic violence?"

"Mind your own fucking business," Sandy said to Roger. Roger ignored her.

"Do either of you want to return to the Cluff homestead?" Roger asked Mindy and Melissa. "I will walk back with you."

Neither woman responded.

"Please let me know that you understood what I just said. I asked you if you wanted to go back and stay with the Cluff's."

Both women shook their heads.

"You want to stay with your partners?"

Both women nodded their heads.

Roger shrugged and walked over to where his pack lay on the ground and sat down to eat his lunch. As he ate, he considered what he should do. He felt Sandy and Florence were probably capable of physical violence and possibly dangerous to him—and definitely to Melissa and Mindy. Clinically, this was fascinating. Sandy and Florence seemed utterly devoid of the human capacity for empathy. Unable to feel what others were feeling or to put themselves in another person's position. This phenomenon was not new to him. In his clinical practice, he came to estimate that roughly 1 in 6 American women of European descent— approximately 15% of the female population—experienced a condition—he did not use the term "suffer from a condition"— he came to call "heterosexual dysphoria," and these women were, almost universally, constrained in their ability to feel empathy— especially towards men. Too, men seemed to elicit a disgust response in these women. A smaller fraction of these women professed to be "lesbians," whatever the heck that was. Nature gave human females an extra helping of empathy to assist them with infant care and the nurturing of children. But this human element, by all outward appearances, was absent in Sandy and Florence. The typical human response to a room, or in this case a farm, filled with children was to smile and engage with the children and to feel the warmth and vitality of youth and the future of humanity standing before them. Roger noticed that Mindy and Melissa responded to the Cluff children in this manner, while Florence and Sandy were stone-faced and uncomfortable or perhaps even irritated by the presence of the children.

Florence and Sandy tucked into their food, grotesquely unaware of the contrast between the hate they possessed for Enoch and his family and the beautiful expression of fellowship that the Cluff family made in packing them food for their hike. It occurred to Roger that these women did not have the benefit of the maturation process of being a parent or of having to provide for a spouse and family. Raising children is an essential element in the socialization process—especially for women. But Mindy and Melissa were not parents and seemed capable of empathy. Roger would need to think about this some more—but later. It was late November, and the days were short. They needed to make some more progress and to find a place to sleep for the night. Roger ate sparingly of his pack to stretch his provisions as long as possible. There was always the pemmican, but that would have to wait until a time when he was starving. He tied up his pack on his stick and started walking without a word to the women, and without a word between them, the women scrambled to tie their packs and catch up to Roger.

In mid-afternoon, they came upon a sign that said:

Annie's Consignment Store
Arts & Crafts — Candles & Quilts
Ahead on Left

About a mile ahead the road headed down into a hollow. From the top of the hill they could see down to the bottom of the hollow, and as promised, they saw the store on the left and a short bridge over a creek a little further down the road. On their left, at the top of the hill, there was a long gravel driveway leading into a cattle farm. Far down the path, a woman was walking toward them. They paused to wait for her. As the woman came closer, they could see that she was elderly and that she was pulling a small wagon a little bigger than the typical little red wagon that children played with. The woman saw them but didn't wave. She just lowered her head and pulled harder. When she got to the road where they were standing Roger saw that she had a load of firewood in the wagon. The woman stopped at the edge of the road and took in the man and the four women waiting for her there.

"Are you looking for somebody?"

"What?" said Roger. "Uh, Excuse me. No. We are bound for Shady Grove."

"Oh. I thought maybe you had kin here and didn't know where to find them. We've had a few stragglers come walking in here looking for some of the old folks. Shady Grove's about 30 miles that way." And she pointed in the direction they had been walking.

At the mention of "30 miles," the women's hearts sank.

"We were wondering if Annie's Consignment Store might still be operating."

"Why?" The old woman enjoyed a chuckle. "You got anything worth trading?"

"We need a place to shelter for the night."

"Why are you headed to Shady Grove? You got kin there?"

"No, just a friend of mine."

"What's his name?"

"Philip Troyer."

"Is that so? I've been doing business with Philip for 20 years. I get all of the leather goods for my store from the Troyer family."

So, this was "Annie." Roger was familiar with this sort of slow give and take of the rural people living in the American south. She was "feeling him out." Roger would not be the one to seek an end to the process.

"Well, I have known Philip for quite a while. But not that long."

"Where are you comin' from?"

"We spent the last two nights at the Mormon settlement about fifteen miles back that way. Before that, I was traveling when the power went down. I met these women at a campsite outside of Napoleon, Tennessee, and we stayed there for three weeks waiting, hoping the power would come back on. But we ran out of food."

"Yea. I think everybody expected the power to come back on any minute. Been a lot of minutes!" The woman enjoyed another chuckle.

"Yes," replied Roger. "I guess it's more than a few minutes. Twenty-six days and a couple of hours."

"I stopped counting. You say you stayed with the Mormons?"

"Yes. Last night and the night before."

"What was his name?"

"Enoch Cluff."

"Okay. I believe what you say is so. I'm Annie. You can camp out in my store if you don't mind doing a little work."

"My name is Roger; and this is Sandy, Mindy, Florence, and Melissa. Of course, we don't mind working! And we've got some food we don't mind sharing."

"Is that so! Well, I ain't hard up just yet. The only one I got to feed is me, and at my age, I don't eat that much. Come on. No point standing around making small talk anymore. Let's go."

Annie's consignment shop, home, and critter barn was a ramshackle wood structure—with some of it on stone stilts, and some of it on poles, barn style, and built piecemeal over the years above the highwater mark of the creek's small floodplain. The store might have been a mill or logging cabin—and considering the creek in the backyard, a mill would be a good guess—in the early part of the 20th century. The attached apartment and living-quarters addition on the north side was probably built in the latter part of the 20th century, going by the building materials and windows. A critter barn to shelter small livestock—laying hens, meat poultry, rabbits, a few goats or sheep—and perhaps a lone family milk cow back when a family might have lived here— hung off the southwest corner. Shade trees, now bare, stood on either side of the building along the street. A broad and cluttered porch faced the road, and there were two signs, one on either side of the door. One sign said, *We Buy Junk and Sell Antiques.* The other sign said, *For Every Christmas Tree Lit Before Thanksgiving, An Elf Drowns a Baby Reindeer.*

Annie had a lively—if dark—sense of humor.

To Roger's keen eye, the place was both welcoming and smacked of rural poverty. The home attested to the strong moral fiber of someone who was barely eking out a living but who had not fallen into the ruin of despair and self-destruction in spite of life's challenges. Their first image of a stringy elderly woman hauling a utility wagon full of stove wood down a long rural gravel driveway fit perfectly to this place.

"Hold on a second," Annie said when they got to the south side of the building. She peeled off with her wagon down a well-worn path and left it under cover of the critter barn, so that it wouldn't get wet. "I'm expecting rain," she continued as she returned to them. "I can feel it in my joints. Come on in."

And with that, Annie led her guests up the porch stairs and signaled for them to follow her into the store. Immediately in front of them in the center of the large single room of the store was a wood cook stove, to the left, an improvised wall made of blankets and tapestries hung from small hooks screwed into the wood paneling of the ceiling. Roger surmised that this was constructed to keep the heat from the stove on the right, or north, side of the store. To the right, he could see an open door and guessed that was Annie's living quarters and bedroom. Just outside of that door was a small table and a couple of chairs. Along the walls were dozens of framed photographs. The empty store shelves had been pushed to the back wall leaving a large open area around the stove. It was warm and safe and dry inside Annie's establishment.

"Well, you are looking at the accommodations. Beats the heck out of sleeping out in the cold though," said Annie. "And your timing is good. Tomorrow is Thanksgiving! And since it is going to rain and I doubt you will want to be walking in it, we might as well set here all comfy and cook us up a bird. I got ducks and a couple of turkeys. I don't want to have to feed them, and some won't make it through the winter anyway. I got to kill them and put them in jars. So, while the stove is hot for the oven and I got me some help, I figure now is a good time to do a little soup and stew canning. How's that sound?"

"Like manna from heaven," Roger replied.

"Good!" Annie exclaimed and clapped her hands together in celebration. "Put your bags on those shelves anywhere you can make room. The outhouse is through that door." Annie pointed to a door on the west side of the room directly across from the front door. "And there are burdock leaves everywhere out back. Paper products are in short supply if you catch my meaning. Here, take these buckets and follow the road down to the creek and bring back some water and we'll warm it up on the stove, so that you can wash later."

That evening, as Annie heated home-canned duck soup and cooked rice and chatted with the women around the stove, Roger took in the framed photos mounted on every inch of spare wall space around the store. With each passing photo, Roger's excitement continued to climb. What a story these photos told! How was it possible that the humanities department at Vanderbilt University had never heard of this woman who lived, in a manner of speaking, right in their backyard? He reached to take down one of the photos so that he might better see it in the dim late afternoon light at the window—and noticed that his hands were trembling. And it wasn't just from hunger, although he was famished—this was incredible. Overwhelming. Or in the vernacular of the photos, "Out of sight!"

The women called Roger to the table for the meal. Three folding chairs were added to the two wooden spoke backed chairs at the table. An excellent supper of duck soup with rice and canned green beans and some refried cornbread from their satchels was waiting at the table, with the oatmeal cookies held in reserve for dessert. Roger was invited to sit in one of the wooden chairs, and as he took his seat, he noticed a book on the table. He picked it up.

"*Meditations*," the seminal work and classic of antiquity by Roman emperor and Stoic philosopher, Marcus Aurelius. Roger looked up at Annie with an expression that said: *Who are you!?*

"If you like to read, I have a good selection here to pick from," Annie said to Roger in her Kentucky twang. There was an amused look on her face.

Roger didn't know what to say. "Thank you; I'd like that," was the best he could come up with. "But I have to ask you, and I hope you don't mind talking about it over dinner. And of course, it can wait."

Annie laughed. "There ain't much else to do around here but talk. Unless your friends would rather sit around in the dark like bumps on a log."

"You lost me," said Sandy.

"Those pictures," said Roger. "That's you, isn't it? 'Summer of Love,' Haight-Asbury. That would be the summer of 1967. The DNC Convention, Chicago 1968. Woodstock, summer of 1969. Abbie Hoffman, Jerry Rubin, Allen Ginsberg. You traveled in rarified company!"

"Yes," Annie replied, with a shocked look on her face. "That's me. But you are too young to know all of this. You wouldn't have been born yet. How would you know all of those people and places?"

"Well, before the power went out, I was a tenured professor of sociology at Vanderbilt University. My doctoral thesis was titled, 'The Post-Modernist's influences on the American counter-culture of the 1960's.' What a resource you would have been!"

"Whew, you scared the shit out of me!" Annie said with obvious relief. "I was afraid my past had caught up with me. Or a psychedelic flashback."

"I am sorry," said Roger, smiling at that last comment. "I am just so excited! I was trembling as I looked at your pictures!"

"So, you're famous?" asked Melissa.

"Hardly," replied Annie. "No one around here but me and your professor friend here seems to know anything about the events of that time."

"But your accent," said Roger. "Pure Kentucky twang."

"I was born and raised on a small holding outside of Edinburgh, Kentucky, 20 miles north of Shady Grove."

"But you were there in San Francisco. Were you a musician? There are a lot of photos of you with some bands that went on to become very famous."

"I moved to San Francisco after I graduated college in the spring of '67. I was 21. I played a little mandolin."

"You were very pretty. Perhaps 'beautiful' is a better description."

"If I wasn't, I don't think all those VIP's would have had much interest in me."

"Typical," said Sandy.

"What's that?" asked Annie.

"A bunch of middle-aged men taking advantage of a young girl," replied Sandy. "They should be ashamed of themselves. But they never are."

"No one took advantage of me, young lady," Annie replied flatly. "And 21 ain't no girl. I was a grown woman. I've done almost everything there is to do at least once, and most things twice. But I never did anything I didn't want to do."

Roger could tell he was just going to love Annie.

"Could you start from the beginning? You said you moved to San Francisco in the summer of '67 after graduating from college?"

"Yes. I drove out to California with a classmate of mine from Washington University."

"In Saint Louis?!" Roger asked.

"Yes."

"What did you study?"

"I took a double major. I was awarded a degree in Mathematics and a degree in Philosophy."

Roger slumped back in his chair, crossed his arms, and said, "Holy shit."

"What the hell are you doing here then?" asked Sandy.

Roger looked at Sandy as if she had just leaned over to one side of her chair and farted loudly, and then back to Annie so that she could see him roll his eyes. Annie looked back and forth between the two of them with a strange smile on her face.

"I came home after my husband died," Annie told Sandy.

"Whatever you say," said Sandy.

"Hold on, Annie. I'm sorry," said Roger. Then Roger turned to Sandy and said, "Please. Give it a rest, huh?" Then back to Annie. "So, you moved out to the Bay Area with a college friend and met many people who would go on to have a meaningful impact on American society of the time."

"I was very young and immature, and I was caught up in the moment. I was a flower child. A hippie. And I was very popular."

"I'll say," said Roger.

"Well, youth and beauty don't last," Annie continued. "And neither does idealism. These are a phenomenon of youth. History is filled with events where pretty young women are keeping company with idealistic and self-important men. Eventually, all of it fades, and then you are left within the confines of human existence—aging and then death. You have to color your life in as best you can, but not with self-destructive excess, or you'll bring on the end of the story sooner than it needs to get here. Life is brief and meaningless enough as it is. Most of the people in those pictures are long since dead, and very few of them made 'old bones,' as my father used to say. What did they accomplish? What lasting effect did they have? I didn't want to be a groupie for some rock band. And I didn't want to spend my life at protests in between court dates and stints in jail. But I did want to matter. I wanted to live a life of meaning…"

"Me too!" Melissa interrupted. Annie smiled at her and reached for Melissa's hand and held it.

"Have you ever heard of, 'The Homestead?'" Annie asked Roger.

"The largest commune in American history?" asked Roger. "Sure! We spent a summer there in southern Tennessee studying their socio-economic strategy a couple of years before the summer I spent with the Shady Grove Mennonites."

"I notice that you are heading to the Mennonite settlement and not to 'The Homestead.'"

Roger took a deep breath before responding, "Indeed."

"Wait," said Florence. "You lived in a commune? We lived in a commune! That's where we all met!"

"I'm sorry to hear that."

Florence stiffened and said, "What do you mean?"

"I wasted ten years of my life, the best years of my life, trying to mold a collection of hundreds—and at one point over a thousand—of dysfunctional people into a functioning community. And it was a complete waste of time and effort. I guess that's the arrogance of youth for you."

"Hold on," Roger said. "When were you at 'The Homestead?'"

"From its inception in 1973. Hundreds of us were living in California at the time. We pooled what little money we had and bought nearly a thousand acres in rural Tennessee, back when they were practically giving land away. Looking back on it, it was one disaster and disgraceful failure after another."

"What do you mean?" asked Sandy. "What was so disgraceful about it?"

"Mankind has been living in family units within a larger community or tribe since Homo Sapiens climbed down from the trees. We insisted we had a better way, and that we were smarter than the collective wisdom embodied in the evolution of the billions upon billions of people who have ever lived. That there was no objective reality, and that reality could be subjectively constructed into any shape we wished it to be. Well, if that is true, nothing we did lend any evidence to support it."

"I can hear your philosophical training," said Roger.

Annie smiled. "Yes. 'Argumentum ad logicam,' if I remember correctly—it's been a long time. An invalid argument is not proof that something is false. Still, Derrida can go fuck himself. I stand with George Orwell—I despise people who use Latin and big words to sound intellectual."

Roger was breathless. He despised the Intelligentsia and Derrida and loved Orwell—this was fantastic! "Please, go on," Roger said. "I am sorry to interrupt."

"There isn't much to say. All I can do is recount the failures— compounded by immature stupidity—that we endured. And I wasted ten years of my young life there." And here Annie turned to Melissa who was still holding her hand and said, "Something I hope you won't do."

"I'm sorry you feel that way," said Florence. "But there is more than one way to live a life."

"Perhaps," Annie said in a sad voice. "But there is only one way for life to go on. We must bear and raise children. You are going to die, Florence. We are mortal. Our paths might seem infinite, but they all lead to the same place and a finite end. There is only one path to the future for mankind. I was the community's first midwife. I must have delivered a hundred babies! And yet, I never had children of my own. And now, I have no future, and I am all alone. I wanted to live a life of meaning—and I blew it. It's too late for me." Here Annie turned to Melissa so that she would know that Annie was talking to her. "But it's not too late for you."

Florence slammed her hands on the table and stood up. "Why don't you mind your own business?"

Annie looked up at Florence and said, "It's not too late for you either." Annie let that sink in for a few moments before she added, "Why don't you sit down and finish your supper?"

Annie smiled at Melissa again and patted the hand she held before removing her hands and addressing her own meal. There was a strained silence around the table.

"Wow! Were you the first midwife there? 'The Homestead' commune single-handedly re-established the legitimacy of midwifery in the United States. That alone is an incredible success story."

"Well, there is that," Annie said and went back to her supper. She didn't seem interested in pursuing this line of conversation.

Roger recovered quickly. "You mentioned that you lost your husband," Roger said. "I am sorry."

"Oh, it's been many years—so long, I can't remember what Baldy's voice sounded like. They say that is the first thing you forget."

Florence sat back down and kept her eyes on her plate. Annie and Roger glanced over to her for a moment.

"How did you come to be here?" Roger asked.

"And why didn't you have babies if you wanted them so much?" Florence hissed without looking up.

"I met my husband—his name was Baldwin, and everyone called him 'Baldy' because he wasn't—while in Nashville on a business trip for 'The Homestead.' I was 35 years old, and after more than ten years at 'The Homestead,' disillusioned doesn't even begin to cover the range of emotions that I was feeling at the time. We met in a restaurant, and he invited me to see some musician friends of his performing at a local dive. I went home with him that night, and I never left. And I never went back to 'The Homestead.' We were married at city hall a few months later. He was a musician and had worked for some of the big acts, but he was then in his mid-40's, and a changing of the guard on Music Row left him out in the cold. When he was young, he paid his dues, and the reward by the big labels back then for all those years on the road for aging musicians was steady studio work. But when the old bigwigs got pushed out by the new bigwigs, they gave the studio work to their people. So, we got jobs at an expensive steakhouse restaurant and tried to save some money to start a family, but month after month, nothing happened. I was too old—this was before the fertility treatments of today, and of course, those sorts of treatments create other problems. The years went by, and we just accepted it. We had a happy life. We traveled, and we took winters off and lived in Mexico. One year, upon returning, Baldy got sick. We thought it might be a parasite he picked up in Mexico. He went to the doctor and got some medication, but it didn't work. After a few more doctors and bunch more tests, he was diagnosed with pancreatic cancer. He died three months later. I was 51 years old.

"I had no one left in the world but my father. My husband, mother, and brother had passed. So, I went to live with my father, who was 80 at the time and not well. My father was so glad to have me home. I think he died then on purpose, so he wouldn't have to do it alone. Baldy left me a small life-insurance policy and my father's estate left me a little something, and I bought this store and property and a pick-up truck with the money.

"And then I realized I was all alone. That I will die alone and that my parents never had any grandchildren."

"What about your brother?" asked Sandy. "It is not your responsibility to provide your parents with grandchildren. It's your life."

"My younger brother was a homosexual."

"We say LGBTQ now," Sandy interrupted.

"He moved to New York City after graduating from high school in 1976," Annie continued without missing a beat. "He came home when he got sick and died of complications from AIDS in 1984. My family line will die with me."

Silence—other than the tick-tock of a cuckoo clock that none of the guests noticed before.

"So, you see," continued Annie. "I am a walking cautionary tale. It's your life. You must make your own decisions. But I think they should be informed decisions. Not the uninformed, me-too decisions we often reach when we limit our lives and experiences to living in an echo chamber with people who don't challenge us."

Annie turned to Florence and then to Sandy to make it clear that she was now speaking to them. Roger wondered why it was that everyone ignored Mindy.

"In the end, and the end will come, what is it you will leave behind? Your stone-cold anger, resentment, and indignation at the unfairness of the world? You have a choice. You can be the *Stones in the Garden* or the life-giving seeds of Truth and Beauty."

Annie paused and took a deep breath before continuing. "Who is going to bury me?" Annie asked in a whisper. "I'm all alone."

Later that evening as Roger was preparing to turn in for the night Annie appeared in a hat, coat, and boots from her apartment and signaled Roger to come to her.

"I have to go see to my evening chores," Annie said.

"Would you like some help?" Roger interrupted.

"No, but thanks. I do this every night, and I know my way around in the dark. You're more likely to get yourself hurt than to be of any help. You're welcome to pick out a book if you like. My favorites are on the bookshelf in the apartment, but there are lots stacked on the other side of those shelves pushed up against the back wall you can't see from here. There is room to walk behind there if you need to."

"Thank you. That's a good idea. I am not sleepy."

"It's only 6 o'clock. It gets dark early this time of year. You go ahead. I'll be back soon."

Annie lit a hurricane lamp and walked out the front door. Roger watched her through the glass in the front door and noticed that she didn't go behind the house to her critter barn but turned right on the road and walked up the hill towards the place where they first met Annie. When she disappeared from view, Roger took the lamp from the table and walked into Annie's living quarters. The first room was a large rectangle with a kitchenette built into the north wall, with two doors on the left, the first to a bathroom and the second to a small bedroom. The wall on the right was faced with built-in wood-framed bookshelves painted white. Books, mostly hardcover, lined the shelves. Roger started at the center and held his lamp up to see the titles as he tilted his head to the right to make it easier to read them.

The Count of Monte Cristo, The Protestant Work Ethic and the Spirit of Capitalism, Don Quixote, Huckleberry Finn, 1984, Lolita, Frankenstein, Das Kapital, Candide, Gone with the Wind, Les Misérables, The Moon is a Harsh Mistress, The Meaning of Relativity.

"Holy shit," Roger whispered to himself.

"What?" whispered Melissa from behind Roger, startling him. When Roger turned he saw that Melissa and Florence were standing behind him.

"Christmas! You scared the shit out of me!"

"Sorry," Melissa replied, giggling. "What's 'holy shit?'"

"Have you read any of these?" Roger asked.

"No," Flo and Mel replied in unison.

"Well, Annie has. I think she's read all of them—this is a 'holy shit' if ever I saw one."

"Maybe she just likes to read," said Florence.

Roger ignored Florence and staggered to his right and took in a title here and there.

Stranger in a Strange Land, A Brief History of Time, Beyond Good and Evil, The History of Western Philosophy, Fight Club, The King James Bible, Atlas Shrugged. Elements of Geometry. The list compiling in his head went on and on.

"What the hell? This little old lady has been sitting up here, all alone, knitting quilts and dipping candles—and reading everything that ever mattered in the history of western civilization? What the hell? What the *hell!*?"

Roger reversed course along the wall, picked a title, returned the lamp to the table and took a seat and began to read.

A little less than an hour later, Annie returned and went directly to her apartment without engaging her guests, dropping an egg basket with a dozen eggs on the table as she went, and closed the door behind her. As she walked past, Roger thought her face looked as if she had been crying.

Annie appeared from her sleeping quarters at first light, fully dressed and with a hat and coat on. Roger was already up and reading at the table. He looked up from his book.

"You can get breakfast working. There are lard and canned potatoes on the other side of those blankets. Onions go good with potatoes," Annie said and pointed to the makeshift wall of blankets and tapestries. "I will be back just as soon as I can get my chores done." She walked briskly to the front door.

Roger laid kindling and stove billets on the coals in the woodstove firebox, opened the dampers, and closed the firebox door. The stove would need a half hour to get hot enough to cook. Then he pushed past the tapestry closest to the stove and into the other half of the store. At least a hundred jars of canned vegetables lined a shelf along the far wall and Roger figured the jars packed with white must be the potatoes. He walked to them and grabbed a jar and pulled a large onion off of a braid of onions and brought them to the kitchen table where the egg basket waited. The women were just getting up from their sleeping bags.

Roger called to them. "We'll need a bucket of water."

"I'm on it," Florence replied.

Roger made no other preparations and sat down to read his book and let the stove heat up, give time for the women to use the outhouse, and for Annie to return. Her morning chores must be lighter than her evening chores because this time she was back in fifteen minutes. She appeared at the door, stumbled into the house and crossed the room and collapsed in a chair at the table. She looked up at her guests and said, "I need you to help me bury someone."

Annie led her guests in silence up the hill and down the gravel driveway where they first met the day before to an old farmhouse. They saw him, or rather his body, facing a fireplace where the ashes still glowed in a recliner in the great room just past an odd entrance foyer to the farmhouse. A large tan blanket made of the same synthetic material used for ski jacket insulation doubled over and draped on him to keep him warm. No open mouth. No staring eyes. He looked like he was sleeping. Roger walked to him and picked up his hand and felt for a pulse at the wrist. The body was still warm, and there was no rigor mortis. Feeling none, Roger felt for a pulse at the neck. Nothing. Roger opened an eye with his thumb. The pupil was large and fixed and stared straight ahead. Roger closed the eye.

"He must have just passed this morning," said Roger. "But he is gone," and as he said this, he nodded his head over and over as if to assure himself that the man was dead, and they were not about to make a terrible mistake and bury him alive. "He's gone."

They wrapped the man in the tan blanket and used Annie's red utility wagon to move his body and buried him in a shallow grave in the soft ground of the pasture bottom. And though they took turns in digging and filling the grave, most of the work fell to Roger. When the job was done, Annie looked around at her guests and said, "Thank you. We already said our good-byes." Melissa came forward and embraced Annie. When the embrace broke, Melissa began to weep as they held each other by their forearms. Then Annie shook her, just a little, just enough to get Melissa to look up.

"This your first burial?" asked Annie.

Melissa sobbed and shook her head. Annie plowed ahead.

"Probably the most important thing you will ever see. Only the sight of the birth of your children will exceed this in importance—this is how the journey ends for all of us. It is important to know this. Know it, not just to think it—to know death at this intimate level. You're going to be okay. We're all going to be okay—until we're not. He had a long, beautiful, and productive life. His name was Wallace Burns. He was a good man. And I will miss him terribly."

And here Annie paused and raised her voice to speak to all of them.

"And on that sad day when we die meals must be served, babies will dirty their diapers and need changing, cows milked, fires lit, water hauled, dishes washed, and laundry done. We die, but life goes on. I knew his time was short when I saw him last night. But when I got home, I killed a turkey for today's Thanksgiving supper. It's hanging up in the critter barn, gutted and half plucked. Because life must go on." Then, after a pause as if to hammer the point home, Annie continued, "Come on. Let's go cook up some breakfast and get that bird in the oven."

Annie let go of Melissa's forearms, walked to her little red wagon and grabbing the handle, as she turned for home it started to rain.

The rain kept at it all day Thursday—Thanksgiving—and Friday. Annie didn't seem to mind having company, but she didn't seem interested in talking, either. Roger helped by slaughtering and scalding the barnyard poultry that Annie wanted to put into canning jars for the winter, and the women helped with the plucking and pressure canning. There was a substantial pantry at Wallace's, and after several weeks of ground field-corn and quack-grass roots, the last five days—the first two spent with the fecund Mormons and the previous three with Annie the hermetic philosopher, midwife, and healer—of rest and plenty rejuvenated their spirits.

Annie always woke at first light to attend to her morning chores. Roger was ready and waiting Saturday morning and was out the door before her.

"You got something on your mind?" asked Annie as she passed Roger down the stairs and on her way to feed her two milk goats.

"I think I am ready to go. I'd like for you to come with us."

"On a 30-mile hike in freezing weather to someplace I ain't expected? At my age? No thanks. I'm well fixed here."

"But you're alone."

"Well, that's true enough," replied Annie. "And it'll be true no matter where I go. Ain't no one looking for a little old lady to take care of. You could stay here. Wallace's house is empty, and you won't starve or freeze to death this winter if you took up residence there. From what I understand, the bodies of the people who were caught out on the road when the lights went out are strewn up and down the highways."

Roger recounted the scene of the woman's body in the car and what was probably the child's remains in the road.

"People can't survive without food, and the cold of winter will hasten the process. I had a real eye-opener myself over at my neighbor's chicken farm. Maybe I should take you there. You might be more inclined towards Wallace's place after seeing that."

"I might take you up on that. There's another reason I have to go to Philip Troyer's. I have twin sons. They are 23-years-old, and they are both U.S. Navy officers. We always kidded around that if the world ever came to an end, we would meet up in Shady Grove. They spent a lot of time at the Troyer farm there one summer when they were kids. Well, if this isn't the end of the world, it's damn close. I don't know where my sons are at the moment. But at the very least, I have to leave word with the Shady Grove Mennonites where I am. It's the best chance I've got to see my sons again."

"Well, that makes sense. You got a wife somewhere?" Annie asked.

"No," Roger said. "We've been divorced since they were seven-years-old. She remarried and moved to San Diego when the boys were in the Naval Academy. But back to the chicken farm? What's so important about a chicken farm?"

"Wallace's friend had four chicken houses. Well, the chicken houses are still there. But the chickens are all dead. You know anything about poultry farming?"

Roger shrugged and shook his head. "Not a thing."

"Baby chicks are raised in huge barns called 'chicken houses.' Long round barns that look like giant greenhouses or framed barns sheathed in metal with huge fans with heaters at each end for ventilation. The chicks are hatched in a specialized hatchery and delivered by truck to the chicken houses. Private farmers own these chicken houses: they are under contract with the meat packers. Their farms are always along the trucking routes between the feed mills, and the meat packers: where the birds get slaughtered, processed and packed. A chicken house will hold 10,000 to 25,000 birds, and a chick will grow from about an ounce in weight to six to 10 pounds in less than eight weeks. That takes a lot of feed. The houses have to be warm, and that takes a lot of fuel. Waste products pile up very quickly and must be disposed of in a timely fashion, or the birds will die.

"After the lights went out, the feed and propane trucks stopped coming to the farm. Within a couple of days, the farmer had 50,000 dead chickens on his hands. They did their best, thinking the power would come back on, and cleared the chicken houses of the bird carcasses with a front-end loader. But what do you do with 50,000 dead chickens? You can imagine the sanitation issues. The farmer had to abandon the farm, or he and his family would have died of disease. We could smell it here, ten miles away, when the wind was right, and it is still leaking into the surface water that all of us have to drink now. It is the same thing for the hog farmers. Hogs are raised in hoop houses or metal barns, just like chickens. They need the feed trucks to deliver feed, or they will die. Now you know why they call these farms 'confined animal feeding operations.'

"Well, the cities are little more than chicken or hog houses— but with people. People get hatched at a hospital, and then they are delivered to climate-controlled houses. They depend on shipments of grain, sometimes in the form of bread, rice, or pasta, and sometime in the form of grain fed chicken, pork, beef, or dairy. Without the grain, the residents of the cities will die, just like the chickens and the hogs. And they will die even faster if they are cold."

Roger took a seat on one of the splitting stumps just outside the critter barn.

"Holy shit," Roger muttered, lowering his face into his hands with his elbows on his knees. "So even if they got the grid up and running tomorrow the famine would continue, at least through this winter."

Annie felt she had said enough and remained silent. After a few minutes, Roger raised his head and continued.

"I can't do anything about any of that. I just have to hope the Navy has a contingency plan for something like this and that I will see my sons again one day."

"I didn't bring this up before because y'all didn't look so hot when I first met you," Annie said. She wanted to change the subject. "I get the sense that you would rather not spend the winter with these women."

Roger scoffed. "I would rather beat my toes off with a hammer than spend the winter alone with these women."

Annie laughed at the image.

"Could you see yourself spending the winter alone with Melissa?" she asked.

"I'm a little old for her. Besides, I don't think I'm her type. I think Florence is more her type."

"I think you're wrong there on both counts—she's not cut from the same cloth as Florence and Sandy, and neither is Mindy. Melissa is starting to understand that she needs a man, that she's going to want a man, and that the pickings are slim."

Roger wouldn't take the bait. "I never thought about cities as grain dependent chicken houses—but now that you have explained it this way, well, I think your analysis is spot on. But society will reform, Annie. Lives will be lost, but the knowledge we have gained will endure."

"That's another reason you are drawn to Shady Grove, isn't it?"

"Well, it is not just the settlement at Shady Grove. We will need a critical mass of people, and we will also need a great deal of practical knowledge and skills, tillable land, and water. The region has dozens of communities that would fit the bill. But that's just survival. Mankind needs culture, political science, law, philosophy, music, and art. We need intellectuals and free thinkers. We need people like you."

"Well, we can talk about that another time. Maybe in the spring—if we're still alive. And you're not going anywhere today. Tomorrow is Sunday, in case you've lost track of the days of the week. The Mennonites will not welcome you on the

Sabbath for sure, so unless you want to sit around in the cold in your tent, you best leave Monday and arrive there on Tuesday. Worst case, they will feed you and turn you around and send you back here. But at least you can leave word for your boys. In the meantime, why don't you take my wagon up to Wallace's woodshed and bring us back a load of firewood?"

Monday morning dawned bright and crisp. If winter wasn't here just yet, she was rapping her knuckles with evil intent on autumn's door. A hard frost covered the grass like a cold and course carpet the texture of salt and silk. Mist rose from the places the sun reached through the bare trees to burn off the frost, swirling in small clouds and then vanishing into the air. After a bountiful breakfast of eggs scrambled with canned sausage, potatoes, and pickled hot peppers and a side of corn grits, Annie presented them with a care package for themselves and something for each of them to carry for someone else.

"The worst that will happen is that the Mennonites will not welcome you. In that case, you are welcome back here. Wallace's house is empty, and there are enough provisions there to get us through to spring."

"I can't thank you enough," said Roger.

"Well, hold on a second," replied Annie. "I ain't done. There is something that I want you to do for me. Come on outside and let's talk while your friends get their act together."

Roger pulled his backpack on and noticed that it was more substantial than it was when he arrived. Anyway, it was a lot heavier. Annie gave Roger Wallace's handgun.

"There is a couple that I am friendly with that lives a quarter of a mile off of 41E about ten miles south of Shady Grove. You should get there by mid-afternoon, so it might work out that you will have someplace warm and dry to sleep tonight. I want you to check on them and give them the jars I packed in each of your backpacks that I marked for them."

"Okay," replied Roger. "Who are they?"

"Just two lost souls who spent their entire lives at the crossroads of the wrong place and the wrong time. They mean well, but they couldn't find their own ass with both hands. Not even if they had someone to hold a flashlight for them. I met them a few years back at the annual horse-drawn equipment auction they hold every April in Shady Grove. Two aging hippies without a brain between them, and even less money."

"Money wouldn't help them at the moment," Roger said. "Yea, but for a lot of people having money 'Before' means having the stuff you need to survive 'After.'"

There they were again. "Before" and "After." Annie continued.

"These two, like quite a few others, showed up out here in the country after listening to crazy people on the Internet talk about how great it is to go 'off-grid' and 'live off the land.' Fucking idiots. Retards."

Sometimes Annie sounded like an old bag lady picking fights at a bus stop.

"They scrapped together some money and bought a few worthless wooded acres from an unscrupulous logging company after all of the marketable timber was cut for five times what it will be worth in 40 years when the trees grow back. Then they went into hock and bought a piece-of-shit pre-fab log cabin and made the mortgage payments with the money from their disability checks."

"They are disabled!?" asked Roger.

"No! Ain't you been listening to me? Almost everyone out here in rural America—except for the Mennonites, Amish, and Mormons, and the big landowners—is pulling a check from the government. Social security, welfare, disability, whatever. Either that or they work for the government. And most of them have probably already died or are on their way out. I expect my friends are still alive. Not because they've got any smarts or skills—trust me when I tell you they do not have the slightest bit of either— but because they are paranoid. Maybe even delusional."

"Oh, great. And you want me to go and stay with them?"

"I thought you said you 'couldn't thank me enough?'"

Roger chuckled at himself and said, "How quickly we forget, huh?"

"It's alright," Annie said. "Self-preservation is more important than gratitude. And I ain't asked you to stay there. I asked you to check up on them and give them the jars of sausage I packed and tell them I am thinking about them. Maybe they will invite you to sleep there for the night. Those two don't have an evil bone in their bodies. Of course, they don't have any brains either. But they do strike me as lucky."

Roger was skeptical. "Oh, yea? How's that?"

"Well, for one, I don't think they will have to make any more mortgage payments on their cabin!" Annie said with a joyful laugh. "Until a few months ago, they'd been living in an insulated room that they built on the property under an old chicken coop that was about to collapse. I doubt they made more than two payments. They got a wood stove. Not a wood cook stove, mind you, but at least they won't freeze, and they can boil water and heat things up on the top. And they buy oatmeal, rice, beans, and such in bulk. They have spent a lifetime living in desperate privation, so they're used to it, and seem to know how to do it. I expect they are still alive."

Here, Annie paused for dramatic effect to get Roger's attention.

"But there is something else I need to tell you," Annie continued. "You need to brace yourself for what you are going to see on 41E."

"How's that?"

"From what I have gathered from some of our neighbors, the fields along the highways are a grizzly sight. Like what you saw over by the Mormons times a hundred. You are going to have to harden your heart. You are in no position to be a hero—this is every man for himself. A bout of diarrhea would be a death sentence in this weather. That's why you're carrying so much water. You can't drink the surface water, or you will get sick."

"Do your friends have a well?"

"No, but neither do I. We both have rainwater cisterns. The water from the creek I use for washing—and only after I boil it on the stove—because my cistern is small. They'll have plenty of clean water this time of year."

"What do you want me to tell them?"

"Tell them that Wallace has passed away but that I am okay," replied Annie. "And tell them to keep their head down for the winter and that we will get together in early spring. Here's a hand-drawn map, mailbox number, and their names."

When Annie finished speaking, she handed Roger a folded piece of brown paper.

The women appeared from the back of the building on the critter-barn side after visiting the outhouse. They said goodbye and thank-you to Annie in age order. When Melissa's turn came, she and Annie embraced, and Annie whispered in her ear. When they parted, both women were teary-eyed.

Annie walked up onto her porch, waved and said, "I'm not partial to long good-byes," and then disappeared inside her front door.

Chapter 9

A clear path rose before them with running water to the left and an impenetrable line of trees and scrub to the right. The bright early morning autumn sunshine spilled forth to their delight upon the road before them and warmed their shoulders. The beautiful and liberating effect that a full belly has upon the mind of man, a state of mind best appreciated by people who have experienced the real pangs of true hunger and who no longer take this satisfaction for granted, prompted a spring in their step.

A half hour into their day the terrain turned into a mild but long decline. On the north side of the road, a cement spillway emerged out of the tree line pouring water into a culvert that drained into the creek. At the top of the spillway was a cement trace channeling the water into its tight confines for some mechanical purpose, though they couldn't see anything turning in the flow of the sluice gate. But this was no weekend-warrior-do-it-yourself project. With an earthen berm at least 100-yards wide to hold a ten-acre lake back from tumbling unimpeded into the creek and the tons of poured concrete of the spillway it was clear that someone invested a great deal into the engineering and construction of the project.

Sandy hiked up the grade next to the water.

"There is a big house right on the water up here!" Sandy called down to the others.

"Sandy!" called Roger. "Come down from there!"

"Why?"

"Because we are not looking for trouble!"

Sandy descended to the road and caught up with Roger. "What trouble?"

"In the current environment, I think it is a good idea to stay off of private property unless you know the people, or are invited."

"'Private property?'" interjected Florence. "I don't believe in 'property.'"

"Me neither," added Sandy.

Roger considered this for a while. Then he asked a question.

"This morning, when you went to the pile of shoes by the door, did you put the same shoes on as the day before and the day before that? Or did you take whatever shoes appealed to you?"

"Of course, I put my shoes on!" said Sandy.

"I know where you are going with that," said Florence. "Don't be silly. We're talking about money and land and the means of production—not shoes."

"Fair enough," replied Roger. "So, you believe in private property rights for a particular object—shoes—but not for other objects?"

"Well, not just shoes obviously," said Florence. "Personal stuff."

"Okay. So, you believe in property rights when it comes to objects you define as 'personal stuff.' What about your body?"

"What do you mean?" Sandy snarled.

"Take it easy, Sandy. I know this is an issue that is near and dear to you. Do you believe that we, mankind, have exclusive rights to and agency over our bodies?"

"Yes," Sandy and Florence echoed together as they walked on either side of Roger with Melissa leading and Mindy taking up the rear.

"And that a woman has the right to say 'No?' to sex at any time for any reason?"

"Yea, Roger," said Sandy, obviously becoming irritated. "Are you trying to make me angry?"

"Not at all," said Roger. "Stay with me, please. And try not to get angry—this is an intellectual exercise. Think before you answer. Why do women have the right to say 'No'? What is the moral foundation of this right, and why do we use the term, 'right'"?

"Well, it's her body," Florence answered.

"Yes, it is! It is *her* body! And she enjoys the right to the exclusive use, possession, and enjoyment of her body. Now, who, or what, does your body belong to?"

"Roger," said Sandy. "Stop twisting words and asking questions. Just get to the point."

"Hold on, Sandy. I am not twisting words. I made no declaration. You said you don't believe in private property. I am merely establishing that the idea of private property as not the object itself but an abstract that describes a set of rights an individual has to an object or a thing or, in the case of intellectual property, an idea—and even to your body. But let me ask you another question. Is your body your life?"

"You lost me," Sandy said. Florence decided to drop out of the discussion and let Sandy take it from here.

"I'll restate," Roger said. "Is there a difference between your body and your life?"

"I don't understand what you want me to say."

"Well, I don't want you to say anything on my account. I hope you come to understand that your right to the exclusive possession, enjoyment, and use of your body comes from your inalienable right to your life, as does my right to the exclusive possession, enjoyment, and use of the fruit of the efforts of my life—the rights that I have to the objects people confuse with private property. Private property is an abstract, a right, and not an object or thing."

"Bullshit," Sandy spat. "That's just capitalism bullshit."

"No. It is the accumulated wisdom of over 2,000 years of philosophy and law, going back at least to the ancient Greeks."

"The Greeks were full of shit too. They held slaves and women couldn't vote."

"You are changing the subject, Sandy. I am patiently pointing out that your sense of private property as an object or objects is not the definition of private property in law, society, and history. It is man's ability to reciprocate and recognize the rights of others that separates us from the beasts. You keep insisting that you have rights, but you do not want to reciprocate, and you express that by insisting that private property are objects that you can seize via government force rather than part and parcel of the collection of the inalienable rights held by a human being; this is just another manifestation of the post-Modernist assertion that there is no objective truth or reality."

"I am not changing the subject, Roger. You are. We were talking about private property versus collectivism, and suddenly it's about a woman's right to say no to being raped and her reproductive rights."

"Listen to you! And I haven't got to collectivism or abortion just yet. You toss around the word 'rights' as easily as you do your sunk premises whenever it suits you. And when it doesn't, you expect everyone around you to wander off with you on the magical mystery tour of your subjective reality. It's white when white works for you. And then it's black or green or red. Whatever fits into the revolving door of your worldview. But without the objective rule of law, we are soon back to Henry the VIII, cutting off heads and disemboweling those who don't see things through the political and social kaleidoscope of a tyrant— or a mob. They're the same thing. Civilized people must insist on logical consistency or all is lost."

"Hey, Roger?" said a voice from behind. Roger looked over his shoulder to be sure. The voice belonged to Mindy.

"Yes, Mindy?"

"If I understand you, you are saying that a woman's right to say 'No' is derived from her sovereignty as an individual?"

"Mindy, all of her rights, or his, as the case may be—our human rights—arise from our existence and sovereignty. Our lives are ours by natural right. Nature brought us into existence— feel free to use G-d or Providence if you like—and we are endowed by virtue of our existence with natural rights and responsibilities. To live and to let live, unmolested and unharmed by others. The only morally legitimate exception to that is the use of retaliatory force to protect us from people who would violate our rights. If that is true, if we own our lives, then we own our bodies as well as the efforts, products, and results of our lives— that is, our rights to private property."

And here Roger stopped and waved his arms about him and spun around once. The women halted and formed a semi-circle in front of him.

"There is air all around us. Does anyone have the exclusive rights to possess, enjoy, and exploit the air? Is air someone's private property?"

"Of course not." This time it was Melissa's turn to join the discussion.

"Why not?"

"Because air is free."

"Yes! Yes!" Roger was feigning an erotic experience. "And what is the difference between the air around us and your next breath?!"

The women looked at each other and laughed at the comical pleasure Roger seemed to be taking from all of this. There were smiles all around. And then a few moments of awkward silence. Finally, "Huh?" came from somewhere.

"The air is free! But your next breath and every breath you take belongs to you because you worked for it. You earned it, and you deserve it. Because you have a right to it, to work for that next breath because you have a natural right to life. It is as immoral to impugn your natural rights to the exclusive use and enjoyment of your private property—you sacrificed the limited time of your life in exchange for the exclusive rights to enjoy these objects—as it is to impugn your natural rights to the agency over your body. And while the air we breathe and the water that falls from the sky is free—and by 'free,' I mean unbound and immune to claim—that is not true of water in a pond that someone dug on the land they acquired lawfully or pumped from a well by the sweat of their brow. That water—unlike rain—is private property, in that someone has exclusive rights to possess, enjoy, and exploit it."

"What if someone is starving?" asked Sandy. "Or dying of thirst? Don't they have rights?"

"You're terrified aren't you, Sandy?" Roger's eyes bored into Sandy's. "You are so very fearful that you wasted your life in anger at existence that you must resist the unassailable logic and moral authority of natural law and retreat to the ramparts of the margins to initiate another attack. Unable to support your hardened and internalized belief systems you must change the subject and commence another argument. And when people like you have power, they use their power to censor and shut down debate by force to defend ideas they cannot support with reason and logic."

The mood went from jovial amusement at Roger's antics to a tense silence.

"Come on, Sandy," Roger pleaded. "I could never have hoped to be able to reach you 'Before.' And I am shocked we got as far as we did in this exchange. You are going to have to make some adjustments, and the first thing you are going to have to do is to stop insisting that you have the moral high-ground—because you most certainly do not. You are going to have to learn to trade value propositions without resorting to or relying on coercion, and you are going to need the good-will of the very people you are conditioned to despise if you are going to survive." Roger scoffed loudly and swatted his hand at the air and strode off. "Ah! Come on! We've made some progress, but we've still got a way to go."

Up ahead was a road sign that said:

State Road 41E
North to Shady Grove, KY, Turn Right
South to Cumberland, TN, Turn Left

*****

A dark single bulb traffic signal swayed in the breeze at the intersection of 41E. The four corners were undeveloped but with the ground graded flat in anticipation of a future commercial enterprise. A sign said, "Available." Well, that didn't pan out. Though it was close to solar noon, their shadows stretched in front of them. Roger guessed they had a little over five hours of light left, and he hoped to make it to Annie's friends' home in less than three and a half hours. That would give them time to inspect the area before deciding where to sleep for the night.

While not a six-lane interstate highway, 41E was a major artery through this part of rural America—emphasis on the past tense. Today, nothing moved on the road for as far as they could see in either direction. Walking north on the east side of the highway, they could see another traffic signal at the top of a long hill about a mile away.

"What do you say we make for that traffic signal at the top of the hill and take five?" Roger suggested.

There was no response. This morning the hike felt invigorating. Ten miles and 4 hours later, and it was one-foot-in-front-of-the-other with no time or energy for chit-chat. The walk down the grade to a bridge over a canyon and another small river was pleasant enough, but the hike up to the traffic signal was long and physically taxing. They were not out for a walk after work. They were half-way into a twenty-mile forced march on a cold day unsure about where they would spend the long and bitter night ahead.

As they got closer to the top of the hill, a figure appeared on the east side of the highway directly in their path. Nothing was threatening about this figure. It seemed to be a woman, and she seemed to be waiting for them. When they got closer, the woman waved to them and then walked to the northeast of the intersection and disappeared from view. Alarmed by this, Roger suggested that they cross the highway to the west side. They did so, but after marching another hundred yards uphill, they could see the woman again. She was standing and waving to them, signaling them to come to her, and standing on a curb between an egress on either side—one on 41E and the other on the north side of the intersecting highway—of a gas station and convenience store. A sign for a country fried chicken franchise stood unlit beneath the price sign of the various grades of fuel.

When they entered the intersection, the woman called to them. "Help me! Please!"

"I don't think we should stop here," said Roger. "There isn't anything we can do for her."

But Sandy was already crossing the intersection on her way to the woman. The rest of the party remained on the other side of 41E. Mindy looked back and forth from Roger and Sandy, unsure of what to do. Florence decided to follow Sandy, and that clinched it for Mindy who followed on Florence's heals. Roger kept walking north. Melissa caught up with him and grabbed his hand to stop him.

"Please," she whispered as Roger turned to face her. Her eyes pleaded with him. Melissa did not let go of Roger's hand and led him across the street following the other women in their party who were following the stranger to a car in the parking lot. When

Sandy and Florence got to the car, they turned around suddenly and darted back the way they had come, met up with Mindy, and stopped. Roger and Melissa stopped where they were, about 25 yards from where Sandy, Florence, and Mindy were now standing.

"Please help us!" the woman from the road cried. "Please! We need help! We need help!"

Florence looked back to Melissa and Melissa dropped Roger's hand.

"There's a dead kid in that car!" Florence shouted back to Roger and Melissa.

"Oh, no," Roger said to himself as much as anyone. He could see it all. This woman has been here for lord-knows how long, waiting for help. Her child dies of starvation, dehydration, exposure or dysentery—it doesn't matter—and she's gone mad. Roger looked back to the woman. From this distance, Roger can see that she is emaciated, with sunken eyes and blistered lips. What did Annie say to him when they were leaving?

From what I have gathered from some of our neighbors, the fields along the highways are a grizzly sight. Like what you saw over by the Mormons times a hundred. You are going to have to harden your heart. You are in no position to be a hero.

Roger grabbed Melissa's hand and said, "We are not in any position to save anyone but ourselves; this is a self-rescue mission. Some people will survive this; most people will not. Come with me if you want to live."

Melissa hesitated, but only for a second. She called back to Florence, "Let's go!"

Florence, Sandy, and Mindy looked back and saw Melissa holding Roger's hand and walking away.

Sandy gave Florence a second to say something, but she was speechless. "Where the fuck are you going, Melissa?! And with him?!" Sandy screamed.

Roger stopped, shed his backpack onto the ground, and reached into it with both hands producing a large semi-automatic pistol in his right hand and an unidentifiable object in his left. Roger stomped over to Sandy, Mindy, and Florence, pointing the barrel of the firearm directly at Sandy's face. Her expression went from rage to abject fear in an instant.

"Okay, Sandy," Roger shouted. "Give her your food!"

"What?!"

"I think you heard me, Sandy. I said, give that woman all of your food."

"What? Why?!"

"Because she is starving! Now, give it to her, or I am going to blow your head off."

Florence and Mindy backed slowly away from Sandy and Roger.

"And give her your coat! Can't you see she is cold, you heartless bitch?"

"I'm not..." was all that came out of Sandy's mouth. She looked to Mindy and Florence, her face pleading with them to do something.

"What the hell are you two waiting for?" Roger asked Mindy and Florence. "Give this woman your sleeping bags!"

"Roger," Mindy said in her mild voice. "You are not making any sense! If we give her our sleeping bags, we will freeze. We won't survive!"

Roger dropped the hand holding the gun to his side and said, "You mean to tell me you that your rights to life and property and any responsibility you might have to others are yours alone to determine? And you are picking this moment to exercise your right of self-determination? Even if it means that this woman will suffer? Well, what do you know? In spite of yourselves, your nobility lurks just beneath the surface."

He held up his left hand and displayed the ammo clip for the handgun and then dry fired the weapon so that all would know the gun was not loaded. He turned around and walked to Melissa, offered her his hand and said, "You coming? 'Cause I'm leaving."

Melissa took his hand and walked towards the road without looking back.

About a minute later Sandy, Mindy, and Florence gathered themselves and, ignoring the cries of the woman they just met, followed Roger and Melissa without leaving any of their private property behind.

Chapter 10

Shady Grove was a small incorporated city in the state of Kentucky with a population of 4,500. It was also the county seat in a rural county with a population of nearly 20,000. There were little industry and no major corporate employers in the county. The biggest employer was the state and county governments—the various law enforcement agencies, the county jail, the county school system, the courthouse. For all intents and purposes, the "War on Drugs" was the largest employer in rural America. And if you could get a government job you took a government job—even if it meant kicking your neighbor's door down in the middle of the night, threatening to murder him with firearms, and putting him in a cage for a "crime" that had no victim. Human Beings throughout history have always done strange and immoral things for money and status.

There were a couple of fast food restaurants along the highway and several more downtown. A few people commuted to Nashville. And there were several professional practices in the county—two accountants and two dentists, to be exact. The rest of the residents were retirees getting by on social security or single mothers with children eking out an existence from public assistance and the transient men that accompany them—most of whom had criminal records care of the "War on Drugs" that made finding employment difficult. And then there were the nearly 1,500 members of the Mennonite community living in a settlement about ten miles outside of the city limits. But they did have the same post office address—Shady Grove. Hence the label, the Shady Grove Mennonite community. Some people called them "horse-and-buggy Mennonites," others called them "Old Order Mennonites." They referred to themselves as, "Mennonites," with no qualifiers. The thousands of visitors that came to visit their settlement each year thought they were "Amish," but they can be forgiven their error as the Amish and Mennonites descended from the same Anabaptists who fled Europe for William Penn's experiment with religious freedom in colonial Pennsylvania.

They were a unique lot, the Mennonites living outside of Shady Grove. Nearly 50 years earlier, several Anabaptist groups, both Mennonite and Amish, coalesced around a leader who felt that their church groups were becoming too worldly. Forty families bought grass and forest land along the Kentucky-Tennessee border and set to work as farmers and artisans. By outward appearances, the Anabaptists eschewed electricity and all motorized vehicles, equipment, implements, and tools. Horses provided most of the power to farm, mill, and transport but there were two water-wheel powered sawmills in the settlement. Unlike the Anabaptist groups that they descended from, these families rejected tradition in favor of intention. Their decision to rebuff the use of electricity was not due to their traditions. No, the decision to exclude electric power and motorized contrivances from their lives were made *intentionally*—and there is a big difference. Of course, there was plenty of tradition in their rules for living, the "*Ordnung.*" And though there was no written list, all thoroughly understand the code of conduct that church members were expected to live by. They believed in the teachings and divinity of Jesus of Nazareth and a literal interpretation of the Bible. A critical philosophical tenant of Anabaptist life and practice was Gelassenheit—yielding, letting go, and submission to the will of G-d. Gelassenheit manifests itself in the individual as a tranquil and serene bearing and personal composure. They dressed plainly and believed that they must present a calm and modest appearance to their neighbors and their Lord, deal fairly in commerce, practice simplicity and integrity at all times, and live in community with one another.

After the brutality they suffered in Europe, the people living in the Mennonite settlement outside of Shady Grove, Kentucky, lived in peace with—and apart from—the world for a dozen generations here in America. They could have never imagined the trials and tests that Providence would send their way.

Chapter 11

On average, at any given moment nearly 20 million Americans are behind the wheel of their personal vehicle and almost 1 million big-rig trucks. That number swells during the morning and evening rush hours and shrinks during the hours between midnight and 5 am. The average vehicle's fuel tank is just over half full. 42,000 FAA supervised flights take off and land with over 2.5 million passengers onboard. And while the airports have backup generators for air-traffic-control, radar, and runway lights to land the planes in the air safely, once landed those planes were grounded indefinitely, stranding over a million people far from home during the worst humanitarian crisis in history. These data points might seem obvious, but the repercussions of these circumstances for people caught out on the road in the immediate aftermath of the complete and total shut-down of the American power grid were inconceivable. Indescribable. Unthinkable.

The nation lost electrical power and communications in the early evening on Halloween—Trick or Treat! —and the weather in the continental United States east of the Mississippi River during November was unseasonably cold and wet. A blast of cold air out of Canada left overnight temperatures in the mid-teens for the entire third week of November as far south as Nashville. The upshot of it was that by early December a quarter of the population had already succumbed, and exit visas were imminent for another 25% who wouldn't be around for eggnog and a kiss under the mistletoe. You couldn't even say they would be "pushing up daisies" or "on the other side of the grass" or any of the other morbid epigrams men like to say as they "whistle past the cemetery," because most of them would rot where they fell and died.

Roger, Melissa, Sandy, Florence, and Mindy were walking through a lesser sample of the catastrophe. Abandoned vehicles littered the highway, left by their drivers where they ran out of fuel. The bodies of these unfortunate people, some dressed in shorts and flip-flops, who just happened to be traveling when

World War III broke out and winter set in, lay where they fell. Thankfully, that was on the shoulders and fields beside the road leaving the pavement—for the most part—free of death and decay. Roger walked directly on the yellow centerline to maintain as much distance as possible from the depressing spectacle of suffering and loss surrounding them as his mind wandered in worry between his sons and the students who traveled with him to the Garden of Eden commune. They reached the intersection Roger was looking for four hours after solar noon at this latitude. Abstracts, such as "Central Time Zone," lost their meaning. If they had a copy of "The Farmer's Almanac" they would have known that sunrise was 6:40:26 am, solar noon 11:34:32 am, and sunset 4:28:38 with a half hour of twilight on either end, and the day would be 9 hours and 48 minutes in length. Of course, in the future noon would mean noon, when the sun had reached its zenith, and all times would be local. None of them had a wristwatch as they relied on their cell phones for the time. Optimists all, they still carried their cellphone in their backpacks.

Looking down at the piece of brown-paper-bag Annie drew her map on Roger turned west onto a small road carved in the side of the woods. A half mile of moderate incline and Roger saw the landmark Annie described, a small quarry etched into a wooded hill. There should be a mailbox on the other side of the road a hundred yards further west with the number "300" on it, but there was no mailbox to be seen. But there was a gravel drive artificially covered with forest debris leading north into the woods. When Roger came closer to inspect the driveway, he noticed a square shaped hole in the ground adjacent to the road and the drive.

"We're here," Roger said.

"Thank G-d," said Melissa. "I'm exhausted."

Florence glared at Melissa but said nothing.

"I don't know these people," Roger said. "But it looks to me like they took their mailbox out of the ground and piled brush along the entrance to their driveway, so they might not be partial to visitors. Annie asked me to stop by and give them a message and the jars we are carrying for them. Maybe they will put us up for the night, or maybe we will be sleeping in our tents. But I think we've had enough walking for today."

"Amen to that," Sandy said.

The woods swallowed them the moment they stepped onto the driveway. Bare trees and forest mists on either side, it felt like they were walking in a high-ceilinged tunnel, and while it was late afternoon out on the road, twilight descended upon them here in the woods. After a couple of twists and turns they came out in a small clearing about a quarter of a mile from the road, and the twilight lifted, and it was late afternoon once more. A small cabin stood at the farthest part of the turnaround loop of the gravel driveway. There was a small shed to the left of the cabin and a poultry yard with cedar posts and chicken wire to contain the birds were arranged next to the house on the right. A tall leafless shade tree stood between the house and the coop. All of the chickens and ducks were lined up against the coop fence nearest the house paying rapt attention to two people who appeared to be walking in circles in front of the cabin. Roger signaled in silence for his party to stop, but there was no need. They were frozen in place. And not by fear. They were far enough away that the couple in front of the cabin was no immediate threat, and they didn't appear armed.

"What the fuck are they doing?" Sandy whispered.

No one answered, and after the women traded glances and shrugs, they looked to Roger and saw that he was smiling from ear to ear.

"They're dancing," Roger said and laughed. "I think. It looks like a cross between Tai Chi and Cirque Du Sole performed by people with absolutely no talent."

A portly middle-aged couple, both with shoulder length unruly grey hair and dressed in tie-dyed t-shirts were dancing in slow motion across their front lawn, jumping onto a miniature trampoline, and then swinging—well, sort of swinging; they dragged their feet on the ground and kept falling and laughing—on a rope hanging from the shade tree, then repeating the routine. The chickens and ducks seemed mesmerized by the dancers, as were Roger and his companions. After several passes through their sequence, they did several full rotations just slightly faster than slow motion with their arms spread and their faces turned toward the sky before falling into a pile of leaves and giggling hysterically. It was infectious, and the new arrivals couldn't contain their laughter.

"Something's wrong with them," said Sandy. "They're not right in the head."

"Yea?" laughed Florence. "Fuck that. I want what they're having!"

"I think Annie tried to warn me about this… but I misunderstood," Roger said. "I hate to interrupt them." Roger hesitated, and then called to the couple. "Hello!"

They stopped laughing and struggled to sit upright; it took them a couple of tries.

"Who said that!?" the man shouted, still unable to right himself.

"Hello!" Roger repeated. "We are friends of Annie Ackroyd! She sent us to check on you! We mean you no harm!"

The man squinted in Roger's direction. Then he patted the front of his t-shirt with both hands, located a pocket, and retrieved a pair of glasses.

"Look, Andrea! It appears we have company!"

And then he fell back in the leaves again giggling hysterically.

"Hi!" the woman called and waved to them before she too fell back into the leaves in hysterics.

"Oh, boy!" Roger said as he chuckled. "This is not what I was expecting." Roger paused and looked around at the women in his party—all smiling broadly—and said, "I think we will be okay. They don't look dangerous to me."

Roger walked over to the couple laying in the leaves. The man looked up at him and said, "Wow! You're really tall, man! You don't look like you're from the IRS!" he burst out laughing again and turned to his companion lying next to him and said, "He doesn't look like IRS to me! Bwahahahaha!!!"

"Let me guess! You're from the government, and you're here to help us?!" the woman asked before she too fell into diabolical laughter.

Now the two of them were moving their arms and legs in unison, and the man said, "Can you guess what we're doing now? We are making snow angels! Bwahahaha!"

"But with leaves! Bwahahaha!!" the woman he called Andrea cried out.

"Okay, okay, okay…" the man on the ground said. "Help me up."

Roger gave him his hand and pulled him off the ground like a sack of potatoes.

"Thank you, Annie's friend! I'm Billy and this Andrea! I'm sorry we're not making sense. We're all fucked up. Mushroom tea. Would you like some? We've got some fine spleef too!"

Billy looked like what Roger imagined Ben Franklin looked like at 65 years of age.

"Spleef?" Roger asked.

"Weed. You know, Marijuana?"

"Annie was worried about you two," Roger replied. "But I get the sense you two are doing fine. My name is Roger Little; this is Melissa, Sandy, Mindy, and Florence."

Florence noticed that Roger introduced Melissa first and her last.

"Annie sent you all the way to check up on us? Wow! Far out, man."

Andrea was out of the leaves and standing with the help of Melissa and Mindy.

"We are on our way to the Troyer farm in the Shady Grove Mennonite settlement," Roger said. "Annie asked us to check in on you. She said she expected you would still be alive."

"Duuuude!" Billy said. "Don't be a buzzkill. Of course, we're alive! Cripes! I'm tripping my ass off. I'm all fucked up!" and he burst out laughing again.

"Be quiet, Billy." The woman stepped between Billy and Roger. "Hi! I'm Andrea." And she held out her hand.

Roger smiled and took her hand and noticed in the fading light that her pupils were completely dilated. He replied.

"I get the feeling this is going to be an evening to remember."

Chapter 12

Annie's concern for her friends Billy and Andrea was misplaced as they were uniquely adapted to the current circumstances. Billy had a thriving marijuana and psychedelic mushroom business, and his contacts from this enterprise proved invaluable in the times "After." Roger wondered how it was that Billy's customers didn't just kill him and take his stash, and Billy mentioned that this was indeed a concern. But Billy was able to communicate to his customers that the price of marijuana, mushrooms, and all other homebrewed or concocted drugs or medicines or alcohol was on its way to zero: now that the government ceased creating black markets via prohibition. But like any other agricultural commodity consumers would need people with expertise to farm these crops and teach others how to do so—especially since it was easy to confuse mushroom species and a single misidentification could kill you. Andrea and Billy traded most of their stash with their customers for necessities, including a terrifying man by the name of Lonard— "don't call me Leonard; I hate to be called Leonard"—Hedges at such a reasonable rate of exchange that there was no incentive to do them any harm. And now Billy and Andrea were well provisioned for the winter—for food, that is; they were desperately low on firewood despite living in the middle of a forest—and they planned on making a living as marijuana farmers come spring.

Hedges had been a guest of the county jail awaiting trial on drug and weapons charges. On the fourth day "After," the county jailer felt he had no choice but to free the 18 hungry men and two women in his custody. The sheriff was so furious with the jailer for releasing the inmates without checking with him that his deputy thought he might shoot the jailer then and there.

"What the hell, Clarence?!" Sheriff Don Daily roared at the jailer, Clarence Crane. "You just gotdam let 'em go?! Are you out of your fucking mind??!!"

"What the hell d'ju expect me to do, Don?!" Clarence responded. "They were starving! Should I just leave them in their cells to die? They all got kin living here in the county. I don't need to be getting killed over this job."

"What? Are you hand to mouth over here, Clarence!? Don't you got a pantry full of food?!"

"Yea, we did, Don. But I got to sleep, just like you. And the guards, cook, and other people working here emptied the storeroom and never came back. I got no lights, no heat, no hot water, no food, and no idea when I will get resupplied. I haven't seen you for days, and the phone and radios ain't working. So, I made the decision not to starve 20 inmates to death. What would you have said to me if you came here in a few days and we had 20 bodies rotting in the cells?"

In the first days "After," people expected that the power would come back on at any time, and the sheriff and his deputies maintained their patrol cars to try to help the stranded motorists on 41E with fuel pumped with a generator from one of the local gas stations that did not sell out in the immediate aftermath. On the sixth day "After," they found the bodies of the sheriff, his second in command, and the local criminal court judge in the court square; hacked to pieces. After that, the remaining law enforcement officers working for the county sheriff and the Shady Grove city police department fled or went into hiding. It didn't matter much. By early December half of the former inmates and former officers were dead, many by their own hand, or knocking on death's door. By the end of March, it would be closer to 90%. Cold and hunger is a deadly combination.

"How do you know all of this?" Roger asked Billy. Billy was nursing the after-effects of the mushrooms the night before. He was moving and speaking a lot slower than usual.

"A woman who lives up the road is friendly with Andrea. She worked for the county. It's a small community."

"Does this Lonard Hedges have a gang?" Roger asked Billy

"I don't know," Billy replied "He didn't come here with anybody. But he is young and strong and fucking scary. And I get the sense he ain't afraid—of anything."

"And he came up in here with a bag full of provisions asking if he could trade for some weed?" Roger asked.

"Not exactly. He came here looking for some pot. This was a week 'After.' I gave him a couple of ounces and told him what my plans were and that I knew how to grow good weed and safe mushrooms. He took the pot and said, 'I'll bring you something fair for this.' And then he left. I was just glad to be alive, and to get him the hell out of here. The next day he came back, and my heart dropped out my ass. But he gave us ten pounds of flour, two of salt, a huge bag of corn meal, and a no. 10 can of vegetable shortening. And that was the last we saw of anybody. Go figure, eh? It turns out, he's an honest thug."

"He walked up here carrying all that?" Roger asked.

"No. He came up in here on a dirt bike with a big army duffle bag on his back, handed the food over and said he would stop by sometime. But I haven't seen him or any of my regular customers since."

"Huh! How about that!" Roger said with a will-wonders-ever-cease look on his face.

"Yea," said Billy. "It was kinda strange and a little scary, but the more I think about it, the more I think he just wanted some weed."

"It sure looks that way. And you don't know that he killed the sheriff."

"Well, someone killed three men with ties to local law enforcement. He was the only inmate being held on multiple felony charges. We just haven't got that many bad hombres here."

Roger planned on leaving that morning for the final push up to his friend's farm, but nature intervened. Florence and Sandy got their monthly period.

Roger and Billy got up early so that Roger could help him gather some larger pieces of windfall and deadfall firewood. Billy didn't have a chainsaw. He didn't even have a decent timber saw. Billy was using an ax, and a typical carpenter's crosscut saw to cut his stove wood into a size that would fit in the stove's firebox. Before he left for the woods, Roger packed his sleeping bag and backpack and left them outside next to the shade tree. When the men returned, Andrea was ready for them with an egg on cornbread sandwich. Roger thanked Andrea and hollered out for the women to move out; they had a long walk ahead of them. Melissa stepped outside of the cabin without her backpack and walked over to where Roger and Billy were eating their breakfast and stood next to Andrea for support.

"Roger, we can't go today," Melissa said. Roger waited, but she did not explain. After a few moments, Roger lowered his head towards Melissa.

"Come again?" Roger asked. "What are you talking about? We've got what? Less than eight miles to go? What's the problem?"

Melissa looked away from Roger's penetrating stare. So, Andrea spoke up.

"Two of the girls got their periods this morning," Andrea said.

Roger shook his head once, and his eyes pointed up into his brow as if he didn't comprehend what was said. He shook his head once more and then looked at Melissa.

"So, what?" Roger was stupefied. "What's that gotta do with this 'we can't go today' stuff?"

"Roger, dear," Andrea put her hand on Roger's forearm. "They don't have any sanitary materials, and at my age, I don't stock such things anymore."

Roger had to suppress a laugh. Andrea was the hippie version of Harriot of Ozzie and Harriet fame.

"Look! Periods happen," Roger said to Melissa. "What's to say that as soon as they're done that you or Mindy won't get your period? And then the weather might not cooperate. I am not waiting around hoping for the perfect day in between the menstrual cycles of four women. It might be months before we leave."

"He's got a point," Billy said from the periphery.

"Shut up, Billy," Andrea said, turning to Billy and giving him the hairy eyeball. "Mind your own business." Billy shrank from Andrea's glare.

Roger took Melissa by the arm and led her away to speak privately.

"You're right," Melissa blurted out before he could speak. "I usually get my period a couple of days after Florence gets hers."

"I don't even understand what the freaking problem is. Don't women go jogging and swimming when they have their periods?"

Melissa smirked at Roger's ignorance. "Yea... like when we have tampons and access to toilets and showers."

"Well, you must have had at least one period since the whole thing went down. How did you handle it then?"

"We were still at the Garden of Eden—not marching from dawn till dusk. And we used up the last of our sanitary napkins. There we had an outhouse and access to warm water to keep clean. Do you know what a mess this would be for a woman, hiking all day in blue jeans without tampons or napkins?"

"I forgot about this."

"Yea, well it's not the kind of thing a man has to worry about, is it?"

"No," said Roger, a little breathless. "I meant the incredible freedom that women gained with the invention of the toilet, tampons, indoor plumbing, and access to warm water and privacy. I forgot about this. Look, contrary to what your crazy friends may have told you, the social and political gains that women made during the 20th century didn't come about from brave Feminists marching around for women's rights. Technology and sanitation freed women—not Feminism. I just had a brain fart: I forgot about this."

"About what?" Melissa asked. "That women have periods? And stop repeating yourself!"

Roger was lost in thought and rubbing the back of his neck as he searched his mind.

"Hey!" Melissa shouted and pulled his arm so that he would have to face her.

"No... no... look; I've got a lot going on," Roger said, a bit absentmindedly. Then he snapped out of it. "Do you understand where we are? What the situation is?"

"What—the hell! —are you talking about?!"

"Look, we have to survive. Of course, that's first. But we have to reconstitute and recast a functioning society. Clean water, sanitation, law, and order, with escaped felons, murdered law enforcement officers, aging hippies and potheads, and women who can't walk—or work, for that matter—during their period? We've got a lot of work ahead of us." Roger was shaking his head and running his fingers and hand through his mustache and beard—he hadn't shaved in five weeks—and staring blankly at the ground. "I don't know if we are going to survive this. I just don't know if we are going to make it."

Melissa dove into his body and wrapped her arms around him. She was crying. "Please don't say that. You're frightening me!"

Melissa was a foot shorter than he was, but she fit perfectly in his arms, and he enjoyed holding her like this, and Roger held her in that warm embrace until she stopped crying. After some time, she willed herself to leave the warmth of his body and looked up into his eyes and said, "We should leave. Today. Now. You and me. And Mindy if she wants to. Sandy and Florence can catch up when they're ready."

The screaming match inside the cabin would have woke the dead along 41E. Roger was glad he was standing in the circle of the turnaround in front of Billy and Andrea's home, far from the fray. He wanted nothing to do with this. They were letting it all hang out, but so far, no one came crashing through the front window. Then the door opened, and Andrea and Billy stepped out of their cabin followed by Melissa and Mindy, both of them packed and strapped for the hike.

Andrea approached Roger and smiled kindly. "You better go," she said as she nodded and squinched up her face and took his hand in her right hand and patted it with her left.

"They are welcome to stay here," Billy said. "We could use a good long walk. We'll bring them to the harness maker's shop at the Mennonites when they are ready to go."

Roger nodded and said, "I'm sorry about this. Thank you for putting us up. It was a pleasure."

Melissa and Mindy said their goodbyes to Billy and Andrea. Then Melissa turned away and grabbed Roger's hand and held it tightly as they walked down the gravel drive to the woods.

Florence watched them through the window until they disappeared behind the trees and thought that she might get sick.

Chapter 13

Contrary to popular belief, there isn't much work to be done around a typical small farm from late fall through early spring. The livestock in the barn need feeding, the cow milked, and the rest of the time was spent harvesting, cutting, splitting, and stacking firewood until the evening feeding. Before the industrial revolution, there just wasn't much in the way of machinery to maintain and repair. As the industrial revolution took hold in agriculture, the percentage of the population working on farms plummeted from one in three to one in a hundred. And the people who remained on a working farm had a bit more to do, and more opportunities outside of agriculture to earn extra income. The socio-economic model of the Shady Grove Mennonites was very close to the model of colonial New England, but with several essential components missing. Unlike the Amish living in the region, the Mennonites endeavored to stay away from off-farm employment—this left them with far less of a cash income, and that forced them to be very creative both in self-sufficiency and in the manufacture of artisanal goods at home when not working the farm. Of course, over time they became just as dependent on industrial manufacturers for cloth, leather, finished metal products, machinery, hardware, and glass as every other American. A practical people, they realized their liabilities quickly. Though figuring out what to do about it seemed to be taking a little longer.

Philip Troyer was the harness maker for the settlement. Horses cannot work and pull equipment without a harness, bridle, and reins. It occurred to Philip as he took stock in his shop that he was not a harness maker at all. He was a harness assembler. He bought all of the thread, leather, synthetic fabric, buckles, belts, and metal fasteners, spikes, and studs to assemble a harness through a catalog from an Amish manufacturer in Lancaster, Pennsylvania. These materials got delivered by truck, and the trucks were not running. He had enough materials on hand to repair several dozen harnesses, but the community had over 500 workhorses and over 300 buggy horses—this was a big problem.

Leather wore out. Parts broke. One thousand five hundred people lived in the community, and Philip knew it would be impossible to feed them all without traction to work the crop fields. He assumed the community's buggy makers were fretting over similar issues.

But these challenges were insignificant within the essence of a new overarching paradox in their worldview— "In the world but not of it," taken to the extreme—that the new circumstances presented. No one in their community had ever even heard of Aristotle or his middle way, and the idea that vice is an excess of virtue would be as incomprehensible to the Anabaptists as a bottle of ketchup on a table in a pricey French restaurant to a gourmet. Their faith called on them to go and live separately from the people of the world, but there was a fly in that ointment. They were forced to confront the harsh truth that the wall they built between their community and the people of the outside world was rather low and that plenty of goods and services passed over that barrier in both directions. Philip approached this problem from every conceivable direction. He worked at this hour after hour, and though he backtracked through the maze in his mind to reconsider every possible change, of course, he arrived at the same place—nowhere. Their people intentionally limited their interactions with the outside world, and in the weeks and months "After" this was the difference between living and dying as they were not immediately dependent on outside suppliers for food, water, and heat—the things most necessary to survive a long, cold winter. But what about next year? And the year after? Would there be anyone left to separate themselves from? And if not, where would they get the know-how to provide their people with all of the goods and services they depended on the outside world for?

And the English! They were so clever! They had every material comfort imaginable. But it wasn't enough. They had to build ships and planes to carry men and weapons and bombs all over the world to defend their conveniences and comforts. And now they are starving and freezing by the millions here at home.

Philip sat down at his desk that he kept tucked in a small corner office—more like a large closet—of his workshop. His office was a place of refuge for Philip as well as the place he kept his paperwork. It suddenly occurred to him that paperwork was probably a thing of the past. Not that he had very much compared to the people living out there in American society. But it was now zero: no more sales tax reports, no more property tax bills; this was a mixed blessing. There were also no more livestock feed bills or income from leather work for outsiders. They wanted to live apart, and now they were entirely on their own.

"Dad!" Philip's youngest son, Ezra, screamed up the stairwell from the front door. "Three people are walking up the driveway," Ezra said in their German dialect. "One of them looks like Roger Little!"

Philip rose from his chair and slid down the wall and out of his cubbyhole to a window on the south side of his workshop building. He was on the second floor—where they did their measuring, cutting, and sowing—and looking down the hill of their driveway that ran between two livestock ponds, he saw a very tall man followed by two women. Philip couldn't make out his features from this distance, but his gait looked familiar and he knew only two men that tall, so it was likely Roger Little or Jason Thomas, an Englishman who lived in an Amish community a day or two's ride to the north. As the man came closer, Philip recognized Roger Little.

"Well, perhaps the good Lord works in mysterious ways," Philip said to himself as he went down the steps and out the door.

Roger, Melissa, and Mindy stopped for a moment at the entrance to the Troyer farm.

"Please remember to be mindful of their sensibilities at all times. I don't know how this is going to go, or how we are going to be received. I hope to petition them for shelter and assistance for the winter. They are good and devout people of faith, but they live very differently from anything you've ever seen, including the Mormons."

"You don't need to worry about us," said Mindy.

Roger took that to mean that he did have something to worry about when Sandy and Florence arrived, but let it go. He had enough on his mind.

Chapter 14

Roger was surprised at the warmth of the welcome he received. He and Philip had always been friendly, more than mere acquaintances, admittedly, but they were hardly close friends. For Philip, Roger was an economic and social connection to the society at large beyond Shady Grove. And for Roger, Philip was a gateway into a fascinating society constructed on an astonishing foundation of faith, philosophy, and community filled with paradoxes and inconsistencies: but which nevertheless had evolved and survived in a tiny universe parallel to the giant one that Roger inhabited.

A visit to Philip's homestead was a break from the oppressive gauntlet of the job, car, commute, apartment, shopping, electronic entertainment, and restaurant hamster-wheel that made up Roger's experience of reality. Here, at the Troyer family homestead, he had often sought refuge from the storm—working firewood at the Christmas break, tapping maple trees and cooking syrup over an outdoor woodfire in mid-winter, working a team of horses in a hayfield on a beautiful spring day, and sweltering in the heat of summer getting the hay into the barn. The Troyer family welcomed him to their table. They dined on a modest fare, the European peasant foods of stews and soups and simple bread. Roger would have done anything to live like this; to work exposed to the elements and return home to the solace of a simple meal and warmth of a woodfire and soft light of a kerosene lamp or candle. Anything, perhaps but give up the prestige and comforts that came with a tenured professor's position. He always felt Philip's lifestyle was the peach out of reach, hanging so low that he could smell its enchanting scent and see its mouthwatering colors, close enough that with a mighty leap into the unknown he might have had it, but too afraid to dare to leave the sureness of the ground beneath his feet.

That first night, Mindy and Melissa were given quarters in the home of a family who ran one of the community's four dairies, milking sixteen Jersey cows by hand at 4 am and again at 4 pm. Roger was settled in a small one-room cabin built on Philip's property by the Troyer's fourth son, Matthew, to house his leather workshop—it seemed the entire family worked leather—since Matthew had gone to court a woman in another Mennonite community over 400 miles away in Missouri. The cabin was a bit drafty and not well insulated, but it had a new wood cook stove, a twin bed, and mattress with sheets, blankets, two pillows, a wooden milk-crate for a nightstand complete with a candle in a jar, and a wood-fired hot water kettle a few steps outside the door. Roger's sense of and demand for comfort was brought to heel over the past five weeks, and as he looked his quarters over, he felt overwhelming gratitude.

The cabin had a shower of sorts. The bottom half of a 55-gallon metal drum sat perched on a heavy wood frame over a galvanized livestock tank. The metal drum had a shower head screwed into the bottom of it, and the livestock tank sported a drain. Two shower curtains hung from a circular bracket, and a stepping stool and a step ladder stood folded in the tub next to a bar of soap in a metal basket affixed to the livestock tank. Roger figured that Matthew could not reach the shower head without the stool and used the ladder to fill the metal drum with hot water. The ingenuity of these people and their solutions to practical problems never ceased to amaze him.

It occurred to Roger as he gathered wood from the shed for the stove and kettle and carried two buckets of water that he pumped by hand from the well that the famously slow pace of life of the people living here that drew visitors by the tens of thousands was not an option. In the absence of electricity, hot and cold running water, central heating, and fossil fuel powered engines life is different in many respects, and the slow pace of life is just one of these differences. Going from one paradigm to the other in the space of a day was a shock. But everything is relative, and after five weeks of sleeping rough Roger turned into the soft bed in the warm cabin sure he was in heaven.

Roger woke and dressed before first light and headed down to the barn complex to wait for Philip. After a while, he heard the men, Philip and the two unmarried sons still living at home, as they left the house for the morning chores of feeding and checking on the well-being of the livestock. They completed their tasks in the twilight between first light and sunrise and then headed back to the house where Philip's daughters served them breakfast. The women did not join them, and Roger assumed that they had already eaten.

"So, tell us," said Philip. "I think it is fair to say that we are dying of curiosity." Philip and his sons, Ezra and Jonah, leaned toward Roger.

Roger told them he was traveling and met these women at a campsite the day the electric power went down—which was true; there was no reason to mention the nature of the campground—and that he decided to stay there rather than return to Nashville. He recounted how they were running out of food, their decision to leave, meeting the Cluff's, Annie Ackroyd, and Billy and Andrea, and their experiences on the road.

When Roger finished his tale, Philip pushed back from the table, crossed his legs and let his arms fall to his side and said, "Whew. That is some story. You're lucky to be alive."

"I never felt that I was in danger, but without the kindness and generosity of the people we met along the way, I suppose we would have died."

Roger repeated Annie's anecdote about the chicken and hog houses to Philip.

Philip shook his head and said, "Yes, Annie is quite a character, isn't she?"

There was a pause in the conversation, and all of the men stared at nothing on the table in front of them. After a while, Philip broke the silence.

"Okay. Well, now what? I mean, there isn't anything we can do about it. What's done is done."

"Well, first things first. I need to survive the winter. I came here hoping that I might make myself useful in exchange for food and a warm place to sleep. I realize that you don't want outside influence, so that you won't want me around for long. But I won't survive the winter out there. I need your help."

Philip noticed he didn't say "we."

"At any other time, outside influence would be my foremost concern. Right now, I think we are all a little off balance. And I think you are here for a reason. But getting back to survival, what is going to happen to the people out there?"

Roger didn't hesitate. "Most of them are going to die. But even if 90% perish over the winter, Kentucky and Tennessee will still have a million survivors. Life will go on. But what kind of life? Will we sink into barbarism, raiding and killing each other? Or can we reestablish an intelligent civilization again before that happens?"

"You think 90% of the people will die?

"At least. Maybe 95%. It all depends on what kind of winter we have. They don't have a way to stay warm, and they don't have any food. Without snow removal equipment a serious snowstorm could kill everyone within its field in a matter of weeks."

"Oohoo!" Philip was not dramatic—this was shocking to him. "All of this, just from the loss of electricity?"

"Yes. It is hard to imagine. We built nuclear bombs and massive armies and navies to defend our nation from an invasion that could never have happened only to build our empire out of the loose sand of dependence on a system that a child could kick over or a small wave might wash away."

Philip's elbows were on the table with his hands laced together in front of him. He looked to his sons, first to Jonah and then Ezra, and then back to Roger. "'The water prevailed upon the earth one hundred and fifty days.'"

"The Flood," replied Roger, nodding his head. "I guess that's the closest biblical event to what is unfolding here. One hundred and fifty days without electric power and in a thousand years people will still remember this as 'The Famine.' *The Seven Years of Famine* will not even rate an honorable mention."

An uneventful week of unseasonably cold weather passed. Roger convinced the Bishop and Deacons not to slaughter the cattle and to use the strategy that many of the western states employ: "fence out" rather than "fence in." Instead of fencing the beef cattle inside of pastures they would fence the cattle out of the crop fields and let the cows graze anywhere they pleased.

Roger worked on a crew of men who were gathering the barbed wire and posts from the pastures and redeploying them around the crop fields. Hogs would remain confined for this year, and they would revisit turning them out next year. But for now, they had enough corn from the surrounding industrial farms for their hogs and milk cows for this winter; they just had to go out and get it.

Philip's son Ezra was driving a buggy with a hot lunch for the men working on Roger's fencing crew. When the men saw him, they stopped what they were doing and gathered around the large horse-drawn wagon they used to move men and material and sat along its edge.

Ezra pulled up and signaled Roger to come over to his side of the buggy.

"Your friends arrived at my father's workshop about a half an hour ago," Ezra said. "There are two men with them that you didn't mention—Karl and Evan. They seem to know the women. My father wants to know if you were expecting them."

"No, I wasn't expecting anyone else," replied Roger. "They must have left the campsite after us and followed us here. I told your father when I arrived that I told the people walking with me that there might not be a place here for them. Maybe I should go back with you and tell him he is under no obligation."

"No, that's okay. I'll tell my father what you said. Do you have work for them here on the fencing crew?"

"Ezra, I expect we could put them to work all winter; this is a big job."

Ezra smiled at that. "Well, if they are willing to work, it's just another couple of plates around the table." And then Ezra slapped the reins, and his horse ran for home.

The new arrivals were quartered separately, with Sandy and Florence joining Mindy and Melissa at the dairy and Karl and Evan lodged at the home of Daniel Hoover.

That evening, Roger heard the cabin door open and turned to see Melissa step inside with her backpack. The moment of truth had arrived—or at least a moment of truth. It is impossible to tell

112

the difference until after the fact. With Florence's arrival, Roger felt that Melissa would have to make a decision, and here it was. Roger gave her a gentle smile. They had not seen each other since they arrived a week earlier.

"This place... this community..." Melissa stammered. "This is just incredible."

Roger felt a flood of relief. He had thought about this moment often, to be sure, but Melissa would have to close the distance. Roger wouldn't meet her with so much as a single step, never mind meeting her halfway.

Yes, it is," Roger said. "And yes, they are. They have that effect on people. I once said that the best way to describe them is to imagine a village of Samurai Warriors, but with workhorses and plows instead of warhorses and weapons."

Melissa breathed a soft laugh and nodded. "That's perfect. Well, for the men anyway. I just spent two hours with Mrs. Fisher and three of their daughters cooking and cleaning up and then the evening milking—and not a moment of discontent between them. Don't they know that cooking is drudgery?"

That got a chuckle out of Roger.

"Yep. They make you feel pretty inadequate, don't they? Just wait. It gets a lot worse."

Melissa did not respond to that. She met his gaze directly, blinked a few times, but didn't look away, her mouth slightly open. After a few moments like that, Melissa stepped in and placed her body close to his.

"Do you want me?" Her voice was soft and thick.

Roger sighed. "That's a silly question, Melissa. You're a beautiful young woman. Of course, I am powerfully attracted to you. But what do you want with me? Think about that before you answer."

"I want a man. A real man. Like you."

"I'm flattered. But do you want a man 'like' me? Or do you want me?"

"I don't know," Melissa playfully replied as she put her arms around Roger and hugged him tightly. "I haven't had you yet." She did not look up at Roger but snuggled her head into his chest.

"Are you sure about this?" He was breathing deep, and his heart was pounding.

She bit his nipple through his shirt and then kissed his neck before whispering up towards his ear.

"Yes, Roger. I'm sure."

Melissa left Roger's cabin before the morning twilight showed itself but not before they indulged themselves for the third time and walked to the Fisher's for breakfast and the morning milking duties. She arrived at the kitchen just as one of the Fisher girls came outside to fetch kindling and stove billets. The Fisher family women never said a word, but Melissa had the feeling that they knew she didn't sleep there last night.

After Melissa left the cabin, Roger ruminated over their passions. Nothing seemed amiss. She seemed comfortable with him and appeared to revel in his affections. From his training and clinical experience, Roger knew that women were far more complicated and elastic than men in these matters. But beyond the sex, Melissa seemed to enjoy touching and kissing his body. Lesbians typically experienced an extreme disgust response to the idea of sex with a man and an erect penis. He remembered a lesbian patient of his who described the male penis as "like a kind of tumor," and an erection as "a malignant growth." She was visibly and viscerally disgusted by the image.

Disgust is a powerful human emotion, and it has an essential evolutionary job—it keeps us safe from spoiled, dangerous and poisonous foods, as well as dead bodies, excrement, insects, et al. so that we might survive long enough to pass on our genes to the next generation. Of course, Lesbians were not mainly concerned with passing on their genes. It seemed to Roger that their disgust response to males played a central role in preventing these women from reproducing, which to his mind was what nature intended. Along with pathological response to the only human beings who could impregnate them, it was his consistent clinical observation that these women typically scored extremely low in the ability to feel empathy. Nature gave heterosexual women an extra helping of empathy—compared to men—to help them care

114

for and raise infants and small children and get along with their male sexual partners. It would seem that nature felt that an extra dose of empathy was unnecessary in women who existentially rejected men as potential sexual partners. Roger referred to the disgust response as "heterosexual dysphoria," and was sure that Melissa didn't exhibit that condition in the slightest.

That next night, and every night for the next week, Melissa slipped away again under cover of darkness to spend the long December nights in Roger's cabin and the warmth of his bed, and then back to the dairy before dawn. After the morning milking on the third Monday since their arrival, Melissa went again to Roger's cabin. The day before, a Sunday, it rained and sleeted all day, leaving the ground too wet and muddy for fencing work. They thought they were sufficiently discreet.

There was a loud knocking on the door. Melissa and Roger looked at each other. *Who the hell can that be?*

Roger dressed quickly. All Melissa had to do was pull her long dress over her head. Roger opened the door. There, standing on the small porch of the cabin was the Mennonite Bishop. His eyes were stern, his face severe.

"Roger Little and Melissa!?" the Bishop asked in a firm-but-not-harsh voice. "I don't know the last name. You two have taken to living under one roof!"

Roger was dumbfounded. And terrified. Were they about to ask them to leave? When it appeared that Roger had nothing to say the Bishop continued.

"Do you intend to persist in sharing a bed?" the Bishop asked. "Are you hand in hand?"

"Well, I…I…" Roger stammered.

The Bishop gave Roger a few moments to stand and deliver. When Roger did not, the Bishop continued.

"Then by the power vested in me: May you love and cherish each other in good times and in bad, in plenty and in want, and may G-d bless your union and make it fruitful! I declare you two to be man and wife in the name of Jesus Christ. 'What therefore G-d hath joined together, let no man put asunder.' Good day to you."

When he finished speaking, the Bishop turned and walked off of the porch and down to the hitching post, untied his horse and got into his buggy and rode off.

Roger watched him until his buggy began to move away, and then stepped back into the cabin and closed the door. Melissa and Roger looked at each other with expressions that crossed somewhere between stunned and highly amused.

"Holy shit! I think he just married us," Roger said.

Melissa came to Roger and put her arms around his neck and said, "I guess I don't have to sneak back to the Fisher's for the evening milking." Then she stepped back from Roger and pulled her long Anabaptist dress over her head, took his hand, and pulled him to the bed.

Chapter 15

Thirty miles to the north of Shady Grove, near the Sulphur Springs state park, Ellen and Jenny Thomas, married respectively to the brothers Jason and Walter, were sharing a quiet moment in the kitchen. Jason and Ellen moved to the region nearly fifteen years ago from New York City via South Florida. The Thomas family spent the first ten years on a smallholding just outside the Shady Grove Mennonite community; for the last nearly five years, the Thomas family lived on a two-hundred-acre cattle farm next to the small Amish Settlement in a larger farming community near the park.

After three years of trial and error, Jason was failing miserably as a farmer—until he befriended the Troyer family and the Mennonites of Shady Grove. Jason quickly noticed that the Mennonite community was thriving—by every measure—while the rest of rural America appeared in desperate condition. Jason studied their socio-economic strategies and copied many of them. He learned to farm with horses, raise enough food during the growing season to feed the family all year, and to remove all of the calls and demands on his time that appeared in the form of bills in his mailbox each month. The peace of mind that came without all of the pressures to conform to modernity was a life-changing experience. Jason had the wherewithal from a lifetime of scrimping and saving to acquire enough land to make a go of it. With his new-found confidence in his abilities and the skills he learned from the Mennonites, he took the plunge, sold his smallholding at Shady Grove and bought a fair-sized spread thirty miles north near Sulphur Springs by cobbling together several parcels of land with an Amish farm and home. Of course, Jason and Ellen brought electricity into the farmhouse first thing—but only to power a refrigerator and an internet connection. The farmhouse and domestic hot water were heated with wood, Ellen cooked on an Amish wood cook stove, and the barns and outbuildings remained without electric power. For electric power tools, Jason used a gasoline generator. The family had a dozen kerosene lamps and lanterns.

The Thomas family lived simply, and life was good. And then the power went out, and the mad scramble for survival began. Without electric power, the cities were death traps. Jason's son, Roone and girlfriend Pilar, walked three-hundred miles to Jason's farm from their college in Atlanta. Jason's good friend of many years, Rabbi Martin Weiss and his wife Miriam, and daughters Hanna, and Aviva walked out of New York City in the hours before the blackout started. They arrived the following day at the home of Walter and Jenny Thomas where they hoped to rest before continuing their journey north and away from the city. There they found Walter, Jenny, and their son, Manny and pregnant wife, Danielle packing the contents of his gas station's convenience grocery store onto his sailboat along the Hudson River in Tarrytown, N.Y. With winter fast approaching, Martin Weiss made the fateful—and fortunate—decision to throw his lot in with Walter, and after a harrowing month's long journey by sail and foot, the erstwhile traveling companions made it to Jason's farm.

A little more than a week after Walter's arrival to his brother's farm, McCoy O'Neil and his son Trevor sought refuge and assistance at the Thomas homestead. The O'Neil men were traveling with eight starving teenaged girls they found camped out at the Elizabethtown high school, forty miles south of Louisville. Until that time, the Thomas family hardly knew McCoy O'Neil, but what they thought they knew they did not like. The Thomas clan was coming around to a different opinion of the man, but they had not fully arrived on that yet. Even after more than a month, many people, including the Thomas family, were hoping for a rescue for the entire system, though Jason and Walter were not counting on it.

After three days of non-stop eating and hot water for bathing at the Thomas homestead, the girls seemed well enough to make the last of the ride to the O'Neil farm. More importantly, they looked like they wanted to make the trip. Miriam Weiss, the wife of Jason's friend Martin Weiss, questioned severely the girls and the wisdom of eight teenagers traveling with unknown men—but she was harshly rebuked by the girls who believed that if it were not for McCoy and Trevor, they would have starved to death.

Still, the women of the Thomas clan wanted to know how the girls were fairing at the O'Neil homestead and dispatched Jason and Walter to check on them.

McCoy stepped out of his workshop to meet Jason and Walter. A little over a month ago, Jason would have been reluctant to set foot on McCoy's farm. Now, they were almost friends. This was Jason's second visit.

"Yankee! To what do I owe the pleasure?!" McCoy seemed to enjoy teasing Jason. After all, he was the first New Yorker that anyone could remember moving into the county.

"Hello, McCoy," Jason said. "I brought my mechanically inclined brother to check out your operation."

McCoy greeted Jason's brother. "What you got to say for yourself there, Walter?"

"I'm good, McCoy. You doin' alright?" Walter picked up the local lingo quickly, but his accent didn't do it justice. He sounded like someone in the Witness Protection Program trying to fit in and doing a poor job.

"Every day this side of the grass is a good day." McCoy enjoyed a mordant sense of humor.

While Jason went to visit with McCoy's wife and check on the girls, McCoy showed Walter around the production facilities. Their first stop was at the old Case 970 diesel tractor that powered the shop's PTO driven generator.

"That's 90 horse-power. We can cut and weld anything," McCoy said. "Come on. I'll show you what we are making."

"Where are you getting your diesel to run that tractor?" Walter asked.

"This is Kentucky," McCoy said. "We have coal and oil here. We've got two stripper-wells on our farm, and there are dozens in the county."

"Yea, but how do you power the pumps?"

McCoy led Walter to the other side of the workshop and pointed to the nodding-donkey oil jack off in the distance.

"Right now, I've got a two-horse treadmill and a team of draft horses I borrowed from Abraham. We can lift 50-gallons per day.

That's plenty for now, but I wouldn't want to have to do it this way for long. So, we are building a windmill to run the pump and lift the oil. Come on; I'll show you."

McCoy led Walter into the workshop. The first thing Walter noticed in the shop was the plastic sheet in the roof for light. There were a dozen young men there working on the manufacture of wood stoves, hot water kettles, and the windmill. Walter spent a career in the trucking and gas-station business, and he spoke the language of motors, generators, welders, and metal better than he spoke English.

"We don't have enough oil to power a bunch of tractors and cars, but we have enough to keep us in kerosene for lamps and diesel to run the generator for an hour or two each day," McCoy said. "Gasoline is a by-product and the quality is good enough to run chainsaws and a few small generators."

Jason joined McCoy and Walter in the workshop.

"Satisfied there, Yankee?"

"Our wives needed to know the girls were okay."

"So, they risked your neck on a long ride in dangerous times to check on a bunch of strangers. If anything happened to you two, your wives would be in bad shape."

Jason just shrugged.

"How are you refining the crude oil?" Walter asked.

"Come on," McCoy said and took off for the door. Jason already saw the refining operation on his first visit here and stayed behind to watch the men fabricating the metal into usable parts. McCoy showed Walter the one-thousand-gallon propane tank they converted to a crude oil cooker.

"We skim the products the same way you skim butter from milk or fat from soup. The top is mostly natural gasoline. The next layer is the distillates: kerosene and diesel and heavy oil."

"Good grief, that is smart," Walter said.

"It is not very efficient. But we can extract fifteen to twenty gallons of total product—half gasoline and half usable distillates—per day from fifty gallons of crude."

"What do you do with the remaining sludge?"

"We use it to cook the crude oil," McCoy said.

"Oh."

After a few minutes more going over the refining process, McCoy called to Jason from the door, and Walter and Jason followed McCoy into his "office," a small outbuilding where McCoy sought refuge and where he had constructed a traditional "study" filled with books.

They sat at the table in the kitchenette off of the study.

"I'm not just here to check on the girls," Jason said to McCoy.

"Okay. What's goin' on?"

"Abraham is worried that all of the corn seed we have is hybrid and won't mature and produce ears."

McCoy just looked at Jason, the expression of a growing realization spreading across his face.

"Oh, shoot! He's probably right."

Walter looked at Jason and McCoy and their expressions of concern. "What?! What's the problem?" Corn is not a major crop in metro New York.

"The corn in the fields is all hybrid and genetically modified. Maybe it will produce ears. Maybe it will be as sterile as a mule." Mules are a hybrid between a male donkey and a female horse and are unable to reproduce. "Do we want to find out in the fall that we don't have enough food to get through winter?"

"Yep, that's the situation," Jason said with no enthusiasm. "We have vegetable seed coming out of our ears. But we can't survive on vegetables. We need to find grain seed. Spring will be here before you know it."

"Something tells me you have an idea," McCoy said.

"The Old Order Mennonites down in Shady Grove believe in living separately from the world. My bet is they will have heirloom corn seed—they would never allow themselves to depend on outsiders for something so critical. I think; or I hope."

"Shoot, the Amish believe the same thing. Why don't they have heirloom seed?"

"There is a big difference between the Amish around here and the Old Order Mennonites or the Swartzentruber Old Order Amish. They might dress the same, speak the same language, and use a horse and buggy. The Old Order churches are far more hardcore. It's a whole different breed of cat."

"Well," McCoy said. "They used to be your neighbors. I expect you know them. It's a day there and a day back. As soon as the weather turns lets you and me take a ride down there and see your friends."

Chapter 16

The Mennonite community took Roger and Melissa's sudden marriage in stride. The women welcomed Melissa into their homes as an equal. The circumstances of their marriage were not relevant. The Bishop declared them married, and that was that. The following day, Melissa showed up at the Fisher dairy for the morning milking but was shooed off in a kind manner by Mrs. Fisher.

"You're a married woman. Go home and see to your husband! Ruth will find something to keep you occupied and won't interfere with your home."

Married women were not expected to engage in "heavy" work. After all, they might be pregnant. Milking a cow, working in the garden, sewing, and cooking were acceptable tasks, but picking up a bale of hay to feed the milk cow was not while carrying a bucket of water from the well was okay. Heavy work was her husband's responsibility. Of course, some women engaged in whatever chores they wished. There was no prohibition against it. But there were no expectations. If a Mennonite family moved from one house to another, the women in the community would descend on the home to help the family pack. But when moving day came, the men of the community loaded the trucks and moved the equipment, and the women did not lift a finger, other than to point to a particular box and inform one of the men where they wanted it to go.

Florence was beside herself. Sandy and Mindy tried to reason with her to no avail. After the morning milking and chores, Florence walked on the road towards the corn fields and hitched a ride with one of the wagons bringing men and fencing to where they were working. She saw Roger at the edge of a field bounded by the river that ran through the community pounding a t-post into the ground. His back to her, he never saw her coming.

"You fucking rapist!" Florence spat behind Roger.

Roger turned on a dime and shuffled a few steps to his right with his left hand raised—like a boxer—to protect himself. His right hand still held the steel post he just pulled out of the ground.

But Florence made no effort to get physical. She stood her ground.

"Jesus!" Roger purged between clenched teeth. "You scared the shit out of me!"

"Oh, yes? Well, imagine how Melissa feels when you're raping her!"

All Roger wanted was to end this confrontation. He kept his distance but remained where he was, about five strides from Florence. He had a six-foot-long metal fencing post in his hand. Even if she came at him with a knife, Roger felt he could successfully defend himself. He would have to deal with this at some point.

"Melissa made a decision," Roger said in an appeal to reason. "You need to respect that."

"Bullshit! She has no power here. You've got all the power. She can't give consent. You are nothing but a rapist!" She was wild-eyed and spitting as she spoke.

"What power do I have over Melissa?"

"The power of life and death! She can't survive without you!"

"And you think it's a bad idea for Melissa to ally with me because I might have some utility? Do you have any idea how creepy you sound? Women, and men for that matter have the unlimited natural right to select their mates and sexual partners for any reason they choose! And it appears that women's top criteria are to find the most useful man that her utility can bargain for! His family's wealth, his socio-economic status, and ability to provide for her and her children are at the top of women's list in this regard. And you think that is unfair for *women*? Do you have any idea of the suffering that takes place among men in the bottom half of the scale of mate appeal? No. Because you don't give a damn about men *or* women. It's all about you. Melissa doesn't belong to you—or me. In a year from now, she might leave me a goodbye note and take off with someone else. Maybe she won't even leave a note! And you know what? I will respect her decision."

"Oh, my G-d!" Florence shrieked. "You're treating her like a common prostitute!"

Roger suddenly realized that Florence was hysterical. He should have recognized the manifestations immediately, but she had surprised and frightened him. He tried to calm her.

"Florence, I know this is hard. I understand that you love Melissa. I love her too."

Florence began to weep and wail in earnest. "We should never have come with you," she sobbed.

"If you didn't, you would be dead from exposure by now. And if you remember, it was Melissa who wanted to come with me. She didn't ask any of you to join her. I think Melissa saw something appealing in me when we met at the Garden of Eden commune. Maybe it was utility and value. Maybe it was sexual attraction. Maybe both. Just understand that I have no power here! Melissa holds all of the cards. Talk about a power imbalance! Women have immense power in that they control the keys to the sexual kingdom. Men struggle mightily to be seen by the female aristocracy, but we are little more than peasants working in the kingdom's fields."

There was a moment of silence during which Florence appeared to collect herself. Roger hoped the storm had passed and that Florence could move on. She was a deeply disturbed person, but she was a human being, and she was suffering. Small communities, especially those in temperate climes, cannot survive with a culture where mate pair-bonds were always in flux. That is the primary appeal of urban living—greater sexual selection and a large degree of anonymity to indulge. If they were to remain here in this community, this must get settled. Roger wanted to give Florence a big bite at this apple.

"You don't love her," Florence said in a voice barely over a whisper as she wiped her face. "You just want to fuck her."

Florence's course and ill-mannered accusation stung Roger. What is love? Virile young men generally do not fall in love with older women irrespective of a woman's socio-economic status, high-value women do not accept men who are not in the top socio-economic strata as sexual partners, and a great many unloved people got left behind in the wreckage of human existence. Every clinician who had ever practiced heard this lament, over and over again. Roger cherished sex with Melissa, and yet he told Annie he would rather beat his toes off with a hammer than have Florence, Sandy, or Mindy in his bed. Why Melissa? Could it be that she was young, nubile, and fertile? Men seem to fall in love with the women they want to have sex with and not the other way around.

But now Roger was back to thinking about the mean-spirited woman standing in front of him.

"I do love her. I do, as you say, 'want to fuck her.' And every time I make love to her, I pray she gets pregnant. I want to have a family again, and I think Melissa wants to have a family too. And that is something only a man can give her. Good day," Roger said and then walked away.

Florence collapsed to the ground in a heap wailing away, but Roger was done with this conversation and did not look back. He gave Florence the opportunity to vent her spleen. It was time for everybody to move on.

That evening, Roger and Melissa took their supper at the small table in the cabin. The meal consisted of nearly the same thing, day after day—home-canned ground beef sautéed with onions with either corn cakes or potato cakes, and Sauer kraut or plantain greens. Breakfast was more of the same only with ground pork instead of ground beef. For efficiency and security, the community pooled their poultry into six different chicken houses—one for each church-group of 25 families. Those birds were guarded by dogs and watchmen in shifts each night; such was their value. But chickens lay far fewer eggs during the short days of winter than they do during the rest of the year, and those eggs were shared evenly and used for baking, not for breakfast. Lunch—the biggest meal of the day—consisted of stew and bread, delivered in large crocks to the men in the field. Roger noticed that the monotonous and repetitive diet had a bright side to it. There was no temptation to overeat. He was back to his college weight, and with all of the manual labor, he was just as fit as a fiddle if he did say so himself.

"Florence confronted me in the field today," Roger said.

Melissa froze for a few moments. Finally, her eyes darted to Roger, but her head did not move. "I was afraid of this. I've done everything I can to avoid her. I guess when she couldn't get to me, she got to you."

"I think she said what she had to say. It might be okay now."

"Ugh! I wish, but I don't think so."

"Why do you say that?" asked Roger.

"Florence is extremely controlling. She doesn't give up so easily."

Roger almost asked if that's the way she is then why did Melissa stay with her. But he caught himself. Controlling people control—that's what they do. Roger tried another approach.

"What brought you two together? What was it you found appealing about her?"

"Those are two very different questions."

"You're right. I'm sorry. You are very quick; you know that?"

"If I were so quick, I would have left her long ago."

This time Roger didn't trip over his own feet.

"What brought you two together?"

"I met her a few years ago at a concert," said Melissa. "I was following the band 'Monkey Breath' around on the road after I dropped out of college. I was sleeping in a friend's car. Florence invited me to sleep on her couch. It turned out that it wasn't even her couch. I ended up staying with her for more than two years."

"It couldn't have been all bad."

"No. No, it wasn't. It seemed so fun in the beginning—like I belonged to something; to the family I never really had. We associated with professional protest organizations. They would pay us to show up and protest, mostly for 'women's rights.' Other stuff too. But it was always women. Women this; Women that. 'Abortion.' The 'pay gap.' 'Sexual assault.' That sort of thing. I was one of the 'sisters,' but after a while it got old. We spent a winter out west in the desert at an RV commune. But there was a guy there who liked me, and Flo wanted to split. For the last year, we divided our time between the Garden of Eden and Panama City Beach."

"What's in Panama City?"

"A big LGBTQ community."

"Oh," said Roger. "What about your parents? Why did you drop out of college?"

"My father passed away when I was a sophomore in high school. He'd been sick for several years. We were in bad shape financially. I went to a community college outside of Cincinnati. After that, I went to Ohio State but dropped out after a semester. My mother remarried and moved to Florida. I was all alone and very vulnerable."

"I see. Florence seems to think that I have taken advantage of your vulnerability."

"Women like Florence and Sandy think that all heterosexual sex is rape and all men are rapists. They cannot even begin to imagine that a woman would find a man attractive and that we might want to have sex with a man. Their lives revolve entirely around gender politics. They *hate* men, they even hate gay men, and they don't see anything cute and cuddly about children. Did you see their facial expressions at the Mormon homestead? The only reason I didn't bail out on Florence back there was that I already had my eye on you. I was taken with you the moment you walked into the kitchen at GED. I figured I could always go back to Enoch and be a fourth wife." And here Melissa laughed at the idea. "But I was hoping for something else."

Melissa reached out and held Roger's hand.

"Why would gay women hate gay men?" Roger asked. "I thought they were part of the same political coalition."

"Because they hate men, straight or gay. Gay women are not 'gay' in the way that 'gay' men are 'gay.'"

"Oh, yes? How's that?"

Melissa took in a deep breath. "Gay men will have a dozen lovers over a holiday weekend. Most gay women, especially those over 30, are damn near celibate. Even the young women. They might be fun for a week or two—and then again, they might not—and then they cannot even be bothered to brush their teeth and take a shower before coming to bed. For them, it is all about politics. They live for politics."

"All lovers tire of each other," Roger said. "Even gay men."

"Ha! That shows you what a straight man knows about the LGBTQ lifestyle. Most gay men don't stay around long enough to get tired of anybody. Yea, they might pair off when they get old, and nobody wants them, but they are never monogamous. They practically live on the gay 'dating' apps—but there's no dinner and a movie! Lesbians bond like glue, and then they don't have much—if any! —sex, especially when they get older. That's just the way it is. Florence hasn't tried to please me in months. Mindy says the same thing about Sandy. I've heard this story a thousand times. So, what's the point? Well, in the queer women community, the point is about companionship and a shared interest in the politics of hating men, not a desire to have lots of sex with lots of women. They've got nothing but time—no husband, no children, and often an attenuated relationship with their extended family. While straight men and women were taking the kids to piano and dance lessons, my friends were working at politics. Divorce law, Title IX, family and custody law, etc. They move their agenda forward inch by inch. And it never ends."

"Well, that's not true," Roger replied. "It will end."

"How? When it comes to politics, the radical Feminists were unstoppable. You straight guys were too busy working and coaching Little League and paying for private schools, college tuition, mortgages, and car payments. The radical Feminists had nothing else to do but politics. The only thing that stopped them was the Famine."

"Even without the Famine, the Feminists would have died out. They don't produce children. In two generations, the cultures which promote family and children would be the only people left—and some of those cultures might not value things like liberty and due process. Biologically, the Feminists were a dead-end waiting to happen."

"I guess that's true. It doesn't matter now, I guess. Looking back, I am embarrassed that I fell for the propaganda. But you wanted to know how gay men and lesbians were different. For gay men, it was all about how many lovers they could hook up with that night, and how many times they could get their rocks off. And for queer women, it was all about the politics of hating men, and how they could hurt men politically. When Feminists say, 'Smash the Patriarchy,' what they really mean is, 'Smash All

Men by any Means Necessary.' They *hate* you. Look, I spent more than two years living exclusively in the LGBTQ community. I am just telling you what I saw. These are the dirty little secrets no one wants to talk about, and there is a lot of dirty laundry that never sees the light of day."

"Well," Roger said. "I can tell you that in the university system, the LGBTQ political party controlled the narrative. Anyone who challenged their orthodoxy in any way was branded as 'homophobic,' 'racist,' or 'a bigot.' If you wanted to maintain your career you went along—or else."

"Or hundreds of us will show up as a protest unit and shout you down. If that didn't work, we would throw rocks, use pepper spray, and destroy private property. It was easier for the local police to shut down the speaker."

"So, back to you; why can't you or Sandy initiate intimacy?"

"Well, I guess we could. But there is no 'there' there."

Melissa cackled at her joke, but it went entirely over Roger's head.

"You lost me," Roger said.

"Queer women like Sandy and Florence are often called 'butch.' In Charleston and Panama City they were sometimes called 'gentlemen.' Women like Mindy and I are 'femme.' I think you know what I am talking about."

"Yes, of course. But what was the 'there-there' thing about?"

"Well, if a queer woman is a butch or a gentleman, and her entire sense of style, presentation, and self-perception is masculine, and she wants a femme girlfriend, she has to work for it—just like a man does. Otherwise, she's nothing but a eunuch. They've got it all going on—short hair, manly face, deep voice, thick body, and men's clothes. But they don't have a dick. That's what I meant by there is no there-there."

Roger sat quietly for a while contemplating all that was said.

"Wow, that is a harsh assessment," Roger said. "And it sounds like a hard way to live."

"Yea, it's harsh; it's also perfectly accurate."

"Heterosexuals have their dirty little secrets too. People are people. Relationships are not easy."

Roger sat pensive and silent after that.

"Oh, yea?" Melissa said playfully and jumped into Roger's lap. "Well, Mr. Heterosexual: Where are those secrets hiding?" she asked as she ran her hands under his shirt and then down into his pants. "Because I've been looking for them," she said as she kissed him on his neck, face, and lips. "Maybe I better check you over again."

And then Melissa stood up and pulled Roger by the hand to the bed.

Chapter 17

Every other Sunday, the Mennonites attended church. Unlike most other Christian denominations, worship took place in the homes of the members, not a centralized building or location. There were 150 families in the community, and they distributed further into districts or church groups of 25 families. Accordingly, the Shady Grove Mennonite settlement held six districts. Each family would host a church service in their home for 24 or so other families once per year. On the "off-Sundays," church members were expected to spend time with family and the community. They could visit close neighbors, but even though there was no church gathering, it was still the Sabbath. A day of rest.

Philip Troyer sat alone at his dining table enjoying a cup of cedar and maple syrup tea. And a moment alone with one's thoughts was something to cherish for a man with eleven children. But the youngest, a daughter, was now sixteen, and five of his children were married and out of the house. One son, Matthew, took a bus 400 miles to court a woman who lived in an Old Order Mennonite settlement in Missouri a week before the blackout. Philip's oldest son lived in that settlement with his wife and children, so Philip wasn't worried about Matthew's wellbeing. He just wondered if Matthew would ever make it back home. He might have already married for all Philip knew. Such strange times indeed.

There was a knock at the door at the far side of the house. They rarely used the front door. The side entrance had a mudroom and a long, pegged board coat rack and most of the time this was the entrance the family used.

"Hey!" Philip called in a deep and drawn out growl. It wasn't unfriendly. That's just how he signaled his presence to the people who came to his shop when he was upstairs in his cubbyhole office. He must have forgotten that he was home.

"Philip! It's Roger Little."

"Come in, Roger!"

The door slammed, and Philip could hear Roger in the mudroom. Roger was shoeless when he appeared in the great room that took up most of the first floor in Philip's house. Philip always found this custom amusing.

"Grab the pot there on the stove and pour yourself a cup of tea if you're of a mind: tea is one thing we are not short of yet. Mugs are on the warmer."

Roger knew where everything was and helped himself and came to the table. Philip pointed to the chair next to him and turned his chair to face Roger. Roger did the same. There was a quizzically amused look on Philip's face.

"I understand congratulations are in order!"

"It was quite a surprise; I will tell you that."

"I'll bet. The whole community is talking about it. No one alive can remember the last time we had a 'declaratory marriage.' And never in our history has a Bishop presided over the marriage of people who were not church members."

"Believe me; I was shocked."

"I would imagine so."

"And flattered."

"Well, please know that flattery wasn't the Bishop's motivation," Philip said, crossing his arms in front of him and fixing his gaze under his brow at Roger. "As far as we are concerned, you two are married. Man and wife. I hope that suits you."

"I hope it suits my wife," Roger said.

That caught Philip up short. His countenance went from cloudy to amused.

"Oh, I see. Perhaps the Bishop did you a favor? I wasn't home when all of this happened. We visited my brother-in-law for church on the far side of our settlement and stayed overnight due to the weather. When I heard about it, I couldn't believe my ears. Our Bishop is a man of few words. I can't imagine how he came to this determination—this was a custom of ours in colonial Pennsylvania. I doubt it's happened since then—until you. If a couple snuck off together and closed a door behind them and got caught, the Bishop would ask if they "intended to persist." That was a nice way of asking if the deed was done. If they said yes, the Bishop declared them man and wife. But I guess I don't need to be telling you!"

"Well, that's what he asked us. And he asked if we were 'hand in hand.'"

"I heard. And I heard you were stuttering like a schoolboy."

"He caught me off guard. I'm not complaining. That's why I came to talk to you. You're a church deacon."

"I am, indeed," replied Philip.

"And your people have a culture, a society, and a set of rules to live by."

"Yes, we do."

"But you've been living under the protection of American law and custom."

"What's your point?"

"Those protections are gone," said Roger. "We are going to have to reestablish everything from scratch."

"Ya know, before you came here, I'd been wracking my brain about the future. I felt we would survive the coming winter without too much trouble. But what about next year, and the year after? That is why I said to you the day you arrived that I think you are here for a reason. I think that's why the Bishop married you instead of running you off. And I know you don't believe any of that. So why don't you say what's on your mind."

"I'm grateful to you, and I'm indebted to you. Without your generosity, we wouldn't survive the winter."

"If that's so, you took a foolish risk, didn't you?" asked Philip.

"Perhaps. I know it looks that way. But I don't think there is any other way."

"So! You love this girl."

"Yes, I do. But I am not talking about love. I've been thinking about this from the moment she stole into my cabin. I knew that conducting ourselves the way we did would be unacceptable to you and your community. I knew that you would probably throw me out."

"Shun you," Philip interrupted. "We wouldn't physically accost you. It would be as if you didn't exist, even if you stood right in front of me."

"Yes, I know that. I didn't mean to suggest that you would resort to violence or any overt coercion. But I knew that it would mean that I would lose your friendship, and frankly and far more importantly, your sponsorship and resources. And I knew that we wouldn't survive without your help."

"And still you took this risk," Philip finished for Roger.

Roger nodded his head and stared at the table for a moment.

"And still I took this risk," Roger agreed and slid back and up in his chair. "And I am not a young man. I'm supposed to be able to control my impulses, or so our modern conventional wisdom—and every faculty member at the university—says."

Philip shifted in his seat as if he were uncomfortable.

"Please," Roger continued. "Stay with me for a moment. I am going somewhere with this, somewhere important. I need to talk about this with someone; think this through a little. You're a deacon in your church, a man of the cloth—this should be right up your alley."

"Okay," Philip said. "I'm listening." Philip studied Roger's face. If he had met Moses himself on his walk down from Mt. Sinai, Philip would have expected a similar facial expression on the prophet to the one he saw on his friend's face sitting before him.

"Mankind has experienced vile pestilence, pitiless plagues, and desperate disease. Acts of war so cruel and depraved historians find it difficult to comprehend. Acts of G-d so devastating they changed the course of rivers and washed the land clean of life. But let a small group of fertile young women and men survive, and despite the carnage, sickness, and death all around them, that very night a man will nonetheless gladly fill a woman with his loins and life. And from this issue will be born cities and cultures and nations, and their descendants will go on to discover Truth and Beauty, and knowledge and philosophy and reason. And LIFE! Life will go on! A man's will to live and his will to fill a woman's belly with life is overpowering and relentless. For without it, you and I would not be sitting here. Mankind would have perished long ago. But a man will risk everything for that moment where he might reach the future through his offspring. We are in the midst of one of the great catastrophes of history right now, here, as we speak. No calamity of antiquity or modernity—the slaughter of World War One, the nuclear bombings, the starvation in Ukraine, even the Holocaust—can rival this. And what is it that compels me and dominates my thoughts? The life-giving force of my desire for a woman embodied in my passions and desires, represented in the physical response of arousal and my erections and the delivery of my seed via climax into her body."

An uncomfortable silence followed. After some time, Philip breathed a short chuckle, pulled on his beard, and responded, "I see you've given this some thought. Well, 'A generation goes, and a generation comes, but the earth remains forever.' 'There is nothing new under the sun.'"

"Hmm," was all that Roger could muster. Having bared his soul, he was emotionally exhausted.

"'Hmm?!'" Philip mocked Roger. "What is it with your people? You're a college professor—I stopped going to school when I was 14—and this is just coming to you now? Is it because you live so far from the earth itself, from the soil and the animals and the forests that sustain you? Far from the winter that kills and the spring that brings forth life from the barren ground? Are you surprised by the relationship between your passions and the children that come of them? Potzblitz, man! You people should have spent less time in your ivory towers and more time in my barnyard."

"I'm sorry."

"Oh, I don't mean you," Philip cringed and waved his hand at Roger as if to knock him off his perch. "You're the strangest Englishman I've yet met. Or one of two. And I don't mean to compare man to the beasts. We are made in G-d's image. And even if you don't believe that you seem to understand it in your own strange way. Our passions are a gift from the Creator, and they are the most noble thing about us. If all you did were to provide the seed, you would be no different than the stallions and bulls on my farm, and yet life could not continue without them! But man *is* noble. He lives in community with his fellow man, and toils tirelessly to provide for his woman and their children, and he has crossed oceans on rickety boats and conquered continents to do so. I don't know what happened amongst your people that you have forgotten this. But it doesn't matter anymore. You remember it now. I am glad the Bishop didn't shun you. I am glad that you have found a woman to love. I pray she fills your home with warmth and children."

The two sat in silence for some time.

"Was there something else you wanted to talk to me about?" asked Philip.

"Yes."

"I thought so. Well, it seems we are holding nothing back." They shared a short, nervous laugh. "So, let's have it."

"The whole world is not going to convert and become a Mennonite and live under the Ordnung and your Bishop's decrees. We are going to need to reestablish society. A culture of liberty and respect for the life and rights of the individual, and a separation between religion and the rule of law. Where people are free to live under the Ordnung and the rules of your church if they wish or to believe in Bertrand Russel's teapot."

"Who's teapot?"

"It's not important. What is important is that we live and believe the ideals of liberty and tolerance and the respect for life and property that lured our ancestors to colonial Pennsylvania, yours and mine, and which evolved into the greatest political achievement in the history of mankind—the Constitution of the United States of America. Of course, all of that is gone. Everything we knew is gone, and it's too late to get it back. We'll be starting from the beginning. And we have no idea what political entities are out there and what they are capable of. In the meantime, we need to start with the basics."

"'And having food and raiment let us be therewith content.'"

"Well, with all due respect to Timothy, it's going to take a lot more than that. But we have the beginnings of civilization here in your community."

"How's that?"

"Agriculture and community. If civilization is to continue, it has to produce enough food and children to maintain itself. We must develop a common culture and ethics with the family as the social unit and the individual as the political unit and engender a sense of belonging and responsibility to the greater community. There is a great deal that the outside world can learn from your community. And we must innovate. To do that, we need the right incentives. And that means we need a medium of exchange. Money. Barter won't cut it."

"Why do you mention children? You said children would come no matter what happens."

"I said if young men and women survive, mankind will reissue—but it can take centuries. We don't have that much time before we will spiral down to little more than hunter-gatherers reduced to savagery. The cities are filled with our best and brightest young people—and the cities are death traps. Except for the Anabaptist communities, and maybe the Mormons, rural America is in desperate shape too. These are the circumstances we must work with."

Chapter 18

The winter came on early and harsh, and it stayed that way.
It was now early February, and ice and snow covered the ground
for the last 45 days, and while there was little snow in November
and December those months were no bargain. That kind of snow
cover was common for the northern continental United States, but
it was unheard of in southern Kentucky and northern Tennessee.
The men working on the fencing crews got most of the job done
before the ground froze and the ice on the country roads made it
too dangerous to risk injury to the workhorses. Those animals
were priceless now.

The people living in the Mennonite settlement outside of
Shady Grove settled into their houses and sat by their woodstoves
to keep warm, but they were not completely idle. And here,
Roger proved to be very helpful. The women gathered and spun
and knitted wool with the help of an ingenious contraption that
Roger, Karl, and Evan designed from a photograph in an old
coffee table picture book of a spinning wheel. And the men
would sit by their stoves during the long winter nights and
occupy their hands making cordage.

A treadle can power any narrow-hubbed wheel, but bicycle
wheels were just about perfect. Even better, they seemed to be
abundant. If a family wanted a spinning wheel constructed, they
had to scrounge up the wheel and the hardware and bring it to
Philip's harness shop. There were several woodworkers in the
community, and all of their equipment and tools were powered
by horses walking on an inclined treadmill, or by hand. Treadles
and bobbins and stands were turned out faster than the
"Englishmen," as the community took to calling Roger, Karl, and
Evan could cobble the implement together.

For cordage, Roger showed the men how to strip the inside
bark of trees and twist this material into cords and rope. Luck
smiled on them. Kentucky was one of the few states that
legalized hemp for commercial applications, and there were two
farms in the county with unharvested hemp in the field and some
that were harvested and stored in a barn. But there was no sign of

the occupants of either farm. The men were fast learners, and some of them quickly figured out a process for producing commercial grade rope a half inch in diameter. Rope and cordage and spun wool were mainstays of civilization. And that the ideas for cordage and spinning wheels came from Roger raised his standing in the community. He was not a typically helpless and incompetent Englishman, though no one would say such an unkind thing out loud. But they are only human, and humans recognize the abstracts of value and worth.

The nights were long, and Mr. and Mrs. Little put the time to good use in a near constant state of intimacy. An uneasy truce took hold between Roger and Melissa, and Florence. The "Englishmen" made themselves useful. And everyone bided their time waiting for spring. Every few days in the early part of winter, a member of the community who had been traveling or working away from the community turned up. They were tired and thin but not in terrible condition, but the anecdotes they related about what they saw on their travels was truly disturbing. The highways and roads were an absolute horror show. Roger thought about the dead woman in the car they saw and the roadkill they refused to look just before they got to the Cluff's compound and the woman in the gas station parking lot on 41E with a dead child in her car. And that was before three months of hard winter weather. What did the American urban landscape look like now after more than three months without power? Worse, what did it smell like? Roger was sure he didn't want to know. What he wanted to know more than anything else was that his sons were alive and well. Where were they? What were they doing? What happened out there that the American electrical system was *still down*? Were people starving in Chile, South America, and Australia? Did war spread beyond the Middle East? He broached these issues with Philip several times. Roger envied the comfort that Philip's faith seemed to give him. His answer was always the same.

"Therefore don't worry about tomorrow, because tomorrow will worry about itself. Each day has enough trouble of its own."

In the second week of February, Roger detected a change in the demeanor of the Mennonites. Something big. While the weather warmed a bit, the people of the community were cold. Though the people still spoke with him and brought him wheels and hardware and exchanged these items hand to hand, the warmth was gone, replaced with a frostiness that to Roger was as cold as it was apparent. If the Mennonites had shunned him, they would refuse to give or take something from his hand. Melissa felt it too, but only among the general community. There was no change in her relationship with the Troyer women.

Karl and Evan were back working on the fencing crew as most of the homes that wanted a spinning-wheel already had one, and Roger could keep up with the demand alone. But they enjoyed working together at Philip's workshop and became friends. Roger sought them out to see if they noticed anything. They had.

"I think you should know," Evan said. "Something happened between Florence and one of the women at the dairy."

"'Something?' What do you mean, 'Something?'"

"Well, your guess is as good as mine," replied Evan. "But I think you can figure it out. Florence is not welcome back to the dairy, I can tell you that much. And we've become radioactive to the men on the fencing crew."

Roger's faced flushed, and his heart sank; this was a disaster.

Before he spoke to Philip, Roger wanted Melissa's council. She had a sense of people and a set of street smarts unmatched in his experience. She would have made a fantastic psychologist. He found her in the Troyer greenhouse planting broccoli and cabbage seeds in trays for the cool weather garden. He told her what Evan said.

"Well, what did you expect?" Melissa asked.

"What did I expect? Are you kidding me?! These people are keeping us alive! Without them, we won't survive."

"Didn't you tell Florence that people have the unlimited and natural right to choose their sexual partners and develop relationships as they see fit? Florence didn't do anything different than we did."

"Yes, of course, people have that natural right! And people also have the natural right to end relationships—sexual, social, and familial—for any reason they see fit too! You cannot force people to like you or to agree with you on anything even if it is because the flying spaghetti monster told them so. And the Mennonites have the natural right to end their relationship with us just as you ended your relationship with Florence and began one with me. The Mennonites also have the natural right to their private property. They don't have to share with us. They do so voluntarily, and they can stop doing so at any time. We can't force them to share their resources with us or to accept our sensibilities. Any cure that entails coercion or violence is far worse than the disease."

"Oh, my," Melissa said. Suddenly, she was trembling. Her voice cracked. "I don't think they will shun us over anything that Florence did. Do you?" She stepped close to Roger and hugged him and started crying. Melissa's response was not typical of her and seemed far more emotional than it should be.

"I hope not," Roger said, somewhat taken aback by Melissa's weepy display. "I am on my way to talk to Philip. I just wanted to check in with you first and get your sense of it. I'm sorry to upset you."

"Roger," Melissa said as she hugged him tightly. "I'm pregnant."

Chapter 19

Two men of advancing years rode south in silence, their bodies hardened by labor and modest consumption and seemingly impervious to the pounding of the horses on what in any other time in the previous half-century would have been the adventure of a lifetime. The journey was more than pleasant. It was exhilarating. They took a lonely two-lane highway on the east side of Edinburgh to avoid the miserable spectacle that shrouded state road 41E. In a year, nature would render the bodies of those unfortunate souls back to the earth—ashes to ashes and dust to dust—but for now, there was no reason to confront the horror. They would see plenty enough to dread on the lonesome byway. And though they'd been in the saddle all day, their spirits soared.

Jason Thomas and McCoy O'Neil, two men profoundly unalike pressed together by Providence, sat on their horses as their mounts drank in the swift waters of the river that twisted through the Shady Grove Mennonite settlement. Of course, it was this river—and though the people called it "Spring Creek," it was a river—that appealed to the early Mennonite families who colonized the area. The snake-like coils of the river left a broad and verdant floodplain in some places on either side of its banks and in other places it cut the granite hills in two. The natural beauty of the Kentucky-Tennessee border region flashed all around them, and the fertile ground of the plains and the productive forests of the hills were restful on a man's eyes and brought comfort to his soul.

The horses drank deep and then picked their heads up signaling their satisfaction to their riders. Jason patted his mount, Thunder, on the neck and spoke to the animal in soothing tones. Both men nodded to the other and gave their horses a gentle kick and "click-click" signal to move and set off on the last mile of the ride to Philip Troyer's farm.

Chapter 20

"Hello, Philip!" Roger called up the stairs at Philp's workshop.

"Hey," Philip growled, drawing out the vowel in his usual way.

Roger climbed the steps and found Philip standing at a workbench with an old harness in front of him.

"I've got quite a few old harnesses in the loft of the buggy barn. There is a lot of good leather here," Philip said as he handled the harness.

Roger was grateful for the neutral business-as-usual greeting and Philip's familiar and unassuming manner.

"I imagine that we won't have a shortage of leather soon," Roger said. "The tannery is coming along."

"And we've got you to thank for that, don't we?"

The largest retail outfit in the city of Shady Grove wasn't a big box store or a fast food restaurant. It was a church-run donation center that sought donations from all over the border region and sold the contributions cheap while employing desperate people. Roger remembered that they had quite a collection of books from his many visits into town at Shady Grove over the years. The books didn't seem to sell and were piling up at the back of the store. Roger and Ezra took a buggy into town to visit the store, and as expected, it had been looted. Everything else was gone, but the books remained untouched. As they searched through the collection, they found dozens of useful volumes covering many practical tasks. A book on making leather from cowhide hatched the idea for the tannery, and another spawned the spinning wheel design.

"Philip, I've been getting an odd feeling from the plain people." Roger avoided the term "your people."

"Hmm... sit down, my friend." Philip gestured to the delaminating stool on the other side of the workbench and pulled one up for himself. Roger looked down at the seat and marveled at it. It had been falling apart since the day he met Philip, and it was still here.

"Now what's going on?" asked Philip.

Roger told him that he felt a difference in the way the community dealt with him socially and that he was worried about it and wondered if there was something he did.

"I am sorry to hear that," Philip said. "No, it wasn't anything you did. Something happened over at the dairy. The Fisher's don't want your friend Florence to work there anymore." And here Philip cringed and said, "Ah," and made a gesture with his hands that Roger interpreted as "I don't know how to say this, but..."

Roger waited for Philip to gather his thoughts and form his words.

Finally, Philip spat it out. "Is there something strange about your friends?"

"Well, I hardly know them." Roger felt he needed to equivocate. The last thing he wanted was for Philip to know about Melissa's past relationship with Florence. "I met them the day the blackout began."

"But have you noticed anything strange about them?"

"What do you mean?"

"You know. Strange." Philips face tilted down, and he made a rolling motion with his hand signaling forward movement like he wanted Roger to flesh out what 'strange' meant for him.

Roger imitated the rolling hand motion and asked, "Strange?" as if to say *strange how?*

Philip decided to take the bull by the horns.

"Something weird happened between her and one of the Fisher girls. That's all I want to say about it. We can't have that in the community. Some of my people seem to think that something doesn't seem right with the people you came here with." Philip tried another tack. "Do you think that those men are looking to meet a wife and start a family? How about the women? Are they going to find someone and become productive members of the community? You and Melissa found each other."

"Melissa is pregnant," Roger blurted out.

"Well, well, well!" Philip beamed. "That's wonderful!"

"She just told me."

"Well, that didn't take long. You're going to need a bigger house. And then I hope you fill it up!"

"It hasn't really sunk in yet. I guess the baby will be due in September or October."

"Such a blessing! And that's why I asked you about your friends. We expect our people to see to their needs and affairs. To work hard and produce children who will take care of the parents in their old age and take our place in the community after we pass."

"I understand. I am sure there's no shortage of old people around who'd like to come here and have your community take care of them."

"Oh, it's a harsh truth. As Christians, we are called to love one another. But Jesus was speaking about the members of his tribe, his community. He wasn't talking about the Romans or the Philistines. We wouldn't have a community to pass on to our children if we spent all of our time caring for aging outsiders who do not value our customs and were not inclined to invest in the future and raise children of their own."

"I understand. A community must be self-reinforcing. That means the adults in the community must produce the next generation and provide their offspring with a path to the future. I have spent half of my career studying this. The hypocrisy and self-deception that has captured the professoriate is the most self-destructive belief system since National Socialism and Communism."

"The professwho?"

"I am sorry. The people who are teaching at the universities and colleges."

"Oh, okay."

"The Professoriate in the humanities and social sciences came to be dominated with Leftist ideologues. And childbearing and child-rearing are not their strong suit. Neither is operating in the mart of competitive commerce. Your people do it so effortlessly."

There it was. It just slipped out—*your people.*

Philip scoffed. "Hardly. Compared to your people, we make everything hard on ourselves. But we have our reasons, and in the

146

last thirty years, society has proven us right. There are one hundred and fifty families here. Do you know how many of us have been to prison? Died of an overdose? Committed suicide? Killed someone or got murdered or killed someone while drinking and driving? Or got divorced? Got a tattoo? None. Zero. Zilch. We want to keep it that way. Is it perfect? Of course not. But it's a damned sight better than what we see going on out there."

Roger was shocked with the utterance of "damned." It was almost as if Philip took the Lord's name in vain. Almost. Roger did not respond to that.

"Alright," Philip continued. "Let me think on this."

"Yes, I have to go check on Melissa. She is very upset."

"Go see to your wife and comfort her. 'Therefore a man shall leave his father and his mother and hold fast to his wife, and they shall become one flesh.' And congratulations again!"

"Do you know the Bible by heart?" Roger asked.

"Well, I don't know about that. But I try."

"Dad!" Philip's son Ezra yelled up to his father from the front door of the workshop. "Jason Thomas is riding up the driveway with another fellow!"

Philip dashed for the windows on the other side of the halters and lead ropes along the far wall with Roger on his heels.

"Potzblitz! As I live and breathe!" Philip said. He turned to Roger. "Go now. Leave this with me. I need to speak with this man."

The two riders walked their mounts up the Troyer driveway in the late-winter sunshine. The days were noticeably longer than in the depths of the winter solstice, but the shadows cast by man and horse were still long, shuddering, and otherworldly as they passed over the ground. The men in the saddle bore little resemblance to the gentle and indulgent men they were "Before." For a moment, their appearance was disconcerting to Philip. He had never met McCoy, but he knew Jason well enough. And the man before him looked like a caricature of someone he used to know. But the friendly smile

147

was still there, though framed in the face of sharp corners that Philip hardly recognized. When Jason swung down from his mount, he did so with the fluid ease of a lean cat.

"Well, as I live and breathe! You're alive!" Philip said as Jason approached.

Handshaking in greeting is not a custom the Mennonites practiced, and although Jason knew this, he must have forgotten. But Philip took his hand and gripped it enthusiastically nonetheless.

"Indeed, I am," Jason said. "And thrilled to see you alive and well, my old friend."

The men beamed at one another, clapped the other on the shoulder, and marveled at the wonder of Providence.

"You've lost weight," Philip responded. "I hardly recognized you."

"You, too. When you stepped out from behind your workshop, I thought it was your eldest. Paul, is it?"

"You must want something. No one would confuse me with Paul at my age." They shared a laugh.

"Philip, this is a friend of mine, McCoy O'Neil. He is a man of many talents. His family owns the biggest spread in our community."

"Hello, sir," McCoy said, and he removed his hat.

"Hallo," replied Philip, unconsciously using the Pennsylvania Dutch "Hallo." "Come on. I expect you are tired and hungry. Ezra will see to your horses. Follow me."

After a meal of canned ground beef, mashed potatoes, and cornbread, all washed down with copious volumes of milk served in the house, the men retired to the workshop to talk.

"So," said Philip as soon as his guests sat in their seats. "Tell me." He spread out his hands in a gesture that said, "everything and anything."

"After the power went down, we were unable to communicate with the outside world. We didn't know what was going on, so we met with the other families in the community and set our teeth to the tasks at hand and hoped for the best. There are twenty-five families, and eleven of them are Amish, but unfortunately, like most Amish these days, unlike your community, they don't farm full time. McCoy here has figured out a process to refine the crude oil from the wells in our community into kerosene and diesel, with gasoline as a by-product. My son and his girlfriend walked out of Atlanta and arrived at my place in less than two weeks, but it seemed like two years, and I think I aged ten. About a month "After" my brother arrived at my farm after taking a sailboat from New York to the Carolinas and walking over the Cumberland Pass. I have no idea if my other brothers or my sister and mother are alive."

Jason wondered if it sounded like he was rambling. And of course, he was.

"I'm sorry to hear that. I know how you feel. My son Matthew was in Missouri when it happened. But he was staying in the Mennonite settlement that Paul lives in, so I think he will be okay."

"Yes," Jason said. "I would think he will be fine. And I think we will be okay too."

"What do you mean by 'we?'" asked Philip.

"I mean the people who survived the winter will find their way to the communities like yours and ours. Life will go on."

Both Philip and McCoy lowered their heads and said nothing. Jason looked to one and then the other.

"I take it you don't agree with that assessment, Philip?" Jason asked.

"We've got some challenges ahead of us, to be sure," Philip answered.

"Well, it seems that you and McCoy here are of like minds."

Philip looked to McCoy. McCoy nodded back to him. "Yes, sir," McCoy said to Philip. "That would be a gentle way of putting it. This harvest season we had the luxury of collecting a corn and bean crop that was planted 'Before,' with seed, fuel, and fertilizer we won't have next year. And unlike your community, I think the survivors will have a gaping hole in their demographics. I think an entire generation has gone missing."

"How's that?" asked Philip.

"My experience so far," McCoy said, "tells me that the majority of survivors will be between 16 and 45 years of age. I haven't seen many survivors in the newborn to 15-years-of-age group outside of the Anabaptist communities in the region. We've got no time to lose. We need fertile women, and we need babies."

McCoy's thinking struck Philip like a slap across the face. If what McCoy said was true, in the years to come, outside men would be looking for women, and if the Shady Grove Mennonite community was the only source of women, this is where they will be looking. He tried to put that thought aside for the moment.

"There's a fellow here I think you two should meet." As soon as he said this, an idea struck Philip. Maybe the solution to an immediate problem was sitting right in front of him. He changed the subject. "Before we get into that, I'm thinking you didn't come here just to visit."

"No," Jason replied. "That's true enough. We are in desperate need of a supply of crop seed. I'm looking for heirloom field-corn. And wheat if you've got it. But we need at least 200 pounds of field corn seed if we are to survive the next winter. We have kerosene to trade."

"Well," Philip said. "You're in luck! We've got both. And three breeds of seed potatoes. We saved our field corn that we would have fed for seed and fed the hybrid corn we've harvested to the stock. The wheat ain't nothing special. It's just mixed feed wheat, but it will sprout, and you can take it from there with a little careful husbandry."

McCoy and Jason looked at each other, their eyes wide open. Then they turned back to Philip and unconsciously leaned forward in anticipation, figuring he would want to bargain for a fair supply of kerosene.

"So, what did you have in mind?" Jason asked.

"I will give you 200-pounds of corn seed, 100-pounds of wheat, and 300-pounds of seed potatoes. 100-pounds of each variety."

McCoy and Jason were shocked—this was almost too good to be true.

"In exchange," Philip continued, "we'll want 500-gallons of kerosene, and you've got to take seven people who have been living with us since the Famine started."

The "Famine." Not the "Bombings" or the "Blackout." To them, it was the Famine, and there was "Before" the Famine, and there was "After" the Famine.

"What do you mean, 'take' seven people?" asked McCoy.

"They can't stay here," replied Philip. "They've got to go with you."

"What would we do with them?"

"Find them a house. Get them started. There must be an endless supply of empty houses along the roads up by you."

"Sir," McCoy offered tentatively. "We're down here with our hat in our hand hoping to find enough crop seed so that we will have something to grow to survive on next winter. We're not a big community like y'all are. Seven people will be hard for us to feed in the lean times between now and the first of the spring harvests."

"They will have to tighten their belts and get by with meat, corn, and milk like the rest of us—but they can't stay here. You need our help. Well, we need your help. Believe me, parting with that much seed will not go over easy here, not even for 500-gallons of kerosene. We'll use candles if we have to."

"Is something wrong with them?" McCoy asked unartfully.

Philip just looked at McCoy, his face impassive.

"I mean," McCoy continued with a less aggressive tack, "why are you looking to get rid of them?"

"Look, they're English, like you. They don't fit in here. I know you've got a mish-mash of people up there. They should be able to fit in with you, and it shouldn't be that much of a burden. And you've already met one of them." Philip directed this last comment to Jason.

"I have?"

"Yes. A tall fellow about your height from Vanderbilt University."

"Yes. I remember. The professor."

"That's him. He's got a young wife. She's pregnant. He knows how to do just about anything around this kind of farm because he spent an entire growing season with us some years back, and he's handy as all get out, and so are the two other men in their crew."

Both Jason and McCoy noticed Philip didn't mention anything about the other three people, but since he separated the men by skill, the balance must be women. Both McCoy and Jason came to the same conclusion at the same time. Whoever they were, they lacked a certain appeal.

"How old are the other women?" McCoy asked. He just couldn't help himself.

"I'd say two are in their early 30's. The other is probably in her early 40's."

Jason and McCoy looked at each other and shrugged. It seemed like a strange request, but Philip's proposal was not unreasonable in economic terms. Their community needed corn seed. The wheat and seed potatoes made the offer irresistible.

"Well," Jason said. "We're not in any position to say no. We'll head out in the morning. Give us a few days to get up a team and a wagon and head down to McCoy's to pick up the kerosene. And then we will head this way."

"Take your time and come back in a week," Philip replied. "I need time to round everything up, and we need to give these people some time to get used to the idea."

"Hold on a second," McCoy said. "What if these people don't want to go with us?"

"Well, I'm going to give the professor and his wife a parting gift for all their hard work if they take you up on your kind offer."

"What kind offer?" asked McCoy.

"Your kind offer to take them into your community. With our seed, their labor, and your help your community should be able to feed itself and have something to trade with us in the future."

"Oh," McCoy said. "I get it."

"That leaves a better taste in everyone's mouth," Philip said.

"What's the parting gift?" asked Jason.

"I'm going to give them a buggy and harness, an older buggy mare, and a stud colt. There is no shortage of horses around. I think the people just let their pasture gates open before they died or moved off and let the horses fend for themselves. We've got a corral full of them."

"Well, what about the other five people," McCoy asked. "No parting gift for them?"

"We'll give the men a horse and tack."

"What about the women?"

"That will be up to our women," replied Philip. "But I wouldn't expect much."

Well, there it was. McCoy and Jason got the picture, but they would come to find that they drew the wrong picture.

"I don't know that I have 500-gallons of refined kerosene available immediately," McCoy said. "I am pretty sure I can come up with 300-gallons. I'll deliver the balance in a month if that's okay."

"It's good enough," Philip replied. "We'll put it on your account. I am sure there will be lots of trade going on between us. Now that we've got that settled, why don't you two bunk over in the loft over the buggy barn. Jason knows what I'm talking about. There's a stove in there, and I will have my wife send over some cornbread and milk. I need to have a talk with Roger."

Chapter 21

Roger guided his buggy horse onto the floodplain next to Annie's store. This was his first long buggy ride—just under thirty miles—and now he understood why people were so keen for automobiles. For trips under a half an hour or so, buggy rides are exhilarating. After that, they become exhausting, especially if you don't have someone to take the reins and share the driving. Melissa desperately wanted to come with him, but a long bumpy ride seemed an unnecessary risk for a pregnant woman. She would have to make such a journey soon enough on their move to the Sulphur Springs settlement, the name that McCoy gave to the community surrounding Jason's farm. Melissa relented and agreed that there was no point in tripling that risk with the round trip to Annie's.

It was now the third week in February. Roger rode north with Jason, while McCoy rode alone to his farm, the day after they arrived in Shady Grove to inspect the proposed living arrangement, but he realized that he didn't have much choice in the matter. Philip and Roger had a heart-to-heart talk in which Philip assured Roger that he and Melissa were welcome back to live amongst the Shady Grove Mennonites if things didn't work out in Sulphur Springs, but the other members of the Garden of Eden cadre were not. Still, Roger had to agree with Philip that living as an Englishman alone amongst the Mennonites would not be easy. The Sulphur Springs community had a diverse mix of belief systems, and they were interested in bringing productive families into their community, whereas the Shady Grove Mennonites were not. Roger agreed that this was probably a better fit, at least for him and Melissa, but not because of the multi-culturalism of the community. That way led to disaster, but society would have to be rebuilt with the stones that are within reach. Roger recalled Annie's powerful metaphor. Stones might be inanimate, but civilization was built with barren rocks at least as much as it was on fertile soil and clean water.

There was an old Amish general store on route 318 that Jason's neighbors ran for many years before they got too old to stand all day on the poured concrete floors. The building was empty and would serve to house Roger and Melissa until the Miller's moved to their nephew's property where an apartment addition to the main farmhouse was under construction where the Miller's would spend their final years. At that time, Roger and Melissa would move into the Miller's house. They would have a water well and a good-sized stock barn, woodshed, and workshop steps from their backdoor. Jason and Martin Weiss would be their closest neighbors. More importantly, they would have the foundation of a real, sustainable, and self-reinforcing community. Roger felt exhilaration with the possibilities presented.

Roger tied his horse and called out for Annie. He rounded the building and stepped onto the porch and knocked on the front door—no answer. He opened the door slightly and felt the rush of warm air on his face. With a hot stove, she couldn't be far.

"You lookin' for someone?" Annie said from behind him.

Roger turned and said, "Yea, I've come to get you." Roger spent the next five minutes bringing Annie up to speed on everything that had transpired since he left her place back in December.

"Stop talking!" Annie said. "I'm ready to go! It's been a long winter. Give me a half hour to pack. My books are already in boxes. See what you can fit in the back of that buggy."

"No need to rush. This horse has had enough for one day. We can leave first thing in the morning. And there's plenty of room. I got a cart behind the buggy."

Roger and Annie departed at first light. The morning proved to be cold, but Roger brought two thick wool blankets with him, and they were comfortable enough. By noon the temperature was almost spring-like with just a slight raw edge to the air when the sun snuck behind a cloud. Nature was slowly reclaiming the unnerving spectacle of the aftermath of the crisis for the unfortunate travelers who ran out of fuel along state road 41E. They say that time heals all wounds, but that's not true. Time merely erases all of the signs of suffering and death, and nature takes care of the rest.

"Come summer," Annie mused as she took in the tragic scene, "the grass and the wildflowers will swallow all of this. In a year, except for the junk cars, it'll be like it never even happened."

Roger understood perfectly. Without lawn mowers and weed-whackers and other machinery, the grass will be four feet high in June, and its roots will climb over the bodies along the roads and in the fields. Even the bones will be consumed: ashes to ashes, dust to dust.

"It's hard to wrap your mind around," Roger said.

"You think so?" asked Annie. "I don't find it hard to comprehend. We were due for an old-fashioned ass-kicking. Perhaps overdue. Pandemics, wars, polar vortexes, famines, floods, syphilis, wildfires, hurricanes, you name it. We conquered everything, but we held it all together with electric power. That was the weak link, our utter dependence on electricity to power everything."

"I don't even miss it now."

"That's easy for you to say. You just happened to have a friendly relationship with an agriculturally based religious cult, and they took you in and fed you and kept you warm for the winter. What do you think happened to your colleagues in Nashville? They are not enjoying a sushi dinner before an evening concert with the Nashville Philharmonic. The suffering in places like that must have been inconceivable."

"I can't even imagine," Roger said. His mind went to his sons, and his graduate assistant, Mark and his girlfriend, Jill. Where did they go and what did they do?

"Don't overthink it, Roger. Events can be no other way than the way they are. If anyone survives this besides the Anabaptists and the Mormons, it will be the military. They will just take what they need."

"What about the rest of the world?"

"We will know soon enough. I bet that the U.S. gave as well as it got. It might be quite some time before we know, and I doubt there are humanitarian efforts underway by the international community to help us. We are on our own. There is no point worrying about the big picture. We've got our hands full."

As they approached the Shady Grove settlement, the highway opened wide and clear. The Mennonites organized teams of draft horses and men to move the vehicles abandoned in the middle of the road in a ten-mile radius of the community. If there was a corpse in the vehicle, they did not disturb it. The men drained the vehicles of their engine oil to use for lubricating farm equipment and sometimes stripped them of their wheels and left them on the shoulder of the highway to rust in the rain. Roger imagined that in the years to come the metal would find its way to a productive enterprise. Or maybe he hoped they would. Perhaps they would remain here and get swallowed by the grass too. Roger turned his horse off of 41E and onto route 110. They were still well outside of the settlement, and all of the houses along the road were English. The Mennonites formed teams in early February to go door to door to the homes on the access roads into the settlement. Most of the houses were empty, their occupants long gone. But about one in five of the houses was marked with a spray-painted "HR," indicating human remains in the home, somewhere easily seen from the street, to signal that these were unsafe to enter. When informed of this, Annie merely raised her eyebrows and shrugged and repeated, "Events can be no other way than the way they are."

Chapter 22

The day of Roger and Melissa's departure from the Mennonite settlement at Shady Grove dawned bright and clear. It was the last week of February, and the winter weather broke in a delightful foreshadowing of spring. Of course, winter would be back. March was a fickle month at this latitude. But the night, and now the morning, was as tender and mild as a mother's love. Jason and McCoy had arrived the night before with three massive workhorses hitched to a forecart pulling a 16 x 8-foot hay wagon loaded with a 330-gallon sized tote tank filled to the brim with kerosene. The fuel was offloaded—with great care—with buckets the night before so that the tote tank could return. The seed corn and wheat and potatoes were loaded first and onto the front of the wagon. Enough canned food to last the outcasts for a week got loaded next. The Mennonites provided Roger & Company with a week's supply of soups and stews in quart jars and cornbread that would be easy to prepare on the road and provide comfort and warmth as they settled into their new life. All of this careful consideration made for people who were essentially exiled reminded Roger of the extraordinary humanity of these people. Only Philip and his wife Ruth, and their adult children came to say good-bye. When the last of their worldly possessions were loaded, Evan and Karl mounted their horses, and Sandy, Mindy, Florence, and Annie climbed up on the wagon. McCoy was already in his saddle, and Roger and Melissa were waiting in their buggy with the stud colt that Philip gave them pony-tied to the back. All waited for Jason to say his good-bye and thank-you to Philip. Finally, Jason climbed onto the forecart, picked up the reins, and signaled the workhorses to move out.

"Don't get too comfortable back there, ladies," McCoy said as he rode along beside the wagon. "Y'all can ride downhill and on flat ground, but you will have to get out and walk when climbing hills."

Florence wondered if Melissa would be walking up the hills too. McCoy must have read her mind and called over to Roger and Melissa in the buggy.

"I told the women they would have to get off and walk when we head uphill, but that doesn't include pregnant women. Besides these are my horses, and I am careful not to overwork my horses. That horse is yours to do with as you please."

Annie looked at Florence with an amused look on her face and then looked away when Florence returned her gaze.

"I'll get out and walk," Melissa said to Roger. "I'm not that pregnant, and I will be happy to stretch my legs."

"Lucky you," Roger replied with a smile.

Melissa laced her arm under Roger's arm and pulled herself close and said, "You should take it easy. You're going to need to save your energy for tonight."

McCoy and Jason decided to take 41E north through Edinburgh on the trip home to shave over five miles off of the trip back. Riding a horse to Shady Grove was one thing. Driving workhorses in the lines and pulling a rig was a different story. The party took route 110—the same spoke-road that Roger and Annie came in on two days earlier—out of the community to 41E. Houses dotted the ribbon of land along the way. There were cars in some of the driveways, and mailboxes stood silent guard, waiting for a mail delivery that would never come from a mailman who was probably no longer alive. Here and there, a child's bike or plastic toy lay in a front yard with its unnatural colors fading from the effects of the weather. But there were no people, no dogs, no movement: just the sound of the horses' hooves and the metal rim of the buggy wheels clanging against the pavement. The wagon's rubber tires rode in near silence.

McCoy pointed out the houses with the glaring "HR" marked on them indicating the house contained human remains.

"What's the point of marking the house?" asked Sandy. "So that someone can come back and bury them?"

Jason explained. "The houses without human remains can be stripped and repurposed. The presence of decaying human remains in a house makes that impractical. And if the survival rate is ten percent, each of us would have to bury nine bodies without assistance. If the survival rate is five percent, then you'd

159

have to dig nineteen graves and transport the remains all by yourself. As a practical matter, nature is going to have to handle this. The living has their own problems and must see to themselves. The best thing we can do is keep clear so that we don't get sick."

McCoy kicked his horse up for a few steps to get out of earshot of the wagon and Jason's horse, Thunder, took it upon himself to catch up. Jason marveled at the nature of horses.

"I get the feelin' we bought us a pig in a poke," McCoy said to Jason as he pulled alongside.

Jason shrugged. "I think that couple will fit right in and be an important asset," Jason said, nodding to the buggy where Roger and Melissa huddled together.

"I'm sure they will. But I ain't talking 'bout them."

"Philip said the men were handy. If a Mennonite farmer says that, you can bet they are."

"I ain't talking 'bout them neither. Look, we still got too many men and not enough women. And we need everyone pulling in the same direction."

"Well, maybe they will pull in the same direction—they don't have any choice. Did you hear Philip's appeal to them before we left?"

"No," replied McCoy. "I musta missed that."

"He told them, 'For even when we were with you, this we commanded you, that if any would not work, neither should he eat.' And by the way, we didn't have a choice either. We needed what Philip had, and he needed us to take these people away from his community. His motivations are not important. The way I see it, we entered into a contract with Philip voluntarily, and we have an ethical responsibility to give these people a chance."

McCoy took a deep breath and puffed out his cheeks. "Look, I was the one who told you we couldn't go it alone. We need a community. A real, cooperative, and interdependent community. 'Community,' not just people living in 'proximity.' Ain't that what we said?"

"Yes, indeed. And didn't everyone come to agree with you?"

"Yea, they did!" McCoy was getting excited and animated. "And you know why? Because I make fuckin' sense. A community is made up of its people. And people come from babies. And babies come from women. Do those women look like baby-makers to you? An old lady and three dykes?"

"The older woman is going to live with Roger and Melissa. I imagine she's going to take on the task of surrogate grandmother. There's nothing wrong with that. If anything, that sets a good example for our community. And the man thought enough of her that he traveled sixty miles roundtrip in a buggy to go get her."

"Yes, well, that's his business, and she's his problem. But the Mennonites ain't kicked her out. They kicked the others out. I imagine they got their reasons."

Jason paused for a moment and waited for McCoy to look over and make eye contact.

"I imagine they do, McCoy. But we are not Mennonites. And now we have enough crop seed that if we are careful, we won't starve to death next winter. I reckon we got a bargain." Jason reached out and patted his friend on the back of the shoulder. "Have faith. The growing season is coming up. Between all of us, we have to be expecting a dozen babies right in the middle of it, and that's just the first wave. We are going to have our hands full, and we are going to need all-hands-on-deck."

"I admire you, Yankee. You're always a fucking optimist."

Jason enjoyed a belly laugh.

"Ha! So, it's back to 'Yankee,' is it? Come on, McCoy! We've got bigger fish to fry. We've got a community to feed, grandbabies to raise, fields to prepare, and crops to plant. And every time I look over at those sacks of seeds, I feel better and better about the future."

Chapter 23

A cloak of hushed sadness descended over the group as they picked their way through the abandoned cars and debris that littered the highway through Edinburgh. It didn't look cataclysmic. It looked more like the aftermath of a massive holiday party and parade, and the municipality forgot to clean up afterward. The small city of Edinburgh was established two hundred years ago, and the courthouse square built over a hundred years ago. The by-pass road they traveled on was less than fifty years old, and about a mile from the square and developed in the ugly and obnoxious strip-mall style that dominated America in the post-1960's to serve the needs of motorists and later updated with big-box stores that soon struggled with the onslaught of the internet. For the people, Edinburgh was the land that time forgot. With the advent of industrialized farming the agricultural workers living here in the first half of the 20th century transformed into factory workers in the early part of the second half, but with the automation of the factory, there was no work in the modern economy for the people in the region to turn. Their young people moved off to Chicago, Atlanta, Washington D.C., and New York and the old folks stayed behind and smoked and drank away their social security checks.

The American economy relied on long-distance trucking to deliver the goods to keep the people warm, fed, clothed, hygienic, and entertained. Economic specialization turned America into an economic powerhouse and provided a standard of living unparalleled in human history. Well, that is before our acceptance of specialization created the liability that spawned the greatest existential crisis in human history—Whoops! America's big-rig trucks supplied every single thing the people consumed on a daily basis. The people had no idea how to provide anything for themselves, and they were unaccustomed to privation. The trucks stopped delivering on Halloween, nearly four brutally cold and starving months ago. Events might have unfolded differently— and if "if's and and's were candy and nuts we'd all have a merry

Christmas!"—but they didn't. When the power went out, the people hunkered down and waited for it to come back on. And waited. And then they waited some more. It took a week before anyone seriously considered the possibility that the power would not come back on anytime soon. And then events spiraled out of control.

In the Hollywood version of the apocalypse, the characters turned to violence. But death from hunger, exposure to the cold, and suicide makes for a bummer of a movie. How can the heroine save the day by killing the bad guys if she is near death from hunger and exposure, and the bad guys got nothing left to be bad with? In the real-life version of the apocalypse, the people turned to suicide. And suicide turned out to be exceedingly contagious. Their passage through Edinburgh was the first large-scale exposure that Roger Little and the residents of the Garden of Eden LGBTV commune had to what took place in the towns and cities across much of the industrialized world since Halloween. The buildings were undamaged. No zombies were wandering the roads, no hordes of roving gangs raping and pillaging—there were no people at all! There was only the wind. Everything looked tired. Depressed. Four months' worth of dust and grime covered every car, every store window, every sign.

Jason and McCoy decided to rest and feed the horses in a field on the north side of the commercial strip on the west side of 41E before the final push on to McCoy's farm where they planned to spend the night. The women walked together to the woods on the north end of the field to relieve themselves. The men did so right there in the field. The details regarding bodily functions were another issue that books and movies glossed over in their depictions of survival situations. Toilets fill quickly without water to flush waste away making them useless, and people who have never once squatted to relieve themselves found it almost impossible to do so, especially the overweight and obese, and many of them solved this problem by killing themselves. It takes time to become accustomed to privation, and some people just don't have any patience.

With their ablutions complete, Jason and McCoy unhitched the workhorses from the forecart, removed their bridles and hobbled each animal, and fed them hay and grain in rubber tubs from the feed sacks; all carried on the hay wagon. Roger, Evan, and Karl did the same with their horses. Roger helped Annie and Melissa up onto the hay wagon to rest against the hay bales with a heavy wool blanket wrapped around them. He kissed Melissa on the lips and asked if she was okay, and then took a seat with the men on the ground leaning on their packs. Florence and Sandy joined the men, but Mindy hopped onto the wagon and cuddled next to Melissa and Annie.

Sandy broke the silence.

"The whole city died?" she stated as much as asked.

"No, of course not," replied Jason. "McCoy thinks there are plenty of survivors out there."

"But only those who took immediate and correct action survived," McCoy said. "Whatever y'all did, you must have done it right, and right away."

"Nope," answered Roger. "It was just blind luck." Roger recounted their meeting at the campsite, waiting three weeks for the power to come back on, running out of food, and their improbable hike from there to the Mormon homestead, Annie's home, and the Old Order Mennonite community.

"Yea," McCoy said. "I'd say you had a heck of a run of good luck there. He's got a brother, a nephew, and a friend," and here McCoy hooked a thumb towards Jason, "who sailed down the eastern seaboard from New York and walked across the Cumberland Pass with their families to his farm."

"Holy shit! You're kidding!" Roger said.

"No. He's not kidding," replied Jason. "They did indeed."

"But they left the next morning, and his brother owned a boat and had a gas station convenience store filled with food. Did I mention he was a boy scout? There's bound to be lots of stories like that," said McCoy. "And some lucky ones like yours too, I suppose."

Then back to Sandy. "There's nothing to survive on in the commercial centers like this little town we just passed. To survive the winter, you'd have to evacuate to a place where you could keep warm and fed. If you don't have or know of such a place, you didn't make it. Going only by what we saw around here, the people caught out on the roads traveling away from home died of exposure. The people who stayed home mostly killed themselves. It would make a boring TV series. Just think: What would they call it? 'Everybody's Dead?'"

McCoy enjoyed a good laugh.

"Can you imagine what went on in Nashville, Louisville, or Cincinnati?" Jason asked.

"No," replied Roger. "I can't."

Jason continued, "If you waited around for the electric power to come back on and for the authorities to distribute food and water, you didn't survive the winter. If you left and didn't have a place to go, you died on the roads. Think about it. A family of four makes a run for grandpa's farm. They run out of gas. One of the kids gets sick. Do they leave the child to die and try to save themselves? No parent would do such a thing. They stay with the child, and all of them die. Anyway, that's what it looks like to us."

McCoy nodded in agreement and stared blankly at the ground.

Roger told Jason and McCoy about the dead woman with the pearls and the missing child and the woman on 41E with the dead child in the car.

"That's fucked up," McCoy said.

"But we are still here," Jason said. "And winter is almost over. All of the grain and hay that we and our livestock need to survive next winter will come from the spring growing season. What we do in the next three months must feed us through the rest of the year."

"And that's where we come in? As your new field hands?" Sandy asked with an edge. There was always an edge with Sandy.

"Don't flatter yourself there, toots," McCoy said. "Ten of you couldn't do the work of one Amish girl. What we need from our women are babies."

Sandy regarded McCoy with a smirk on her face. "Don't expect babies from me."

McCoy smirked right back. "Why not. Are you too old?"

"It's none of your fucking business," Sandy replied, venom dripping from every word.

Roger rolled his eyes and lowered his head. Sandy was a walking confrontation just waiting to happen. And McCoy seemed to know how to push her buttons.

"Ah, don't be like that, sister," McCoy said with a big smile. "I am just thinking about the future. We've already settled this issue in our community. Our people are expected to have and raise children to provide our people with a path to the future and to care for us in our old age. There ain't no one else. It's just us. The only social safety net we got is each other, and there ain't no such thing as 'each other' unless we have children. You are not special, sister. You must be in your 40's, right? Think about 20 years from now. Who is going to put food on your table for you when you can no longer fend for yourself?"

McCoy always came out swinging, but he was willing to take a punch too. He sat there, his eyes locked with Sandy's eyes, and waited for her to say what was on her mind. She looked to Florence, and then to Evan and Karl. No one came to her rescue. The enormity of the situation crashed down on Sandy as like an anvil dropped out of a hayloft.

"I'll worry about that then," was all she could come up with.

"Good! I was hoping you'd say that. I want to make it clear to all of you that you are on your own. No one is going to force you to do anything, and you will not force us to do anything. I ain't telling you what to do, but I'm telling you that you ain't special and that you will have to engage in a free and voluntary exchange of value if you want to live in cooperation with us. And you will abide by the culture and traditions we are working hard to establish and become a contributing member of the community. Otherwise, you should keep walking, and we will wish you well. Do any of you have any questions for me?"

Silence.

"Alrighty, then," McCoy said. "I'm gonna catch a few winks." Then to Jason, "Take your time, Jason. I figure it's less than two hours at this pace to my place."

McCoy took his pack and stretched out on the front of the wagon.

Jason looked around at the people from the Garden of Eden. "When I first met McCoy, I thought there was something seriously wrong with the man. But all of us have come to value him as a member of our community. He's not big on small talk, and he is not afraid to speak his mind. I am not going to apologize for him. That's just his way."

"Is he homophobic?" Sandy demanded. Florence, Karl, and Evan raised their eyes to Jason.

"I don't think he's got a mean-spirited bone in his body," replied Jason.

"That's not what I asked."

"Sure, it is. That's exactly what you asked. There's no such thing as 'homophobic.' That's something your political organization came up with to slander people who don't find your sexuality appealing. Well, there are lots of religious groups here that are not going to welcome you. And you don't have any right to force them to pretend that they do. You are going to have to live with that. And they are going to have to live with you."

"People must be free to reject any or all of your sensibilities for any reason they wish," added Roger.

"Exactly so," Jason said. "What they must not do is use force on you for any reason other than to defend their right to life and property."

"But they are bigots!" Florence said.

"So?" asked Jason.

"What do you mean, 'so?!'" asked Sandy. "Are you defending them?"

"Would I defend them from you if you attempted to use violence to coerce their thoughts and sensibilities? Of course, I would! You are not the judge of a universal worldview. If you don't like them, don't engage with them. Didn't any of you read Orwell's '1984?'"

Jason looked from face to face.

Roger smiled and looked around too.

"No?" Jason asked. "Well, what *was* the last book you read? How did you come to the determination that you could justifiably use force to coerce thought compliance?"

"I can't believe I am hearing this!" Florence looked stupefied.

"That's because you have spent your entire life in an echo chamber. Here, we let our people speak their mind. You don't get to reject their argument just because you don't like the conclusion. But you do get to present a counter-argument. Are you asserting that the use of violence to force compliance with your belief system is morally acceptable?"

Florence and Sandy looked at each other in disbelief. Evan and Karl remained uncommitted. Roger was enjoying this immensely.

"Bigotry is evil! Racism is evil! Homophobia is evil!" Sandy shouted.

"Well, perhaps they are. But who gets to define those terms? And who says the people you are pointing and wagging your finger at are practicing any of those?" Roger asked. "What if I think you're a bigot, Sandy? Is it okay if I use violence to correct your thinking?"

"How am I a bigot?"

"Well, you hate men," Roger replied. "Men disgust you. You hate McCoy because he pointed out the pathology of your personality."

"The 'pathology of my personality!?' Because I won't be subjugated to a man and his fucking dick?"

"No. Because you would gladly use violence to force compliance with a worldview that is driven by your foundational disgust response to men and maleness."

"Oh? But you get to determine what is 'pathological?'" Sandy asked Roger.

"Well, pathological has a complicated definition. But in this case, each must determine what is dangerous. Your thoughts and feeling and interpretations of your liabilities within existence—and those of everyone around you—belong to you as a natural right. What you and I don't have the right to do is to use violence or coercion of any kind to force another person to comply with our thinking and belief system. That way lies the slippery slope to damnation."

"I'm not listening to any more of this," Sandy said as she rose from the ground and stormed off.

"You people are nuts," Florence said, and she stomped off after Sandy.

McCoy listened to the entire exchange as he rested his eyes and body on the wagon and roused himself when he heard Florence and Sandy depart and sauntered over to where Jason, Roger, Karl, and Evan were sitting.

"I told you they was crazy," McCoy said to Jason as he sat down on the ground with the men.

Jason made eye contact with Evan and Karl. "Do you guys think we're nuts?"

"Not even a little bit," said Evan.

"No," said Karl.

"Well, we got that going for us," Jason said to McCoy as he gestured to Karl and Evan.

"If I understand the community's philosophy," said Evan. "Your people reject the use of violence to control or influence people's thoughts and beliefs and personal nature."

"And we won't tolerate the use of force or the support for the use of force by others to attempt to control what people think or feel," Jason said. "Violence committed on your behalf and with your endorsement, what McCoy has termed 'violence by proxy,' is just as unacceptable as violence you commit yourself."

Evan and Karl looked at each other for a moment and then turned back to Jason. Both men shrugged.

"That works for us," said Evan. "We're not interested in using force on anyone—or having others use it on us."

"Well, to make that work, as a practical matter, we believe that all of us have a responsibility to find a way to prosper—because desperate people are dangerous. Desperate people do desperate things. Our community is cooperative and interdependent, but we are not a collective. Our first responsibility is to ourselves and our family and then the community."

"Come on, Yankee," McCoy groaned as he got to his feet. "You're starting to sound like a commie organizer in reverse. Let's get the horses up and get going. You can sort all of this out later. But I will tell you right now: Those women are not staying at my place. They are going up with you."

"We haven't made provision for them," Jason protested.

"I didn't say the whole gang. My clan will take Evan and Karl here. You take the women."

"Gee. Thanks," Jason said. "I feel like we're back in elementary school picking teams in the playground—and I got the kids with two left feet."

"Look, I took in Belinda Cutliff when you wanted to get her out of your house." Last year a neighbor of Jason's had a terrible fight with her husband, and he wouldn't let her back in the house. Jason brought her to McCoy, and he took her in. "Well, those two ain't poisoning my people. Maybe you'll get lucky, and they will keep on walking."

Jason didn't respond.

Roger thought, *what about Mindy? No one ever seemed to notice Mindy.*

Chapter 24

The O'Neil family owned the largest productive farm in the five-county region surrounding Edinburgh with five-hundred acres of hay, crop, and pasture ground and two-hundred acres in hardwood timber. The current iteration of the family traced their roots in the region to a Scottish émigré and cattle trader by the name of Samuel Bull who acquired some of the land now owned by the O'Neil's after landing in Philadelphia and making his way down the Blue Ridge to the Cumberland Pass. Samuel Bull was buried on the land he acquired, and the family has interred their dead there ever since, with Bull's obelisk tombstone towering at the center of the family graveyard. The rest of the current day O'Neil spread was cobbled together over the more than two-hundred years since Bull arrived in the region.

McCoy O'Neil came back to the farm with his wife, Theresa, and their children after his father, Peter, suffered a debilitating stroke. His mother, a life-long smoker, had passed away several years earlier from lung cancer, and his brother, Liam, was busy building his construction business. McCoy was struggling with the direction of his life after his forced retirement from the U.S. Army at the rank of Major due to migraines and vision problems. Within months of moving back to the farm his vision improved dramatically, and the migraine headaches vanished. McCoy concluded that something he was doing or exposed to in his previous occupation was absent on the farm, and while he could not be sure, he suspected that fluorescent lighting was the culprit. The only other significant difference as far as his eyes were concerned was exposure to sunlight. On the farm, he worked outside for much of the time, and in his former military and suburban life, he spent all of his time indoors. But he hated fluorescent lighting with a passion, so he decided that was the culprit. In any event, his good health returned. Theresa was born and raised in Edinburgh and what she wanted most from life was to see Edinburgh in her rearview mirror. She resisted the move to the farm and tried her best to hate it, but within a year she had to begrudgingly admit that farm life was starting to agree with her and that her husband and children were thriving. Living on a large farm was nothing like living in the boredom of small-town rural America. Here, there was no time for idle hands—there was always something to do—and the rhythm of the seasons, the fresh food and air, and the physical demands seemed to satisfy their minds and bodies.

Theresa was home on the early afternoon of Halloween working in the kitchen to leave supper on the table for McCoy and their middle child, Lori Anne, preparing to take their youngest child, Mary Anne, to trick-or-treat with her eighth-grade classmates when the news of the nuclear bombings in the Middle East broke. McCoy was out walking the fence-line looking for future escape routes for their cattle, and on a farm of this size, it took a while for Theresa to find him. He wasn't out walking the fences. Theresa found him glued to the TV in his library in one of the outbuildings near the workshop. McCoy was mesmerized by the reports of people pouring out of the world's major cities. Within a half hour, cell phones didn't work, and the internet operated at a crawl, but the cable TV news channels were still on the air. The family gathered for the evening meal and then went back to the TV. When the power went out an hour or two later, McCoy was furious with himself for sitting around and watching the TV instead of making preparations. It wasn't like a family farm with 200 years of operating history doesn't have things like candles, flashlights, and kerosene-lamps somewhere. But finding them in the dark was another story. They used the flashlight app on their cell phones in the mad scramble of the first hours of the blackout, only to find that cell phone batteries don't last long when used in this way. McCoy wanted to save the phones just in case his son, Trevor, or brother, Liam, might call him, even though he knew this could not happen without power to the cell phone towers. His first thought after his anger with himself was that the big east coast cities of the United States would spend the next twelve hours in the dark with people trapped in elevators, subways, trains, and in traffic. He could deal with the inconvenience of cell phone flashlights and candles. He was home. Those poor souls will be shitting in the corner of these conveyances tonight.

That night, McCoy hardly slept. He kept looking over to his clock-radio, fully expecting to see the ghostly illumination of the digital clock face and surprised each time he looked that it was dark. A nuclear war in the Middle East and power outage here in the United States were not likely to be a coincidence, and if this was an orchestrated attack, it might be quite a while before the power came on. Unfortunately, the time when the entire system would expire was probably much nearer than the time when the power would be restored. Nuclear weapons and carrier groups were nothing more than the restaurant in front of the casino—payoffs to the people who pulled strings and leaned on the leavers of power. The money table in the casino was the electrical grid. Total war without firing a shot—well, except for a handful of nuclear bombs in the Middle East. Now, it was a race against time. McCoy felt that they had a week to restore the grid. Maybe two. After that, the suffering will begin in earnest.

McCoy visited with the prominent farming families and the local Amish community in those first days "After" to get a feel for the situation. October is the driest month of the year in this region, and the extended forecast called for a rainy November. The beans could wait until December, but they needed to get the corn in before the wet weather. Eighty percent of the corn crop and twenty percent of the bean crop was harvested "Before" and placed on trucks destined for the feedlots in Oklahoma. This was their cash crop, for which they expected to receive payment by the end of the year. Their own grain bins were empty.

Well, when you're, you're hot, McCoy thought to himself.

His son Trevor made his way home from Western Kentucky University three days "After." McCoy's brother Liam and his son, "Bark," short for Barclay, took another two weeks to complete the journey from Franklin, Tennessee. When they arrived, they were in rough shape, and in another week, they would have been in desperate shape. In addition to close-family, several cousins and family friends, mostly young men, drifted to the McCoy spread over November, and other than Trevor, none of them was in any condition to put in a day's work when they arrived.

A Southern Baptist by tradition, a mechanical engineer by training, a farmer by practice, and a voracious reader by interest, the substance of McCoy clashed with the good-ol'-boy style of McCoy. He was a chess enthusiast, and his chess mind informed him that the current situation would unfold into a crisis of biblical proportions. There were a dozen young single men taking refuge at the McCoy spread. As they regained their strength these men were put to work reclaiming materials from abandoned trucks, houses, and barns and metal fabrication in the shop. There were two oil "stripper-wells" on the farm, and there were dozens more in the county. McCoy developed a basic and course refining process that produced a small but critical volume of distillate fuels, diesel, and kerosene, as well as the natural by-products, primarily gasoline. Enough to run a one hundred horse-power diesel tractor driving a PTO driven generator to power the welding equipment in his shop and trade kerosene with the local Amish and Mennonite communities for labor and other necessities.

After a visit from Jason Thomas and the Amish deacon's youngest son, Noah and the relocation of a local woman, Belinda Cutliff to the O'Neil farm, McCoy was inspired to seek survivors—young women—who would be a good fit for his overwhelmingly male clan. He and his son, Trevor engaged in a daring rescue of eight starving girls from Elizabethtown as well as several lesser rescue operations. That was just over two months ago, and now there was a thriving clan taking shape in and around the O'Neil farm, and associated with the larger Sulphur Springs community.

Chapter 25

Jason and McCoy led their charges onto the long gravel driveway at the O'Neil farm. On their right, a dozen newly constructed cottages, one after the other, stood along the drive. And though the work day was over, the late afternoon sun, though low in the sky, still shone at this time of year. The party passed the last of the cottages and came to the former parking area between McCoy's office and library and the farm's massive workshop building. A small crowd formed around the erstwhile travelers and a pleasant aroma filled the air. McCoy's son Trevor stepped forward and introduced himself. Roger, Melissa, Karl, and Evan were quartered in the first cottage they passed and Sandy, Mindy, Florence, and Annie in the next cabin. Each structure had two small bedrooms at either end with a larger communal room in between, sparsely furnished in early-American-garage-sale. Both were equipped with homemade wood-stoves made from 40 lbs. propane tanks seated horizontally and refitted with a firebox and a loading door, dampers to control airflow, and a short stove pipe that vented through a stoned-wall section, but neither had a kitchen or any sign of cooking utensils.

"There are soft beds in each bedroom," Trevor said. "Might as well make yourselves at home and rest. You'll hear the dinner bell. We've got a sheep on a spit, and we're steaming a goat, and they are almost done. Tonight, we feast." And here Trevor looked down and paused for dramatic effect and added with a wink, "And drink."

"I've never had goat," Roger said.

"I've never even heard of steamed goat," said Evan.

"Oh, man it's good," said Trevor. "When you steam it, it gets so tender the meat just falls off of the bone. We like to wrap it in flatbread and smother it with hot salsa and eat it like a burrito."

"That sounds like heaven," Melissa said.

"It's close," Trevor laughed.

"What are we drinking?" asked Karl.

"We've got corn liquor and hard cider. The cider's been sitting in 55-gallon steel drums, so it's got a little rust in it. Once you get past that, it's the best the best thing since sliced bread. And the liquor will set you right, as long as you don't have to work tomorrow," Trevor concluded with a sly smile. "And I don't have to work tomorrow."

The dinner bell rang.

"Well, you can rest later," Trevor said. "Let's eat!"

The evening temperature was exceptionally mild for this time of year. McCoy called it "grass-growing weather," and explained that sometimes a warm stretch in February or March would last long enough to fool the grass into growing and after a winter of dry hay the livestock couldn't be coaxed to the barn with feed. Of course, this was only the second evening of mild weather, and they would need at least a week for the grass to grow, but it was a welcome break from a particularly miserable and cold winter and a stroke of good luck for their homecoming and planting celebration.

McCoy's brother Liam and his son Bark were busy slicing meat from the sheep while Trevor's wife Tara and Bark's wife Suellen worked the poached goat. Stacks of hot cornbread tortillas waited at a small table to receive the meat and the salsa. There were no plates, and there wasn't much variety—just the bread, meat, and hot tomato sauce—but there was alcohol. And that made all the difference.

After they gorged on the meat and bread, the young people peeled off to socialize among themselves around a small fire in a pit in the grass area in front of the cabins. Roger and his companions from the Garden of Eden commune and Annie Ackroyd sat around the fire on some old chairs McCoy and Liam retrieved from the workshop enjoying some hard cider on a full stomach. Melissa was tired and retired to the cabin. Finally, Jason found his way to the fire.

"What a day!" Annie said to no one in particular.

"And what a meal," Roger said. "I never had goat before. Now I think it is my favorite."

"Hunger makes the best sauce," McCoy said.

"What is this place?" Florence asked.

"This is my family's farm," McCoy answered Florence.

"McCoy's family has lived here for over 200 years," Jason said to Florence.

"All these people are related to you?" Florence asked McCoy.

"Not all, but a lot of the men-folk are kin. Most of the women are survivors. The rest are church members."

"What church is that?" Florence asked.

"Well, "Before," all of us attended the Sunnydale Baptist Church over by Jason's farm. Now, we have a service each Sunday in the workshop."

"I understand that your people built those cabins there just in the last two months?" Roger asked.

"Yes, indeed," replied McCoy. "We framed 'em all in a week. Without electric wiring and plumbing, it ain't no thing. Four outhouses behind them service them. We got ahold of metal roofing material from a chicken house the size of a football field to sheath the exterior and roof and particle board to sheath the floor and interior. We used straw for insulation and tore down a big old tobacco barn along 41E for lumber."

"There are no shortages for anything," Jason said. "Except food."

"Man, ain't that the truth," McCoy added.

Roger cut right to the chase. "So, what are your plans for the Sulphur Springs community?"

"I like the sound of that," Jason said. "It's a catchy name."

"Yea," McCoy said. "Too bad there ain't nobody around to catch it with. But to answer your question, Roger, our first order of business has to be survival. We need to prove—and quickly— that we can farm well enough this growing season to feed everyone in the community for a year. We need to have babies and see to their survival. And we need a critical mass of people— young people—if we are going to make it.

"Why do you need babies?" Mindy asked.

"Look, I ain't looking for a fight with you people."

"No, I don't mean to fight," Mindy said. "I mean that sincerely. Why do you need babies? Won't they be a drain on resources? With no return to the community for more than a decade?"

Roger wasn't sure if he just heard more words from Mindy than he had for the previous nearly four months.

"Well, Imagine this. Imagine 150 of your favorite people relocated to a beautiful tropical island, and that none of these people wanted the burden of bearing and raising children. Maybe they are sterile. Maybe they are low-testosterone intellectual men. Or maybe they are all men or all women who are not interested in the company of the opposite sex. Now, on this island, the fish practically jump into your boat and fruit grows all year round, and the climate is beautiful. It's paradise. And you and your fellow islanders constructed the perfect childless utopia. The only thing required of you was that each one of you had to keep a detailed diary every single day. And you were not to communicate with the outside world until there were only fifteen of you left. So, forty, or fifty years go by, and one hundred and thirty-five of you died, and there are only fifteen of you left. If we came to the island and read the diaries everyone kept, dead and living, what do you think the last several years' entries would say?"

"Why do you want to focus on the last few years?" asked Sandy.

"Because the last entries come at the end of their lives when they are old and dying. People tend to be more truthful as death approaches. But I think the most interesting entries would come from the last to die, with no one around to help them as they look into the abyss and reflect on their life and the life of their dying 'community.' What do you think their diaries would say?"

"How would I know?!" said Florence. "You seem to have all the answers."

"I think the islanders recognized the fatal flaw in their morbid philosophy. I think they realized how vulgar and immature and reckless they were in their youth. And I think at some point the islanders realized it was too late to do anything about it. And I think they got to sit around for the last thirty or forty years of their lives on a beautiful desert island—after their passions and youth and beauty had left them—in abject misery. I think they cursed the stars they were born under. That's what I think their diaries will say."

Annie spoke. "Whitehead said, 'we think in generalities, but we live in detail.' I can tell you from personal experience, that is an excellent thought experiment, McCoy. Painful, but excellent."

"You people keep talking about babies," Sandy said. "I am not interested in having a baby."

"No, I expect not, Sandy," McCoy said. "But what about your old age? What is so special about you that you can evade the burden of the future of humanity and leave the work of forming the next generation to others? Or is that your definition of a strong and independent woman? If you live long, you will eventually become dependent. Why should my children have to provide for you? Isn't that your responsibility? In your old age, you will need to consume the production and resources of the offspring of your contemporaries—all of whom came into existence thanks to a man and his desires for a woman. Our community has less than two hundred souls. If all of us shared your sensibilities, Sandy, in forty years only twenty of us— aged and miserable—would remain."

Sandy raised her voice. "Well, I am not going to have a baby, and I am not going to have sex with a man!"

"As well you should not!" McCoy blasted back. "Most women *want* to have children of their own, and, not coincidently, they are interested in doing the things that will lead to offspring and a future for their family line. Your mothering wires got shorted out along with your sexual wiring. So, you are going to have to find another way of contributing to the community—and it won't be by working to turn our women against the men, Radical Feminist style—or you can keep walking." And here, McCoy gestured down the dark driveway. "And if you start walking now to short-circuit this conversation, do not come back. We don't tolerate censorship. You don't get to tell us what your contribution is going to be unilaterally, and you don't get to make unilateral demands. Whatever it is, it will have to be an exchange of value between willing participants. If you want to live among us, you have to cooperate with us, and we have to be able to depend on you as a contributing member of the community."

Sandy and Florence looked at each other with an expression of shock.

"There is another thing we believe strongly," said Jason. "Everyone gets to speak freely on any subject. McCoy is not thin-skinned. If you've got something you want to say to him, Sandy, now's the time. Speak your mind."

"Gladly," Sandy replied to Jason. Then to McCoy. "How many times do I have to hear about the baby thing?" asked Sandy. "You're obviously trying to anger me."

It seemed that Annie came to Sandy's rescue. "Locke said, 'And such is the nature of the understanding, that it cannot be compelled to the belief of anything by outward force.' In other words, people cannot be compelled to believe something through violence."

"That sounds more like Rand," Roger said.

"I am sure Locke had a great deal of influence on Rand," Annie said.

"Hold that thought for just a minute," McCoy said to Annie and Roger. Then to Sandy. "Do you realize that you do not have any family, Sandy?"

"I have Mindy."

"And that Mindy doesn't have any family? There have always been women like you, Sandy. Women who steadfastly refused men and did not form families of their own. But such women still had the benefit and—more importantly—the *resources* of the family: their parents and grandparents, siblings, nieces and nephews, and others. Lots of those women wound up as the crazy-aunt-in-the-attic—but if they had a family who cared about them, they had an attic to be crazy in. You don't have any of those things. What you have—or what you are stuck with—is what I like to call the 'Feminist Paradox.' Feminists may well hate men, marriage, family, and children—but elderly Feminists are dependent upon the resources and efforts of families and other people's offspring. They will also happily consume inheritances from their parents and ancestors while making no personal sacrifices and providing nothing to future generations."

"Why are you saying this to me?"

"I'm giving you every chance to come to grips with the way things are here before I have to run you off," McCoy replied. "There are no PC police left. You are going to have to stand-and-deliver and make your case if you can. If you can't, then shut up. You don't get to make assertions without clearly stating your supporting argument. Tell me: how you are going to contribute to the community?"

"I can work as hard as any man here can."

"Well, maybe. And maybe not. You look to be in your mid-40's. Do you really think you can do what those young men over there can do? I know I can't. But even if that were true, this strawman you are comparing yourself to is also raising a family. And you are not. Ergo, you are not working as hard as he is, and you are not producing anything nearly so valuable to the community. So, what I want to know is: what are you going to do about that? How are you going to even the score? In a world with seven billion people, that world could tolerate you and your pink hats and your childless man-hating insanity. The new world—and especially our community—does not offer you that luxury. I am trying to communicate something to you here. Are you listening to me?"

There was an uncomfortable silence.

After a while, Mindy spoke. "Well, if I understand you, McCoy, you seem to want to make it clear that community members have an absolute right to speak on any subject. That others have a right to make a counterargument, and that people must support their positions with reason and evidence. Violence, coercion, and even rude behavior in an attempt to silence or intimidate other community members will not be tolerated. Also, there are minimum expectations regarding productive efforts."

Roger was stunned. His only experience with Mindy was as a pet walking in Sandy's shadow.

Annie smiled to herself and slowly nodded her head.

"Good for you, Mindy!" McCoy said. "But that's not entirely accurate. What if Sandy decided to organize marches and encourage the women to strike until all tasks were distributed evenly between men and women—with Sandy as the judge of what's 'even.' What if Sandy spent her time trying to convince the women here that they live under the oppressive sexual demands of men and the responsibility of raising their children? I've just pointed out the life and death nature of children and family to our very survival."

"Either speech is free, or it is not," replied Mindy.

"I am not interested in forcing Sandy to do anything," McCoy said. "But I am interested in the survival of my family and the community. We can't make it alone."

Jason interjected. "Please understand that for the community, that kind of speech would be far worse than yelling 'fire!' in a crowded theatre." Jason turned to Roger and said, "These are the kinds of things that keep coming up that we haven't worked out. There are lots more."

"A community cannot be built around politics," McCoy said. "We are not a political entity."

"Well, I am glad to hear you say that," Mindy replied. "It helps a great deal that you are clear in your expectations. But I think you've spent enough time hammering the baby thing."

"Well, maybe I have." McCoy turned to Sandy. "It ain't nothing personal, Sandy. Or maybe it is. I have to tell you; I don't like people who don't like me first. I'm funny that way."

"Then maybe you two can start over," said Mindy, looking at Sandy.

"If you value liberty and the sovereignty of the individual so much," Sandy said. "Why do you insist that the choice is not mine to make? What if one of the women here refused to shack up with a man? Would you starve her into submission? What if she wanted to have an abortion? You people say you reject the use of coercion. Would you force her to have the baby?"

"You are mixing separate issues, Sandy," Annie said. "Let's take them one at a time."

"Okay. Here's one. It is my body," Sandy said. "So, it is my choice. Roger gave us a fine lecture on our natural rights to private property and agency over our bodies, didn't you, Roger?"

"Well, it appears you only grasped half of the story," Roger said. "You own your life and the rights to your private property. You also own the responsibility of all of your actions and decisions. And then there are the pesky details of ethics, humanity, and personhood. Do you know where that slogan comes from? 'My body, my choice?' It comes from an essay written by Judith Jarvis. Have you read that essay in its entirety?"

"No, I haven't," Sandy replied.

"Are you at all familiar with Jarvis?"

"No."

"Well, then why do you have such powerful opinions? Can you see how you've been programmed? To my mind, Jarvis essay is the product of someone devoid of human empathy. Jarvis does not deny the humanity of the fetus but rather asserts that the fetus is a trespasser, and the mother may kill such with impunity. It is a rather bizarre assertion, one that I think most people have not read and don't understand. I think her essay is a Rorschach test for sociopathology and borderline personality disorder in that if you read it and agree with the validity of Jarvis' premises and assertion, you are likely one or both. Perhaps you should read it before quoting it."

"Hey, McCoy," Annie said. "Roger explained to me your compelling analysis about Feminism and abortion. I'd like to hear it from you."

"Sure. Abortion is about one thing, and one thing only—the socio-economic status of the father of the unborn child. If his socio-economic status is high, the woman will give birth to the child. If the father's socio-economic status is too low, the woman will abort the baby. Women do not abort the children of dot-com billionaires, NBA superstars, or Wall Street hedge-fund managers under any circumstances. No man from the Boston Kennedy clan ever had a child aborted—unless he bribed the mother. But the fetus of a father that comes from a low-status family and who has poor prospects is often doomed by an abortion."

"Well, what did you expect her to do?!" Sandy asked.

"I expect a pregnant woman to do nothing," McCoy said "And let nature take its course. There is no act more unethical than murdering one's child."

"It's not a child," said Sandy.

"Well, there it is. At least you understand that if we recognize the humanity of the child, then it is a person with a right to live. So, you have decided to deny the child it's humanity. The other issue is this disgraceful hypocrisy in Feminist philosophy: Feminism is a collectivist philosophy and rejects marriage, family, private property, and by necessity inheritance."

"Bullshit!" Sandy exclaimed. "Feminism is about equality!"

"Well, that's the pitch, Sandy," McCoy said. "It is also the great lie. Feminist leaders spent most of their time producing propaganda to induce anger and unhappiness in women. And they did a hell of a job. "Before" the Famine, one in three women in America over the age of 35 were taking anti-depressants or anti-psychotic medications just to cope with their existence. Feminism is the most anti-social belief system in history, and the result is our fertility is inadequate, the idea of family has been destroyed, and the few children we manage to produce grow up in broken homes without the influence of a father. Not to mention hundreds of millions of child-murders world-wide. Instead of a father's influence, our kids are subjected to endless propaganda in the public-school system—organized and staffed by Feminists! Feminism sought to sanction the state to eliminate the power imbalances that they assert exist between men and women via abortion."

"Right! This is the part I wanted to hear," Annie said. "Go on."

"Well, on the one hand, we have a philosophy that rejects private property and familial estates and inheritance. On the other hand, the central tenant of the Feminist philosophy is the right to murder their unborn children: the right to an abortion on demand is the absolute foundation of Feminism. But as a practical matter, the life and death decision that each woman makes regarding her unborn child is based on the socio-economic status of the father—and *that* is determined by his property rights and the property rights of his family. But Feminism rejects private property and family."

"Every time I hear you walk someone through that line of reasoning, my stomach turns over," Roger said. "I get sick thinking about it. The philosophy departments of our best universities couldn't see that, but a Kentucky farmer could?"

"No, Roger. They refused to see it," McCoy said.

"I was facetious. In the university-industrial-and-political complex, any professor who dared to challenge the LGBTQ orthodoxy would be an outcast. Even tenured faculty members would find themselves unemployed. Their very life would be in danger."

"It is one of the most disturbing observations I've heard," said Jason.

"Well, spend some time thinking about all of the implications. I bet you will come up with a few I haven't thought of yet. Here's one: Out here in rural America, the men just don't have the social and economic status of the coastal elites. Our women are killing our babies, and abortion is killing rural America. And it's the same story in Black America."

"As a midwife and armchair philosopher, I have a different take on Feminism's unequivocal support for dismembering babies in utero. It has to do with the part men play in procreation. Why do Feminists insist that life begins at birth? The answer is that Feminists must deny that life begins at conception. To say otherwise would be to acknowledge the male's role in creating life, and because childbirth is the province of women. But who can deny that conception is the province of the man? And that it is the male's *active role* of arousal, subsequent penile erection and penetration, and finally orgasm that delivers a path to the future of humanity? If the future of mankind depended on the *passive role* of women or the passions and desires and contributions of Feminists and queer women, then mankind would vanish within a single generation."

"Ugh," Sandy said. "I think I am going to be sick.

But all eyes went to the little old lady sitting by the fire.

"Yes, it would," McCoy replied to Annie. "The moral of the story is as brutal as it is obvious. Those who breed, succeed. The cultures who do not will lose their seat at life's table. Humanity— and every family—is always one generation away from oblivion."

"Children and grandchildren are not an option," Annie continued. "The formation of fecund families is a critical condition for the continued existence of mankind; that's why the ancient religious texts of the great religions were so hard on homosexuality—the practice does not result in issue."

"I am not addressing human sexuality through the lens of bronze age shamans," McCoy said. "I don't give a good fart what the ancient texts say, and I don't care what people like to put in their mouth. Some folks like peanut butter; others prefer peanut brittle. Ain't none of that our business. But when we are talking about the life and death of a Human Being, we must examine the philosophy thoroughly—and then reject its fallacies.

"We are trying to establish a self-reinforcing community, to use Roger's term. And that means we need a steady supply of young people to take our place as we age out and die. It also means we need a common culture and a set of shared expectations regarding personal conduct and responsibility—this ain't no time for rebel-without-a-clue bullshit. We need to successfully engage in procreation, agriculture, production, trade, and commerce."

Everyone gathered here looked into the fire and remained silent for a minute or two. McCoy and Annie's ideas raised the bar and took them all by surprise. Well, except Roger—nothing Annie said would surprise Roger.

"Look," said Florence. "We aren't telling you what to do. We want to live life our way."

"That's bullshit!" McCoy said. "Last I saw, you folks were running around in pink hats, screaming and marching. Who were you talking to? What were you saying? Look, every philosophy and belief system is judged on the major works, speeches, and essays of its leaders and the actions of the people who follow them. I read Julie Bindel, Valarie Solanas, Andrea Dworkin, Robin Morgan, and Linda Gordon; and many others. Would you like me to quote them?"

No," Florence replied. "I don't. You've made your point. Obviously, you are going somewhere with this that applies to us. So, let's have it."

"Okay. Here it is. Feminists coined a political verb, "to objectify," a term of derision directed at the life-giving force of passion and desire that a man—I'm a man—has for a woman. It then follows that what Feminists were insisting on is that the manner in which men achieve and maintain an erection—*the* phenomenon that sustained humanity by filling women with life since the dawn of mankind—must change. Feminists—people who have never had an erection, who have never filled a woman with life, and who do not possess the will or the inclination to sustain and provide for that child and the life of the mother at the most vulnerable time of their lives; the long period of human childhood and the several years of human lactation assert that they have a better way. If only men will change to meet their ideal. And they scorched and salted the very earth and poisoned the water in the wells with their propaganda to accomplish their ridiculous agenda. Don't pull that shit here. Do not fuck with us, and we won't fuck with you. Was that clear enough?"

The McCoy with the good-ol'-boy accent and mannerism was gone. This McCoy was the U.S. Army Major making sure his orders were understood. Florence and McCoy stared each other down. When Florence did not respond, McCoy continued.

"I expect no one has had the balls to stand up to you "Before." Maybe you're in shock, or maybe you're just that pissed-off. Either way, I don't give a shit. Let me know that you understood what I just said."

McCoy leaned forward and bored his eyes into Florence. She blinked.

"I heard you," was all that Florence could muster.

"Outstanding!" McCoy replied to Florence. The hard-ass was gone. The good-ol'-boy was back. "Now, if y'all will excuse me, I think I will catch me some shut-eye."

McCoy rose with a groan and shuffled off, stiff from the long ride.

Roger supposed this would be a good time to interrupt before Sandy and Florence had the opportunity to go ballistic. "So, back to your vision for the community," Roger said to Jason.

"We haven't had time to flesh out a vision just yet," Jason said. "This is not Shady Grove—the Mennonites have an incredible and unique community. The only thing holding us together is our common interest in survival. It's a pretty diverse group. That might sound good for a slogan in a political campaign from 'Before,' but for a small community of fewer than 200 people? I think it is less than ideal. But, look, we're not professors of sociology at a prestigious university. We're open to ideas."

Florence wasn't interested in changing the subject. "You don't find that man oppressive?" she asked Jason.

"McCoy? Well, "Before" I wouldn't say that McCoy was the kind of person I typically socialized with, but it has been my consistent observation that he is both diligent and conscientious, and he has an impressive skill set. We need him. For some reason, he thinks he needs us. I haven't figured that part out yet."

"What do you need him for?" asked Sandy.

"Well, he's got a large clan surrounding him. He knows how to farm at this scale. He's a mechanical engineer by training and turns out an impressive suite of goods from that metal fabricating shop. He's figured out how to produce a modest volume of refined fuels from the local crude oil wells." Jason stopped and gestured to the large metal building a hundred yards behind them. "And he is fearless. McCoy seems to have a strange but firmly rooted moral compass. My wife used to get the willies from McCoy, and now she thinks highly of him. The local prominent farming families seem to hold him in high regard, and it seems that all of them have taken McCoy's 'family-strategy' to heart."

"What?" asked Sandy. "Of collecting young women for their breeding programs?"

Jason didn't take the bait. "I like to think of it as pairing young couples together to form strong families to raise well-adjusted children into functioning adults who will provide mankind—and our community—with a path to the future."

"It still sounds to me like you are running a zoo breeding program," Sandy said.

"Sandy, what is it you want?" Jason asked.

"What do you mean?"

"Well, what is your chief purpose in life? What is it you hope to accomplish in your lifetime? Because my sense of everything you've said and all of my experience with the gender wars informs me that what you really want is to end sexual relations between men and women."

"I want to end the power imbalance between men and women."

"Even if it means the end of the human race?" Jason asked.

"Who says it will? What I want is equal opportunity for women."

"Even if every culture that focuses on making women competitive with men will die out in a generation or two? That social strategy is self-defeating."

"How's that?!"

"To be truly competitive," Jason said. "Women must participate equally in the hard sciences, law, finance, commerce, including small business and the trades, and politics—and not just pretend by studying for degrees in psychology, social work, elementary education, and nursing. All of those tasks were traditionally performed in the home; as they are again now. Your political coalition was successful in having the government extort resources via taxation from the male-dominated fields to subsidize the female-dominated fields in exchange for your votes. But in those male-dominated fields, for every success story, there were a dozen failures. There are no 'failures' in social work or school teaching! Admittedly, it is an arbitrary number for the purposes of rhetoric: But for the women who try to compete in these fields, most will wind up childless; or perhaps some will have an only child. In a generation or two, the cultures who did not participate in that demographic disaster will have bred your culture out of existence. And you and your gang will be back to the crazy-aunt-in-the-attic phenomenon that McCoy mentioned."

Sandy's eyes were bugging out of her head. "You are proving everything we ever said about the Patriarchy!"

"Sandy, have you ever had an intimate relationship with a man?" Roger interjected.

"Of course not!"

"Why not?"

"Don't be disgusting!"

"Well, that's my point, Sandy!" Roger said. "Men disgust you. And the nature of heterosexuality disgusts you. As McCoy already made clear, we cannot build and sustain a community— never mind a culture and a society—around the pathology of your disgust response to men. Nor can we allow the political manifestation of your disgust response, what you call 'Feminism,' to take root here. We cannot build a community around the disgust, hate, and loathing you feel for half of humanity! And as we have already pointed out, you are mortal, and the belief systems and philosophies that do not produce families and children are doomed to extinction—and it will be the very cultures and belief systems that you despise most that will breed your belief system out of existence and perhaps violently crush what little remains at the end. And I should also mention as a personal matter that as a result of your emotional response to men and maleness, you will die childless and alone."

Sandy's eyes flew back and forth between Roger and Jason. "How dare you?!"

"How dare I what?" Roger asked. "Openly examine the sexual and political nature of Feminism?"

"So, Jason," Florence said to get between Sandy and Roger before things got out of hand. "Let me ask you. Why is it that Karl and Evan here are getting a pass on this evening's ass-kicking? Does McCoy have a soft spot in his heart for gay men?"

"Hey," Karl said to Florence. "Leave me out of this debate. You fight your own battles."

"Leave me out of it too," said Evan.

Jason enjoyed a good laugh. "Who knows? That's none of our business. But I think it's a practical issue."

"How's that?" Florence asked.

"McCoy doesn't think that you have much, if anything, in common with Evan and Karl. He is of the opinion that you can have more women than men without much trouble. And that if we have more men than women, we will have difficulty maintaining peace in the community. McCoy figures that Karl and Evan won't respond to a shortage of women with violence. The Mennonites also said that Karl and Evan are very creative and are handy with a set of tools and that all you know how to do is milk cows. So, McCoy wants Evan and Karl to stay here if they are willing, and he wants you, Mindy, and Sandy to settle up on my side of the community. He has a poor opinion of the women's movement of "Before," and he thinks you ladies are going to be more trouble than you're worth. You asked, and there it is."

"Boys will be boys, huh?" Sandy hissed.

"What, exactly, would you like us to do to assure that we have a future? We must form families and produce children!"

"Whatever."

"No, Sandy. It's not 'whatever.' You don't have a solution. You just pretend that you do. I dare you: go set up an LGBTV commune now. See how that works out for you. The truth is, the only real solution—living in a home with a man and raising children—is anathema to you, so you pretend that there is an alternative. But it is our custom to listen to everybody. If you've got a better idea, I would sure like to hear it."

"Well," Sandy began, but Jason cut her off.

"Before you respond with some flippant and programmed remark, why don't you think about it? Write it down, make an assertion and provide us with a set of premises and your reasoning. When we bring our clan together, we will hear you out. But I warn you: come prepared to defend your ideas. Because we let it all hang out. Everyone has a right to make assertions and present evidence, or challenge conclusions and present counter-arguments. Think about that for a minute. You have spent the last twenty years operating in a political environment where you could shout the opposition down or use shame or censorship to silence their ideas. You are not the bully on the playground anymore."

Jason turned to Roger. "As for our ideas about the community, I think we will have a great deal of time to talk about that this spring. We will be working dawn to dusk in the fields until the harvest is in, and starting tomorrow, and through March, we will be working to get next year's firewood in. You will be surprised by how much wood you are going to burn when you heat, cook, and heat domestic hot water with wood."

"And Sandy," Jason said. "I think it is only fair to point out that McCoy took you into his home and fed you, just like the Mormons and Mennonites did. Don't you see that as their recognition of your humanity? Perhaps you could reciprocate. I hope you have half the strength and stamina and cleverness you think you have. And I mean that with all sincerity. Because we need everyone pulling in the same direction—towards the future and the survival of the community."

Chapter 26

It was mid-March. Three weeks had passed since Roger, and the Garden of Eden residents landed in the Sulphur Spring community. Roger and Melissa moved into the Miller's empty house with Annie Ackroyd. They were well fixed from the start with everything needed to run an organized household. But Sandy, Mindy, and Florence were another story. For them, nothing went right. But after the initial challenges, they were quartered in an Amish schoolhouse that Abraham Yoder's community was not using. Evan and Karl remained in the cabin at the O'Neil farm, and from all accounts were fitting in well with the much younger couples living on "Cottage Row," as the driveway into McCoy's place was known. Jason's new arrivals were expecting 55-gallon, stainless-steel hot water kettles from McCoy's workshop, but for now everyone was getting by with rusty steel barrels with the top third removed and placed on top of a masonry firebox. The Garden of Eden women had a homemade outdoor cookstove and an interior heat stove made from the same type of barrel, while Roger and Melissa had the luxury of a real Amish cookstove.

Every day for the past three weeks, except Saturday's, the entire community worked the woodlots for next year's firewood and would continue in this task for at least another week. The Weiss family observed the Saturday Jewish Sabbath, and over the winter the rest of the English families on this side of the community, outside of the Amish, came to celebrate Saturday as their day of rest too. And many began their celebrations at sundown on Friday, something they learned from the Weiss family. The work was strenuous and unrewarding. Yes, the reward would come—next winter—but to say that the work lacked any level of immediate gratification did not do the situation justice. The weather this time of year was often grey and rainy, but the work still had to be done. Jason's brother Walter summed up the circumstances. "It's better to work in forty degrees and rain than to sit home next winter and freeze because it's four degrees and you have no firewood." Walter ran the chainsaw all day—thanks to McCoy and his backyard oil-refining operation—and everyone else packed the cut tree-rounds out of the woods. If the rounds were too big, they were split first and then packed out in pieces, unless it was sweet gum or hickory. When still green, this wood is impossible to split, so Walter left them on the ground in four to six-foot sections to be dragged out of the woods by the horses to lay by the woodshed and dry in the sun. The firewood harvest began late because of the unusually cold winter, but they needed to get it into the sheds before the mosquitos and snakes, and the heat and humidity reclaimed the woodlands for themselves.

In the first days "After," there was the comfort, or perhaps the numbness of disbelief. Then came the arduous expeditions of those who journeyed out of the cities, and the mad scramble of the farmers to survive the first months. But the days were getting longer and warmer. The people could almost taste the spring even if they did not feel its warmth just yet. And now the enormity of their situation was finally crashing down upon the members of the Sulphur Springs community. This is it. This is their life now. If they wanted to cook something, they needed to build a fire first. If they wished to have hot water to wash dishes, do laundry, or bathe, they needed to make fire first. If they were cold, they needed to stoke the fire. And if they wanted to eat in the future, they needed to work hard for it during the growing season. There would be no second chances. Whatever the conditions: Muddy? Deal with it. Drought? Deal with it. Heatwave? Freezing? Blizzard? Bored? Deal with it. Their daily fare was boring and repetitive: ground meat, corn, cheese, and milk. But most of all, they began to grieve for the life–and the loved ones—they lost.

On the third Saturday since their arrival, Jason knocked on the back door of Roger and Melissa's house. The Miller's always used this door. It didn't occur to Jason that Roger and Melissa might not carry on that tradition. There was a little sign tacked up next to the door, a piece of sawn lumber with "The Littles" inscribed in tightly formed connected black circles. There appeared to be some odd texture to the letters, but before he could get a closer look, the door opened, and Melissa beckoned Jason inside. It was hot inside the home, and Jason followed

Melissa into the kitchen through the mudroom. Annie was seated at the table working on something that looked like bread, or maybe muffins.

"Roger! Jason is here!" Melissa called to the great room that spanned most of the front of the house. Then to Jason, "Roger's reading in the living room." And she shooed him in that direction. The two men almost collided in the doorway, their heads almost touching the door jam. They were very tall and about the same height.

"Jason! Sorry for that less than graceful welcome! Come in and have a seat."

"Thank you, Roger. I am sorry to interrupt your Saturday."

"Oh, no! Not at all! We must learn the fine art of visiting again. Especially, now that we have no telephones."

"The Mennonites call it, 'sending word,' or perhaps I should say they still call it that, as we all did at one time."

"Yes, indeed. To what do I owe the pleasure? Were you coming to send word, or were you coming to visit?"

The two shared a chuckle.

"Please, sit." Roger gestured to an Amish rocking chair.

Just then, Annie came in with two mugs and handed one to each man. "Tea," she said, and smiled and walked away.

"Thank you!" the men called in unison after her.

"Try some," Roger said. "I don't know what it is. Annie gathers it wild. It's got a mint taste to it, and she adds a little maple syrup."

Jason sipped his tea. "Wow! That is delicious." He sipped his tea again. "You seem to be getting on well here."

"Yes, well, new love with a beautiful young woman smooths the way forward."

Jason laughed. "Well, there is that. Salud!" He hoisted his tea mug.

"Do you speak Spanish?"

"Not as well as I once did. But that's not why I came." Jason explained that the mood in the community concerned him.

"Yes, well, I have my dark moments too."

Roger explained the situation about his twin sons, both junior officers in the U.S. Navy. "I have to confess; it's not all roses.

195

There are moments where I just don't want to go on. All of us have lost family. Friends. Careers. And lots of people here have nothing to console them. Grieving is a process. And this level of grief is unprecedented. But I would be far more concerned if the people were not going through this process."

"I'm just wondering if there is something we should do," Jason said.

"I think it helps to keep busy," Roger said.

"Well, if it does, then we should be okay. We've been grinding away."

"When the days get longer than the nights, and the gardens start going in, I think that'll help too. But it's a process. People can become accustomed to dreadful privation over time just as they become accustomed to luxury and abundance. In psychology, we use the term 'habituation' to describe the diminished psychological, physical, or behavioral response to a specific stimulus that repeatedly occurs in a person's environment."

"That makes sense."

"'Habituation' is why we had so many suicides when the Famine began."

Jason noticed that Roger was calling the crisis the "Famine," like the Mennonites and Amish do, and not the "Blackout."

"That will never make sense," Jason said.

"Well, I don't know about making sense of it. But I think I understand what happened. The denial response is a powerful motivator, but it cannot stand up to death. Death breaks denial's grip on the survivors. A person can hold on to hope in spite of bare shelves, dark refrigerators, and empty gas tanks, but when someone close to them, like a child, dies; or commits suicide, most likely a spouse, that hope is destroyed making way for anguish and despair. From there, it is not that far to hopelessness and suicide. Especially if they have become physically weak and had the tools for the job on hand."

"You mean like guns?" asked Jason.

"Suicide is a crime of opportunity," Roger replied

"That's great. We've got more guns in the community than the Wild West."

"Has the community lost any children to sickness? Or any adults to suicide?"

"No."

"Well, that doesn't mean we won't. But it's a damn good sign. Is there something specific that concerns you?"

"Yes, there is. The women you traveled with."

"Oh."

"They don't seem to be adjusting well."

"Well, I haven't spent any time with them. So, I don't know. What is your impression?"

"They look forlorn. Deeply depressed—walking around like zombies."

"Are they working?"

"Yes; they are putting up their firewood like everybody else, and they work for Abraham's wife in the greenhouse, but that is more social than work."

"Well, that's a good thing. Socializing is important. But I would imagine those women are having a terrible time of it."

"Why do you say that?" asked Jason.

"Imagine their lives 'Before.' Florence and Mindy are in their 30's. Sandy is in her 40's. Even if they wanted to form families and have children, that time has probably passed. They don't have a home life as you have, and they do not have any of the typical life milestones of middle-age to look forward to—things like the marriage of their children and the birth of grandchildren. Men and women with families go through the trial-by-fire of dealing with a spouse and providing for and raising children. The reward comes later in life. Well, it is later in life for Sandy, and she has no reward to look forward to.

"In a family with three children, twenty years go by before you even pick your head up. That's how busy you are. Remember what I just said about keeping busy? For most of us, creating meaning in our lives comes from our responsibilities to our children, to our wives or husbands, and also to our parents. And now, to a community. And by the way, you've got a wonderful thing going on here. Let me ask you: were the Shady Grove Mennonites the inspiration for the Sulphur Springs community?"

"Yes," Jason replied. "Of course, they were. And we were failing miserably—until the lights went out. I envisioned a cooperative and interdependent community, but it took that kind of crisis to encourage real cooperation. And now, there is no choice. We are dependent on each other for survival."

"It's a funny old world," Roger said.

"It is, indeed."

"And back to our friends from the Garden of Eden. I imagine they are going through one hell of an adjustment. Their entire life revolved around politics. And now that outlet is gone. Such women have had difficulties with their families, especially their fathers, their classmates, and their teachers for as long as they can remember, and later in life, they perceive themselves as victims of persecution. For them, living at the bottom of the social hierarchy, life on a hostile planet is all they have ever known. Males living at the bottom of the social hierarchy from a young age have a similar story of suffering, especially those who, in addition to low socio-economic status, are physically unappealing. But low-status males can move up the social hierarchy and become attractive sexual partners via achievement. That is not true for females. Men don't give a damn about the socio-economic status of their female sexual partners. Women concern themselves almost exclusively with the socio-economic status of their male sexual partners. Think Cinderella and Prince Charming."

"I don't think our friends are concerned with male sexual partners," Jason said.

"No. Probably not. But what I have just described is the hostile world in which these women came of age. Confused by their feelings during their formative years, rejected by their fathers, and invisible to their peers they turned to each other for moral support, and to identity politics and protests to vent their rage at the catastrophe that is their life. And now, quite suddenly in the aftermath of the Famine, they have no political divide to rally around and distract them from the tragedy. No moral support from their fellow-victims-at-the-hands-of-existence. And no idea that they could be seen as valuable by people outside of their identity cohort."

"Do you think it's everybody else's fault?" Jason asked.

"I didn't say that. I said that the people at the bottom of the social hierarchy suffer in ways that the people at the top cannot even begin to comprehend. And I am not suggesting these women developed their identities and sexuality entirely from their environment. I think most of who or what people are is 'essence before existence,' to turn Sartre on his head, at least when it comes to our place in the social/sexual hierarchy. I am saying that things are just the way they are and that there is no other way for things to be. Assigning fault or blame within a determinist mindset sort of defeats the purpose of holding that philosophy."

Jason did not respond to that. He sipped his tea as he processed Roger's commentary.

"I'm not helping you very much, am I?" Roger asked.

"No."

"Well, what did you expect? I'm a psychologist."

The two men shared a laugh.

"Ya know," Roger said. "I am happy to examine the human condition with you until you are blue in the face. I admire your interest in the members of the community. But you said 'cooperative' and 'interdependent,' not 'paternal.' We are responsible for ourselves. I was a clinical psychologist for years, and the only person who benefited from my advice was me, and the only one I ever harmed were my patients' insurance companies. I had no effect on my patients."

"A determinist who came to any other conclusion would lose all of my respect."

"Well, I know you hold for free well. But free will or determinist, we cannot give others something to live for. Not everyone makes good use of the brief and pointless time of their lives. Some people waste their youth and beauty on anger and protest. Others enjoy the warmth of the sun on their bare skin before they wither and die and never have a lucid thought. I would rather beat my toes off with a hammer than spend another moment trying to make someone 'happy.' Because that's why most people seek mental health care. They want to be 'happy.' Either that, or they want validation. The latest nonsense is 'closure.' I wanted to give them a fucking post-it note with the word 'closure' written on it. See? You now have 'closure!' Existence is a bit more complicated than 'happy,' 'validation,' 'closure,' or whatever mind-numbing neurosis people want to prattle on about. Of course, the truly disturbed do not want to be treated, and the more profound the pathology the less they want to change. I have never, not once, met a well-adjusted Feminist with healthy relationships with the men in her environment. And I never met a Feminist who *wanted* healthy relationships with the men in her environment."

"Perhaps we made a mistake bringing them into the community," Jason said.

"Oh, I don't know about that," Roger said. "I think they make an excellent cautionary tale. You are trying to rebuild society, though you call it a community, and society needs kings and beggars, success stories and failures. Charitable people like yourself, and angry, self-absorbed lunatics who wouldn't piss on your chest if your heart was on fire. But most of all, a community—or a society—needs children. And the society must mold the children with an ethos and an identity and a sense of belonging. Your friend McCoy seems to understand perfectly. I understand that you are a Quaker by philosophy?"

"Yes, indeed."

"But not by faith."

"I don't deny anyone's faith," Jason said. "But I don't spend any time thinking about faith, or what I should believe about the things I cannot possibly know. Are you familiar with Wittgenstein?"

"'What we cannot speak of we must pass over in silence.'"

"Yes, indeed."

"And you are a student of history and philosophy. You've studied the ancient Greeks. You seem familiar with Aristotle's modes for persuasion, Ethos, Pathos, and Logos."

"I am."

"You've obviously given this a great deal of thought," Roger said. "And long before the Famine. What was your goal here?"

"I wanted to build a community around the precepts of Simplicity, Integrity, Community, Equality, and Peace."

"The Quaker Testimonies."

"Those are Stoic precepts too," Jason said.

"Yes, they are," said Roger. "So, you've spent some time with Seneca and Marcus Aurelius too, I see. Isn't it a hell of a coincidence that Annie, you, and McCoy are all interested in philosophy?"

"Wait till you spend some time with Martin Weiss."

"There seems to be some survivor bias for philosophers. So much for preppers and survivalists and their guns and bug-out bags."

The two men shared a laugh. Roger continued.

"But, you're in a pickle here. Practicing Simplicity and Integrity is an individual effort; Practicing 'Community' is not. 'Community' requires the goodwill and cooperation of the people in a web of interconnected interdependence. Such a community must have a commonality of purpose, ethics, and acceptable behavior—a community ethos. No people can survive as a 'house divided.' Nor can they survive the reprisals and vendettas that will surely come as a result of identity politics. By the way, did you know that Abraham Lincoln stole that phrase from Thomas Paine's 'Common Sense?' Like you, Paine was a Quaker philosopher who also rejected mysticism."

"I knew he was a Quaker," Jason replied. "I did not know that Lincoln lifted that from Paine."

"I'm sorry," Roger said. "I didn't mean to ramble. I'll try to stay on point. The idea of 'Community' also requires a local mindset for work, play, school, gatherings and traditions, and elder care—unless the ethos is to engage in euthanasia—because not only will we die, but many of us will experience the indignities of old age. It then follows that a community must produce strong and enduring families and babies, mold children in the ethos of the community, and benefit from productive young and mature adults. A community will have non-productive elderly and children to care for. Relations by blood and marriage, the type of 'marriage' that produces children, will dominate.

"This is not to say that everyone must produce children. There are people who, by their nature, will not give birth to a practically significant number of children. Such people will get old and frail and will need the offspring of others to care for them in their old age. As McCoy pointed out, to be fair and interdependent, the childless must make other contributions that are of equal value to the community during their productive years—that is the production, accumulation, and maintenance of capital. To reject this is to accept violence and coercion—the theft of resources from other people's offspring at the point of a gun. McCoy—or was that you? —made another brilliant observation: a free people must not resort to force, coercion, and violence to achieve personal, moral, or political agendas, *and they must not hire other people or task the state to do such dirty work for them*. Might—even a majority—does not make right. The community must not countenance its destruction from within. It is not a coincidence that the childless LGBTQ cadre so highly values socialism and collectivism. Such people are not invested in the future of humanity and are not concerned with building wealth to be passed down to the next generation. They don't have a 'next generation.' Too, Feminism dominates the LGBTQ demographic, and I would assert that Feminism's founding document is Fredric Engels' *The Origin of the Family, Private Property and the State*. Engels was Karl Marx's protégé and partner in crime. And I am convinced that the reason the LGBTQ community is so anti-Capitalism is due to the condemnation of homosexuality in the Bible. Are you familiar Max Weber?"

"No."

"That's amazing to me. Here, you are one of the most well-read people I've met outside of academia, and you've never heard of Weber? I think that is because the progressives have worked hard to blackout his work and ideas. Anyway, in the early 20th century, he wrote one of the most essential books in the history of Western Civilization—*The Protestant Ethic and the Spirit of Capitalism*. It was one of the most cited philosophical works in modern history. In that book, Weber makes more than a few brilliant and poignant observations, but I think the most prominent of those was his assertion that "Capitalism" is an idea that could not, and did not, happen without the social transformations that came about with the Protestant Reformation.

And specifically, Calvinism. And Calvin believed in predestination."

"Holy smokes…"

"Yea, I can see the light bulbs are going off in your head! Calvinism believed that homosexuals were predestined to be damned by G-d. Well, if Christianity in general, and Protestantism and Calvinism in particular, are the source, the wellspring of ideas that gave us Capitalism, and those belief systems despised homosexuals and homosexuality, then it makes perfect sense to me that the LGBTQ community would reject not only Christianity but the foundation of Western Civilization—Capitalism. And with it, all of the rational structures—canonical law, free-labor, the sanctity of private property, and the republican form of government—that sustains it all. Of course, you'd think that this demographic would also reject Islam, but consistency was never their strong suit, and I think that is moot for our purposes. We need to help such people understand the realities of the situation—if possible. Humanity's political struggles between its great religions and human sexuality and our urges and desires are not new."

Roger waited to see if Jason wanted to say something. Jason shook his head and said, "Go on."

"For nearly one-thousand years, Western civilization had a place, a 'safe space' if you will, for the LGBTQ people of the time. The Roman Catholic Church. Does that offend you?"

Jason shook his head and frowned. "I went to Catholic school for nine years. Back when all of the grade school teachers were nuns."

"Wow!"

"Yea. They were nuts—violent, and completely lacking in empathy, especially when it came to boys. I have to say; it was pretty awful."

Roger threw up his hands and shook his head. "And you have such patience for Sandy and Florence! Anyway, throughout history, the hypocrisy of the Church was apparent to the cognitive elite and the aristocracy. But the Church gave legitimacy to the ruling class and did a great job of keeping the masses from rising and killing the landed gentry. So, everyone turned a blind eye to the sexual and social deviants hiding in plain sight as priests and nuns. The system was so well entrenched that it took several hundred years after the Enlightenment for the deviant sexual nature of the Catholic Church to be fully exposed. I don't think it is a coincidence that after the nuns stopped hiding beneath the veil and habit and became Feminist and Lesbian Activists that the Church was outed as the safe-space for male sexual deviants that it was. But human sexual deviation didn't disappear; it just stopped hiding. Sexual deviation became acceptable as religious mysticism retreated under the steam-roller of science."

"And the evolution of the concept of liberty," Jason said.

"And because of our evolving sense of freedom, yes. But humanity still had millions of people who deviated from what society nonetheless felt was the sexual norm who believed they were persecuted, especially during their formative years and their forced participation in the pathological environment of the public-school system. In short, I suspect that many if not most of the LGBTQ population today suffers from post-traumatic-stress-disorder. And that's in addition to the serious issues with identity that seems existential to the condition I refer to as 'heterosexual dysphoria.'"

"Evan and Karl don't seem to have anything in common with Sandy and Florence," Jason said.

Roger nodded his head and smiled knowingly to Jason. "Just because the LGBTQ community banded together for political purposes doesn't mean that lesbians and gay men have any more in common than heterosexual men and women. As someone with extraordinary powers of observation pointed out to me, 'gay' women are not 'gay' in the same way that 'gay' men are 'gay.' The problem that confronts us here is the hardened and internalized political and social belief systems of all of the people in our nascent community, not just the lesbians from the Garden of Eden.

"To develop a community ethos, you seem to believe that we must reject politics and other distractions. I think that's spot on. For now, there can be only one political agenda: The wellbeing and continuity of the community and our way of life—should we ever get around to defining what that is. If we want our community and our way of life to survive, then life and the family must go on, and children must be given life and then formed by their parents and extended family into functioning adults. A community—and its members—must have an ethos of intergenerational stability or the community will not endure. Children must be imbued with values that will perpetuate the community. I do not deny the humanity of people who do not wish to produce children. I am pointing out that in the context of 'Community' such people must make compensating and equal contributions to the wellbeing of the community—or they are not part of the community at all. And they most definitely must not be permitted to harass the people who are forming the next generation—the heterosexuals who produce children—with their political machinations. Feminism, collectivism, and any form of authoritarianism, identity advocacy, or victim construction— anything that harms family formation or encourages family ruin—will be the death of the community, and us. That's why the Mennonites kicked us out. If we wish to have an intentional community, we must make an unflinching examination of this. There are no examples of successful intergenerational communities operating under the belief systems I just mentioned. Our community would not survive them either."

Jason listened intently and stroked his beard but said nothing.

"I'm sorry. I'm not telling you anything you don't already know," Roger said. "I get excited. I've been thinking about this for years. It never occurred to me that I would have the opportunity to be a part of something like this. I can't help but hope that we are the next Athens. Or Vienna."

Jason's mood brightened. "Well, when you put it like that. I'm pretty hopeful myself."

"We've got the beginnings, the foundation, of something good here. Yes, people are suffering now, but most of us will get past that, and the generations to come will only know what we tell them. Hopefully, we will try hard not to inflict our trauma on them."

Chapter 27

It was Saint Patrick's Day. Jason Thomas' clan—his brother Walter and wife, Jenny, his brother's son, Manny, and wife, Danielle, and son Roone, and wife, Pilar, the Weiss family, Roger and Melissa, and Sandy, Mindy, and Florence prepared an acre of ground closest to the well and the cisterns behind Jason's house as their potato and vegetable garden. The heirloom seed corn would get planted later in the spring and broken up into three plots so that they could not lose the entire crop to a tornado. The wheat was already broadcast and raked in two separate plots. But local tradition held that potatoes must be in the ground by Saint Patrick's Day. Jason kept fifty pounds of the seed potatoes and gave one-hundred pounds to Abraham Yoder, the leader of the local Amish church group. He also shared the corn and wheat seed in the same fashion, retaining one-third for his clan and handing the other two-thirds over to the eleven Amish families spread in as many plots. Jason demonstrated how to cut a seed potato so that they might get the most seed plants from each spud. They used a string to mark out thirty rows spaced three feet apart and two-hundred feet long and placed a cut potato seedling every three feet along the line. Jason drove a team of workhorses pulling a garden cultivator equipped with hilling disks to cover the seedlings with earth. Roger and Melissa walked behind the cultivator and marveled at the thing as it pitched dirt over the potatoes and covered the row of raised dirt with old hay. When Jason got to the end of the row, he turned around and started down the adjacent line of seedlings, this time with Roone and Pilar following him to cover the row with hay. The hay would keep the ground warm now when it was still cold and hold moisture when the weather got hot.

"I don't think you need me for this," Melissa said playfully to Roger. "I've some chores at home to do. You stay here and play farmer." She kissed Roger good-bye and took the short-cut through the woods where the trees had been cleared for a gas pipeline installation.

Florence took notice of Melissa's departure.

The Thomas women also departed to fix lunch.

It took the rest of the morning to get all of the potato cuttings planted, and when finished, they found they only had enough cuttings for twenty rows.

"Do you think that's enough to feed us all for a year?" Roone asked Jason as everyone gathered around the last row.

"Well, that depends on the weather. Everything depends on the weather. Welcome to farming."

"That doesn't engender a lot of confidence," Roger said.

"Have faith," Jason said. "We are going to meticulously water, weed, and care for this patch of ground. Abraham has a greenhouse filled with okra seedlings. We will put that in the other ten rows. And we've got a bunch of sweet-potato slips that we'll plant in May. I think altogether we will have plenty of starch."

The dinner bell rang loud and clear, and Jason drove his team to the barn and hitched them to a support pole while everyone else lined up at the rainwater cistern to wash their hands. Florence slipped away and followed the path Melissa took through the woods and out to the road.

Melissa and Annie were preparing a rabbit that Annie shot in their pasture for supper when they heard a knock on the front door. Since most visitors came to the back door, this caught them by surprise.

"Now, who could that be?" asked Annie.

Annie's hands were bloody, and Melissa's weren't. "I'll get it. You're in too deep," Melissa said.

Annie just nodded and smiled and pushed her reading glasses up on the bridge of her nose with the back of her wrist, and hoped she didn't get any blood on her face. When Melissa opened the door, she saw Florence standing about ten feet to the west side of the poured concrete pad front porch.

"Florence! Hi!" Melissa didn't know what else to say. They hadn't talked since she moved into the cabin at the Troyer homestead with Roger.

"Hey, Mel." Florence always called her Mel. "Can I talk to you?"

"Yea, sure. Come in. We're preparing a rabbit out back in the mudroom." Melissa signaled Florence to follow her, but when she got to the kitchen, Melissa saw that Annie was finished cleaning the rabbit and had it in a metal pan on the table and was looking through the jars of canned food she brought from her store. When Annie saw Florence, she put three mugs on the table and bustled over to retrieve the ever-present stainless-steel teapot that sat on the stove.

Melissa gestured to Florence and said, "Please, have a seat."

Annie poured some tea for all and took her mug and stood next to the stove. Melissa sat down and took a sip from her cup and looked expectantly at Florence.

"Does she have to be here?" Florence asked Melissa.

Melissa's face went to stone. "Florence, her name is Annie, and this is her home. Please don't be rude. Whatever you have to say, you can say in front of her."

Florence's eyes went to Annie, but she didn't turn her head, and she didn't say anything to Annie. When her eyes came back to Melissa, Florence said, "I want you to come back to me."

"Florence..." Melissa breathed in exasperation. "We were over long before I met Roger. I've moved on. You have to move on too."

"Come on, Mel. You don't love him! I don't know what you're doing here, but you don't love him."

"No, you're wrong, Florence. I do love Roger."

"How can you say that? That's disgusting."

"Why? Because Roger is a man?"

"Yes! Of course, because Roger is a man! We spent two years together. I *know* you. You couldn't love a man."

"You're wrong, Florence. You don't know me. I don't know what else to say."

"Say you'll come back. You don't have to live like this! Are you out of your mind? After all we've been through?"

"What are you talking about, Florence? What have we been through? We traveled together, and we went to some concerts together, and we crashed on couches and at the Garden of Eden commune together, and we fooled around a little. That's not saying much."

"Fooled around? I loved you! And you humiliated me for a man!"

"You loved me? You couldn't be bothered to get out of bed in the morning to do anything to keep me! You couldn't be bothered to take a shower before you came to bed at night! How many times did we have sex in two years? A dozen times? Two dozen? I get laid that many times in a month now! And he *wants* me— and I want him! I've never experienced anything like it. And I wanted to have a baby!"

"You could have had a baby with me!"

"What? How?!"

"We could have adopted! We could have had a sperm donor!"

"Oh, great! And where would we live? At the commune? On somebody's couch? You wanted to live without money, remember?! You didn't need anything, remember?! You hated 'materialism,' and 'capitalism,' and the 'patriarchy,' remember? 'Zero population growth' to save the planet, remember?!! What could you provide for a mother and child! What were you going to do? Get us on public assistance? Have us live in public housing? Go back to school while I worked at McDonald's? What were you going to do for me? You would have abandoned me."

"What the hell does Roger do for you, Mel?"

Melissa stood up from the table. She turned sideways and smoothed her dress over her belly with her right forearm under her breasts and her left holding her lower abdomen. She nodded her head fiercely at Florence and said, "I am pregnant!"

Florence burst out in tears, weeping and wailing and rocking back and forth in her seat.

Melissa shot a glance over to Annie. When their eyes met, each could see an expression of frightened apprehension in the other.

"Okay!" Florence bellowed and stood up from her chair. "Fine! You've got your baby! You don't need him anymore! Come home! Come back to me!"

Melissa grabbed her own head between her hands. "Are you out of your fucking mind?" Melissa whispered to herself as much as to Florence in disbelief.

"No," Florence replied. "You're the one who is out of their mind! You wanted a baby; now you've got one! You don't have to put up with him and his fucking dick anymore!"

"What the fuck are you talking about!!??" Melissa shrieked at Florence.

"Look, you wanted a baby! I get it! But you don't have to put up with his shit anymore! It's not like you need him to get pregnant; you're already pregnant! Do you really enjoy it when he fucks you? How about when he shoves his dick down your throat or up your ass?! You're not his fucking sex slave. You don't have to put up with that! You're only doing that to please him and to keep him around to take care of you! But you don't need him anymore. I will be there for you! I will take care of you! Roger has served his purpose."

"Oh, my G-d! You fucking crazy bitch! Do you think I would want to go back to a passionless relationship with you? When you can't even get out of bed in the morning to go to work? After you, I can't even believe what this man is willing to do for me! And for what? Because he wants to have sex with me? And it's none of your fucking business what we do in bed!! But I'll tell you this: I'll do anything to keep this man happy—whatever it takes to keep him coming back—because this man loves me and will do anything for me! No, you didn't take much, but you didn't give much either. Roger gives ten times more than he takes. Fuck you and your power imbalances! Work twelve hours a day for me? No problem. Go out in the freezing rain before dawn to milk the goat and feed the horses, so I don't have to? He'll do it. What the fuck did you ever do for me? What the fuck did I ever see in you?!" Now Melissa was really wound up. Her voice rocketed off the walls. "You're not a butch or a gentleman or man or whatever the fuck you pretend to be, you fucking eunuch! Don't tell me what I do and don't enjoy. I'm not like you. I enjoy having a man in my bed and my home. Now fuck off and get out!"

Florence collapsed to the ground and flopped around as she wailed at the top of her lungs. Melissa ran to Annie, and Annie put her arm around her. They watched as Florence writhed on the floor in agony.

"Oh, my word! She's lost it," Annie said. "Let's go! For her safety and ours, come on!"

Annie walked Melissa east on route 318, the two-lane highway that ran through the community, and turned left at the first intersection on the road that would take them into the heart of the Amish settlement. Annie deposited Melissa at the Yoder family greenhouses where she would have the company of the Amish women and walked back to their house. Florence was gone. There was no sign of her on the roads, and in an abundance of caution, Annie looked in the two small closets and good-sized kitchen pantry. No, Florence wasn't here. By the time Annie went back for Melissa and brought her home again, Roger was home, exhausted but happy with the day's efforts.

That night, after a long soak in a hot bath, Roger collapsed on the bed and fell asleep. Melissa kept Annie company in the kitchen as she worked her spinning wheel by the light of a single mason-jar candle.

"I can't believe I never played with one of these before," Annie said. "This is even better than knitting. I love it! It's so satisfying and calming to the soul."

"Annie, I'm glad you were here today."

"Me, too."

"I don't know what might have happened."

"You handled yourself well. Florence is volatile, huh?"

"Controlling, volatile, abusive. I have no idea why I wasted so much time with her."

Annie just shrugged. "You were young. If you've figured it out by now, then you beat me by a mile. And more importantly, by a decade."

"What do you mean?" Melissa asked.

"Well, you're 24 years old. And you've got a roof over your head, food on the table, a man who loves you, and a baby in your belly. It took me until I was 35 to settle down with a man. And 35 is too late. I never had a family; and there is something else the Feminists don't tell you about starting your family late in life: You might not live long enough to raise your children."

"What do you mean?"

"Not everyone makes it to my age. Sometimes people die in their 40's and 50's. If they started their family at 35, then they leave young children and teenagers behind without a mother or father."

"Oh," Melissa's eyes filled with tears. "I never thought about it like that! I should have: my father died when I was 15. He got sick when I was 10."

"That's the downside, the terrible liability they never mentioned when they told us to put off having children. Your father had his children late and died when you were young. And I never had a family."

"I'm sorry Annie! And I know it is a cliché to say, but we're your family now."

"And it's been wonderful!" Annie stopped what she was doing and dropped her hands in her lap, her eyes filled with tears. "These past six weeks have been the best of my life. I just hope that I am not interfering. You two are still newlyweds."

Melissa's face made an expression of empathy. "Don't worry! We're good." Melissa winked and nodded her head over and over and reached out for Annie's hand.

"Tee hee!" Annie cried out. "Well, that's a good thing."

"It's bizarre."

"What's that?"

"I'm like an adult now," Melissa said.

"Yes, you're definitely 'like an adult.'"

"No, I mean it's very different. Roger is up before dawn like he is on a mission. He never loses his focus. Yea, I feel like there are demands on me that I never felt before. But that's because no one ever did a thing for me where I felt they could demand anything in return. Florence never did anything for me, never made any sacrifices. Everything Roger does is for *us*. You heard me today. Florence couldn't get out of bed. She's 34 years old and not 'two nickels to rub together.' My mother used to say that." Melissa paused. "I don't know how to say this."

Annie looked up, but Melissa didn't make eye contact.

"There's no hurry," Annie said.

"When you are in a relationship with another woman, it *is* equal."

Annie looked up to let Melissa know she was listening as she worked her spinning wheel.

"But it's not a good equal. It's equal—as in zero is equal to zero. It doesn't add up to anything. Where with Roger, it's not equal. But it's a whirlwind of activity. I mean work, sex, meals, baths, laundry. It's all going on all the time. And it's not like he's ever told me to do something. But I feel like I should be returning something for all that he gives me. And it feels like we are going somewhere; like we are building something."

"Well, you are," Annie said. "You're building the only thing that matters. And if you think we are busy now, just wait until you see how busy we are when the baby gets here."

Melissa looked up and saw that Annie was crying again. Melissa started to cry again too.

"The world almost came to an end," Melissa said. "I came close to starving to death. I don't know if my mother is even alive: I am worried sick about that. And I feel so guilty because I feel like the luckiest person in the world. All this suffering; people are starving: and I'm having the best time of my life. My childhood sucked; no that's not right—my life sucked. My poor father got sick. My mother got sick of him being sick. And I was sick of being in the middle of it. When my father died, I was overcome with grief: and my mother was overcome with relief. I hated everything. I wasn't even sure I wanted to live. I don't know what the hell I'm saying here."

"It's okay," Annie said. "We're just talking."

"I thought my life was shit; I guess because it was shit. I didn't think anyone would want me. Oh, I knew men would want to fuck me, but it never occurred to me that a man could be an asset in my life. And Florence and all the women we hung around with played that theme over and over and over again. 'Men are no good!' Sandy went to college for Women's Studies. You know what she studied? Porn. In her program, they watched endless hours of heterosexual porn. Can you imagine paying $50,000 a year to watch the kind of porn you don't like? Anyway, after watching all that porn, all of their conclusions about men seemed to boil down to this: All men want to do is fuck and dominate women. But this man! And I'll tell you: He is *all* man, and he is *a lot* of man. But I have no problem with his expectations or whatever you want to call them. He's never asked me to cook for him. He just went about his tasks, and when he came home if I didn't do something about it, there wouldn't be anything to eat. He fills the kettle up every morning and lays fire under it. But he never told me to do the laundry. I just did it. He doesn't come to bed unbathed—stinking like a dirty foot like some people I used to know—and when he comes to bed 'it's on like a pot of neck bones!' as they say in Tennessee. I don't feel 'subjugated.' Not at all. That was Sandy and Florence's favorite word, 'subjugated.' I'm sorry I'm rambling."

"You're doing fine—just speaking your mind. Nothing wrong with that."

"Well, I don't feel 'subjugated.' I feel loved. I feel wanted. I feel pregnant. And it all feels so natural. What the fuck was I doing with Florence? What if I never met Roger? Would I be a pile of dirty clothes and bones on the side of the highway like those poor people we saw on the way here? Would I have died alone?"

Melissa lost her composure and started to weep. Annie put her spindle down and moved her chair next to Melissa and held her.

"Oh, easy, there, easy. We've all been through a lot. You have a wonderful life now. You've got a man with ants-in-his-pants, and he loves you." Melissa laughed through her tears at that. "A home, a family, real friends, and a community that cares about you! We are fortunate beyond comprehension. There is no escaping the miserable catastrophes of life. I'm sorry to hear about your father and your childhood. But if you think about it, Florence brought you to Roger, and he saved your life, and now he is giving you a child. Without Florence, you don't have Roger, you don't have the baby, and I don't have you, and maybe we're both dead out there somewhere on the side of the road. But we're not. We're here, and we're alive in this magical place." And here Annie stopped to make eye contact with Melissa. "What an experience we've had! Is it me? Or is this place incredible?"

"No," Melissa answered. "It's not just you. I feel like we fell out of the sky. I was scared to death when the Mennonites told us we had to leave because I loved it there. But now I feel like this is where we belong."

"Me too, sweetie. With all that has happened, I am shocked at my good fortune that I should experience this in my lifetime."

If they sat still and didn't move, without the hum of the electric appliances of modernity, all was silent. The light of the solitary candle seemed to create the perfect ambiance as the two women sat in quiet contemplation of the vagaries of existence.

Melissa yawned.

"Perhaps you should go to bed. It's been a long day. You need your rest."

Melissa stood up and went to the stove and retrieved some hot water and mixed some cold water from the water bucket and washed her face at the sink.

"Thank you for everything, Annie. And yes, I'm going to go to bed. But not to rest! Good night!"

Annie looked to Melissa, a look of contentment on her face and said, "To life!"

Just before first light, Roger rose from the bed and started for the kitchen. Melissa's voice called from the dark.

"Hey, come back here."

Roger sat down on the edge of the bed.

"You're awake," Roger said. "How are you feeling?"

Melissa answered by reaching up and pulling him down onto the bed and folding her naked body into his as they lay on their sides facing each other.

"I haven't been nauseous in the morning for a while. I think it's past."

"Good." Roger stroked her hair and kissed her.

"I have to tell you something. Florence was here yesterday."

Melissa related the exchange in detail.

"Wow... that's disconcerting."

"I don't think she will come back here. I made it all very clear. There was no room for confusion."

"Oh, I'd say you made yourself clear. I am sorry you went through that, and I am thankful Annie was here."

"She had a frying pan in her hand! I think she was getting ready to bunk Florence on the head if it came to that."

"Well, thank goodness it didn't. Break-ups are very hard. One party usually has the comfort of a new love interest. The person who got dumped does not, and they are suffering. I know you are resentful. But there is nothing to be gained by hurling ugly words and slurs around."

"She had the nerve to come into my home and talk like that!"

"You called here a eunuch."

"It's the truth!"

"Easy... Easy. The truth is not always the 'good.' Or at least it isn't always good to speak the truth—some things you just don't say. They're too hurtful—and so they are better left unsaid. And Florence is not a eunuch. She is a woman. You were angry, and you wanted to hurt her. But this is a touchy subject. Freud said that women suffer from 'penis envy.' The Feminists hated that. Of course, when German psychologist Karen Horney said that men suffer from 'womb envy,' that was okay with the Feminists: Consistency was never their strong suit. There is nothing scientific about psychological theory—they are nothing more than unscientific opinions that the profession tries to legitimize in various unscientific ways. And now it is dominated by Leftist political apparatchiks—or was. They're all dead now, I'm sure. But I think Freud was half right. I think women like Florence and Sandy have a form of 'penis envy.' But I think it manifests itself as the human emotion of 'disgust.' I think they see people who have a penis as somewhat less than human and; they find the people who have a penis 'disgusting.' Think about what people want to do with the things that disgust them: They want to kill bugs and spiders and snakes. They want to clean up and sterilize bio-hazards—vomit, feces, blood—to render them safe; and not 'disgusting.' I think that's how women like Florence and Sandy see men in general and me in particular. I disgust them.

216

Especially now—because as far as Florence is concerned, I am soiling you. But I don't feel that way towards them, and I don't want you to feel that way. They are flawed human beings, just as I am."

"Florence and Sandy hate you. And you don't hate them?"

"Florence may not hate me. There is a strong and complicated reaction going on inside her. She likely suffers from challenging identity issues, and on top of that, exposure to me elicits a disgust response in her. I'm not special in that regard—all men elicit that response. And she confuses that set of emotions with hate. On the other hand, Florence might have *male*-variant, anti-social personality disorder. And there are other stressors in her life: She's lost the life she knew, just as we have. Worse, everything that has happened since we left the Garden of Eden commune has informed Florence of the futile nature of her worldview, personality, and belief system. And then she lost her lover—to a man. Florence is suffering. We've all suffered, but she's been suffering for far longer than we have. Good grief! The more I talk about it, the more frightened I become of her."

"That's what Annie said."

"I think we should put some time and distance between Florence and us," Roger said. "Let's not make things worse."

"I think Annie said that too."

"Yea. There is something special about Annie. Anyway, she gives off a great vibe."

"She said the last six weeks were the best time in her life, in spite of everything."

"I wish I knew where my sons are," Roger said. "But I feel the same way, ever since you stepped into my cabin back at the Troyer farm."

"Well," Melissa said coyly, as she reached her arm around him. "If I had to wait for you, nothing would get done."

Chapter 28

The long winter succumbed to spring in the first week of April; and as Roger predicted the general mood of the people living in the Sulphur Springs community seemed to brighten. The workload fell, at least for now, as they were between the firewood harvest and the spring and summer's all-out war in the gardens and fields against the weeds and pests, and for moisture. The days got longer, and life got easier, now that they were free, at least for a year, of tramping wood out of the forest. Of course, there was still much work to do. The men reclaimed lumber and sheet metal and truck axles and wheels and many other useful items from the roads and byways, and for the most part, Sandy and Florence labored alongside the men on these work-crews. The stunning transformation in their physiques over the past five months had happened gradually; even they didn't seem to notice. Their dull and limited diet and strenuous activities hardened their bodies and shrunk their bellies.

Sandy, no longer the ponderous and morbidly obese colossus who lived at the Garden of Eden commune and spent her days enraged at existence, scampered up and down a ladder at the job site where her work-crew was removing framing timber from the skeleton of a massive livestock barn as if she had been doing this her entire life. Although now forty-two years of age, Sandy rejoiced in her newfound physicality like a teenager who survived the awkward and gangly growth spurt of puberty only to flower into a star athlete.

Florence came into her own too. While never obese, she grew soft and plump in her former life as a sedentary political activist, but after shedding the flab of modernity, Florence took on the Amazonian look of a college track star. She bantered back and forth with the men on her crew with the ease and confidence of someone who had lived among these people since childhood, and not the recent transplant that she was. The men enjoyed her creative insults to their mock advances. A typical exchange might go something like this:

"Hey, you're looking hot there, Florence!"

"Oh, yea? Well, squirt it in the sink. You're not my type."

"Hey, baby, you goin' my way?" Another asked.

"Not if you were the last man on a desert island. Can't you come up with something better than that? You dimwit. No wonder your last two dates were with Rosie *Palm* and Pamala *Hand*erson."

The men roared in laughter and teased the rejected pseudo-suitors. But more importantly, this good-natured ribbing served to endear Florence to the men on her crew. And even though Sandy could not make friends with men as quickly as Florence did, the women's workmates descended on the Amish schoolhouse they were living in and built them a two-stall outhouse, a privacy screen for outdoor baths and pour-over showers, and a front porch complete with roof. Even hardboiled Sandy was moved by the expression of solidarity on the part of the men. Jason heard about the improvements the men erected at the women's living quarters and sought Roger out to tell him about it.

"It's a wonderful development," Roger said. "Of that, there is no doubt. Perhaps the perfect manifestation of mankind's goodwill towards their fellow man when they live in the absence of oppression. You have every reason to feel good about it."

"Roger you have a wonderful way of complicating things. Come again?"

"Do you think men who were oppressed and cowed by Feminist doctrine at their workplace, and who live in fear that the slightest misstep could destroy their career would come to their oppressors in a spirit of benevolence like that?"

"No," Jason said. "Of course not."

"Well, there you have it. Anyway, I am glad you're here. I want to talk to you about something."

"Alright."

"I visited the O'Neil farm for the first time since the day we traveled north from Shady Grove. Did you know they take Sunday's off as their day of rest?"

"So?"

"As do the Amish on our side of the community."

"And?"

"But your clan and the half dozen farms on this side of the community celebrate Saturday as their day of rest. That doesn't sound like a big deal now, but it is a disaster waiting to happen."

"I never gave it any thought," said Jason.

"How long have you been observing Saturday?"

"It was something that just happened over the winter. My family gathered on Sundays for a 'meeting.' We don't have a service. We sit together in silence for a half an hour and then share a meal."

"Yes, yes," Roger said impatiently. "Very nice. But when, and how, did your meeting move over to Saturday?"

"My son, Roone, and my brother, Walt, work on a crew with Martin. Martin is an orthodox Jewish rabbi, and from Friday at sundown until Saturday at sundown Martin and his family observe the Sabbath."

"Right; Got it. I'm familiar with Judaism, Genesis, the whole shebang. How and why did your family move its day of worship or silence or meditation or whatever you call it to Saturday?"

"Well, it just wasn't that important," Jason said. "I mean, that is which day of the week we gather. Any day can be Sunday, or First Day, as most Quakers call it. I am not concerned about using the Pagan or Quaker terms, regarding days of the week."

"*That's* what I was after. Thank you."

Jason didn't respond. After a moment, Roger continued.

"It would help a lot if everyone were as flexible as you. Okay. Well, let's shelve that for a moment so we can think about it. Let's move on to item two on the agenda."

"You've been keeping a list?" Jason asked.

"And checking it twice."

The two men shared a chuckle.

Roger continued. "I wish this were funny. And while I am thrilled to hear that Sandy and Florence are making friends, or at least not making enemies, I have to wonder how long that is going to last."

"What do you mean?" asked Jason.

"Mindy doesn't work with Sandy and Florence. She works at Roscoe Cutliff's dairy and the Yoder's greenhouse and nursery."

"So?"

"Well, Melissa seems to think she is spending an awful lot of time with Roscoe Cutliff."

Jason said nothing and stared at Roger with a blank expression trying to process what he thought he heard.

In the immediate aftermath of the blackout and the onset of the Famine, Roscoe Cutliff locked his wife, Belinda, out of their home after a nasty domestic dispute. Belinda sought help from Jason and Ellen Thomas, but after a week with Belinda, Jason and Ellen couldn't imagine how Roscoe survived sixteen years with her. She was just plain evil. Jason and Abraham Yoder's son, Noah, brought Belinda to her parent's house in Edinburgh, but there was no sign of them. McCoy O'Neil's family took her in, and she lived there for nearly two months. But she and one of the young women McCoy rescued from Elizabethtown, Georgia Fox, stole a horse and ran away. The horse returned the next day with its saddle and bridle still on. Some of the Amish men logging a stand of trees a little over ten miles east thought they saw her on the front lawn of an old farmhouse as they passed by with their teams of horses.

"Are you saying that Mindy and Roscoe are romantically involved?" Jason asked.

"Well, it makes sense, doesn't it?" Roger asked in reply. "Three women are living in that old Amish one-room schoolhouse. One of them is bound to be the odd woman out. Or not. But given the evidence…"

"And you think this is going to set off a big problem between Roscoe and Sandy?"

"I don't know. It depends on what is going on over there. Maybe Sandy wants her out. Maybe she's happy Mindy found someone else. Who knows? I don't socialize with them. Melissa won't even acknowledge Florence's existence. But this might be another disaster waiting to happen; this is the kind of shit that can destroy us and have us at each other's throats."

"What will?" Jason asked. "The machinations and romantic inclinations of childless lesbians?"

"Jason… you can't have a cooperative and interdependent community of people living in goodwill if there is any amount of mate shopping and trading."

"Oh…"

"Yea. Look at the Amish here. Or the Mennonites down in Shady Grove. Ah, for fuck's sake, just look down the street at our orthodox rabbi. All of those groups are extremely successful at living in 'Community' with their fellow tribesmen. And look, it is what it is—these are all examples of in-your-face-tribalism. But look closely at their customs regarding the relationship between the men and the women in their community. Outside of marriage and family, there is no socializing between the genders. The Anabaptists separate their single men and women at their Sunday services. The orthodox Jews don't bother to make a distinction. They separate the men from the women, period."

"Roger, I am not going to tell people where they can sit and where they can't. I am not going to tell people how to live their lives. Nothing is inherently beautiful. Beauty is subjective. That's not true of coercion. There is nothing subjective about it. Coercion is objectively and inherently evil."

"I spent several months with the Mennonites. We attended their services. No one ever told anyone where to sit. I've been to a half-dozen orthodox Jewish weddings. At the service, the men sat downstairs and the women upstairs. At the reception, the men danced with the men, and the women danced with the women. Not once did I see someone in authority giving out citations to people who sat or danced in the wrong place. Where was the coercion?"

"But we don't have the history together that those people have," Jason said.

"That's exactly my point."

"What's your point?" Jason was getting peptic.

"We don't have a history. And we will never gather a history if we do not have an ethos of stability in the family and marriage. In one hundred years, humanity will be a reflection of the cultures that were successful in making children and family their cultural priority. Everything else is doomed to burn out in less than a generation—but they can cause a lot of trouble in the meantime."

"What do you think we should do?" Jason asked. "Excommunicate Mindy for leaving Sandy?"

Roger burst out laughing.

Jason couldn't help but smile at his mirth.

"What?" asked Jason.

"Well, isn't this ironic? Two heterosexual white men pondering the sanctity of a lesbian relationship?"

"Well," Jason was laughing right along with Roger now. "It would be if that's what we were talking about." Jason hesitated. "Is that what we are talking about?"

It took them a minute to collect themselves. After all, the situation was highly amusing.

"We're not talking about lesbian relationships," Roger said. "Because the only relationships that matter to mankind and society are those that produce offspring. We are examining marriage, children, and family. What would our relationship— yours and mine—be like if Ellen left you for me, and Melissa left me for you? Now, imagine that sort of thing taking place across the community. We would be unable to cooperate and depend on one another. That was okay when everyone worked for a corporation or government agency. But do you think we would survive the next winter like that?"

"I take your point."

"Do you remember what it was like when you were eighteen? Twenty? Even thirty? Young men are saturated with the hormones and chemicals mankind needs to procreate and survive, but those hormones and chemicals are not concerned with the survival of other men; they likely evolved to help 'off' the competition. From an evolutionary point of view, that might be okay; maybe even preferable: But not for civilization. Every civilization in history that lasted more than a few years sought to manage this phenomenon. Human Beings are not a troop of chimpanzees, with one dominant male driving off or killing the other males and breeding the females."

"Well, we'd like to think so," Jason said.

"Civilization cannot tolerate the violent inclinations of a small percentage of the male population: That's why we have prisons. Some Feminists, Julie Bindel comes to mind, want collective punishment for men. Let's table that for the moment. There are lots of ways people can live in 'Community' with one another.

223

The members of the criminal gang, MS-13, live in 'Community' with each other just as much as the Shady Grove Mennonites."

"Okay. I got it. On the one hand, Sandy and Mindy do not have children. So, there's 'no harm, no foul.' On the other hand, if they can switch partners on a whim, it sets a disastrous example for the heterosexual couples with children. Mate switching is anathema to small tribal communities."

"Yes, indeed. Women with children are never independent. They are dependent on someone or something to help provide for their needs and care for the child: their mate, the government, or in our case the community, their parents, or their extended family. That strong and independent meme was a mirage. And I didn't say only 'couples.' I think couples are probably best, but plural marriages, line marriages, polygamy, and polyandry might be just fine. The way people choose to arrange their lives is not our business unless it demonstrably harms their children. The important thing is stability."

Roger recounted his experience with the polygamous fundamentalist Mormons that he and the women from the Garden of Eden commune met on their way to Shady Grove.

"Fascinating," Jason said in response.

"They were exceptional people. And they are down there in the middle of nowhere, all alone. I think they would make a wonderful addition to our community."

Chapter 29

The people of the Sulphur Springs community, like people everywhere, went about their lives as if each day was indeed a new day with a new beginning, for the most part, unconnected to the day before. Blissfully unaware that every event that has ever happened in the universe was the inevitable outcome and result of all that preceded it—cause and effect. Philosophers often call this line of reasoning "Reductionism." That all that happens, and that every event, can be reduced to a chain of events leading back to a singular "beginning"—and whatever we might believe that beginning to be, this conclusion is unavoidable if you just give it a little thought. Of course, it is only fair to point out that many philosophers believe that "Reductionism" is one of the most misunderstood, used, and abused notions in the history of critical thinking. But for our purposes here, let's just say that every effect has a cause and that anything that happens today is the result of a chain of unbroken events that occurred in the past. These causal chains embodied in the concept of causality resulted in a visit by the Amish midwife, Emma Schwartz, and her assistant and midwife in training, Miriam Weiss, to the Thomas' homestead.

Danielle Thomas was pregnant—very pregnant—and due any day.

Emma examined Danielle thoroughly, but did not perform an "internal." Her husband, Manny, stood by her side holding her hand. His parents, Walter and Jenny Thomas, cooled their heels in the "main house," the big Amish-built farmhouse that they shared with Jason and Ellen Thomas and their children. The men, Jason and Walter, were brothers. Danielle and Manny's child would be the first baby born in the Thomas family "After." It was understandable that the family was excited—and nervous. The Amish were accustomed to giving birth at home. But for this family, the visceral, life and death experience of birth without the emotional security of a sterile hospital environment and a trained physician was a new development.

Walter summed it up perfectly. "Everything will be fine; as long as nothing goes wrong."

Emma Schwartz had delivered hundreds of babies. But in cases of a suspected "breach," Emma had called for an ambulance and a hospital delivery. But there was no ambulance to call, and there was no hospital to turn to. Emma and Miriam would have to try to manipulate the baby around by pushing on Danielle's extended abdomen. During a break in the action, Miriam explained the situation to the family.

"Unless we can turn the baby, we will have to perform a C-section. We have veterinary tetracycline on hand, but that is the only antibiotic we have—and the needle is for cattle sized patients. The only thing we have for pain is alcohol and marijuana."

"The older woman living with Roger and Melissa is an herbalist," Jason said.

"Well, I don't think you want to depend on some new-age witchcraft freakshow at a time like this." Miriam did not suffer fools very well.

"No, no," Jason replied. "She's not one of those. Roger says she is a brilliant philosopher and mathematician. I sense that she is a woman of science, not hocus-pocus."

"It can't hurt to ask!" cried Jenny.

Walter was already on his way out the door.

"Hey, brother!" Jason cried out. "I'll go. You'd better stay here."

"I will help you hitch Thunder," Walter said.

Annie felt around Danielle's abdomen for ten minutes. Then she stood up and said, "I can't tell one way or the other. But if you're sure, Emma, I think we can convince this baby to turn around, 1, 2, 3. But if it is not a breach now, it will be."

"How are you going to turn the baby?" asked Miriam.

"With ice," Annie replied.

"Ice?"

"Yep. Manny, I know you've got an ice house here. I hope it's got some ice in it."

"It does," Manny replied. "It's full."

"Well, we don't need much. I need a couple of pounds broken up into cube sized chunks or smaller. Wrap it up in a shirt or even a clean sock and bring it here."

Manny departed to retrieve the ice.

"Emma, I have to ask you. How confident are you that this baby is a breach?" Annie asked.

"As sure as I'm standing here."

"Well, okay then. Here we go."

The baby girl came into the world the following morning about an hour after dawn. And it had indeed been a breach. Annie applied the ice to the top of Danielle's extended abdomen just under her breastbone until it was almost unbearable for her. And everyone watched, dumbfounded, as the baby's evident movements against her mother's body to get away from the cold left the fetus in the proper position for a normal delivery.

Bad news travels fast, and many of the young women of the community, including Mindy, spent the night in the Thomas' guest house apartment where Manny and Danielle lived along with Jason's son, Roone, and his pregnant wife, Pilar. The men, including the father-to-be, were not welcome and decamped to the main house leaving the women to engage in the magical and reassuring solidarity that women of childbearing age have enjoyed since man first walked the plains of Africa. Just before first light, the baby "crowned" showing the top of its head in the birth canal. The cheers that poured out of the crowd of women present in the apartment brought tears to the eyes of the men helplessly waiting seated around two candles on the main house's kitchen table despite the light of morning. The baby had indeed turned. Mother and child would survive.

Mindy, with the tears of the overwhelming emotional experience of new life still streaming down her face, left the moving scene of the miracle of birth and walked directly to her place of work at Roscoe Cutliff's dairy. She had missed the morning milking. The cows were back out on the pasture and would not return to the barn until the afternoon milking that started at 4 pm. Mindy knocked on the front door to Roscoe's house. Roscoe opened the door, surprised to see Mindy. He heard about the drama unfolding at the Thomas farm the night before, and several of the older Amish women came to help him with the morning milking chores because the younger women were attending the birth.

"Hey, Mindy. Is everything okay?"

"Yea," Mindy nodded and smiled. "Mother and baby are doing fine."

"Oh, that's good." Roscoe didn't know what else to say. He always found himself tongue-tied in Mindy's presence. The two stood there looking at each other, their faces plastered with shit-eating grins in the awkward hush that followed. Finally, Mindy broke the silence.

"I'm looking for a man." She raised her eyebrows and bit her lower lip.

Roscoe stood aside and opened the door to make way for Mindy.

"Good. I'm looking for a wife."

Chapter 30

The cool-weather-garden vegetables began to trickle out of the gardens in late April, and now they poured out in early May. In another week, no more than two, it would be a landslide. But for right now, the community delighted in fresh broccoli, cabbage, garlic, lettuce, and rutabaga. The garden onions were not ready for harvest, but the "wild garlic" that passed for onion grew abundantly in the hay fields; it was among the earliest of the cool-weather grasses. With the threat of frost now past, the community planted the first rotation in the warm-weather-gardens. By planting in stages, they could manage the harvest and not get overwhelmed at any one time and waste their efforts by leaving vegetables and fruit too long on the vines and plants to spoil. The daytime temperatures were still mild, and the work day in the gardens though long was pleasant enough: But the blast furnace heat of the summer awaited them.

Jason observed that the success of the midwives in the birth of the Thomas girl, the fair spring weather, and the fresh variety in their meals infected the community with newfound optimism. Roger wasn't convinced that these were the only feedbacks at work.

"The people have not been subjected to media advertising for six months," Roger reasoned. "The purpose of advertising is to induce anxiety; and then to provide a solution. Individuals don't know that their lives suck; that they are ugly, stupid, fat, or poor—unless someone is there to remind them over and over again to hammer that message into their brains. Well, that's what advertising does. And not just advertising: Some of the worst offenders during the internet age were the online 'do-gooder' nitwits."

Walter loved Roger's rants and would egg him on. "Go on, Roger! I'm listening!" And then Walter would "shush!" everyone else with a big smile on his face.

"That people's sense of well-being is inversely related to their exposure to media in general and advertising, in particular is well-established. And as time goes on, and their brains forget the misery inflicted on them by advertising…"

"Not to mention damn near starving to death," Walter interrupted.

"And as their experiences and memories of the Famine retreat over time…"

"We're not out of the woods yet, Roger," Jason chimed in. "We exist because it rains. An extended drought would be a disaster."

"Oh…"

"I'm sorry. I don't mean to rain on your parade," Jason said. "Pun intended. I appreciate the enthusiasm."

"Well, the weather notwithstanding, things are certainly looking up."

Roger would remember this moment and wished he had kept his mouth shut rather than tempt fate.

Chapter 31

Sandy had not gotten out of her bed since Mindy left. Florence tried to talk to her, but Sandy withdrew into her blankets. Florence felt that she was just depressed. And depression was certainly afflicting Sandy, but after a few days, it was clear that Sandy's condition was something more than a broken heart: She had thick and phlegmy congestion in her nose and lungs. And she was not the only person in the community suffering like this. Half of the young women, but just a few of the men, were sick and laid up in bed. And after a few days, their condition worsened. Miriam raised the alarm. Her twins, Hanna and Aviva were listless, and pale and had difficulty breathing. Miriam summoned Emma Schwartz, the Amish midwife who took one look at the girls and knew they were in great danger. Emma had visited with the Amish women who took sick. But Miriam's twins were at least two days further into the ailment, and they were deathly ill. Would the other women be this sick in a day or two? Emma departed the Weiss home and went directly to consult with Annie; this was the first that Roger, Melissa, and Annie had heard of the outbreak. Emma had lost a nephew twenty years earlier to pneumonia. The Weiss girls appeared to be in the same condition as her nephew just days before his death.

"And this is afflicting mostly women and girls?" asked Annie.

"Yes, we must have twenty women and girls down in bed over in the Amish settlement. And over here the Weiss girls and Sandy seem to be stricken. I haven't asked over at the Thomas family.

Annie was deep in thought.

"We don't have any anti-biotics other than what we got from the farm store," Emma added.

"Go get the Weiss girls. Bring them here *immediately*," Annie directed Roger. Then to Emma. "Please go check on the Thomas family. See if anyone there is sick. Ask one of the men to go get Sandy out of bed and bring her here."

Emma turned to leave.

"No! Emma, never mind that. There's no time. Go back to your community. Roger will have to check on the Thomas family and Sandy. Here's what you must do. Don't let anyone talk you out of it. See that this gets done."

Annie was writing furiously on a piece of paper. She handed the note to Emma and took her by the arm as she gave Emma instructions in a fast and loud staccato. Then Annie grabbed a bucket and walked out of the back door.

When Annie got back to the house Miriam Weiss and her twins and Jason's son, Roone, and daughter-in-law, Pilar, were waiting for her. She went to the stove and dropped the wild garlic and onion she had gathered into a pot with cream, butter, and milk with a little bit of salt.

"Hey, Melissa, stir this, so it doesn't burn, please. Okay, the rest of you follow me outside. Not you, fellas. You are going to have to make yourself scarce."

Roger looked at her wondering what was going on.

"The girls are going to be doing a little almost-nude sunbathing. So, scram!" Annie said to Roger and Roone and then turned to the women and girls. "The rest of you, follow me outside."

Annie went to the clothesline and stripped a blanket off of the line.

"Strip out of your clothes down to your undies. I want you to lay here and sunbathe, first one side for a half an hour. Then the other."

"How is this going to help?" Miriam pleaded.

"I am just thankful it's May." Annie was talking to herself. "I don't know if this would work in March."

"What is this? Some fucking Pagan ritual??!!"

Annie snapped out of it. "Please, Miriam! Do as I say!"

Pilar was already out of her clothes and sitting on the blanket in her underwear and a t-shirt.

"Lose the t-shirt," Annie said. Pilar hesitated. "Ain't no one here to see you but us. Lose the t-shirt and lay facing the sun."

Pilar complied. She was heavy with child. The Weiss twins still had their clothes on.

Annie addressed Miriam.

"Pagan?! Lady, what in the name of Sam Hill gave you that idea??!! There is a research scientist up at MIT's Computer Science and Artificial Intelligence Lab who asserts that the most important compound in the human body for optimal immune function is Cholesterol Sulfate. Let's call it CS for short. Not Vitamin D. CS. I've read everything that woman has ever published. My bet is she's right. CS is synthesized in the skin when exposed to direct sunlight at midday, provided there is enough Cholesterol and Sulphur in the bloodstream—and that comes from what you eat. The Amish women and your girls dress modestly and don't get much sun on their skin. I don't know about their Sulphur and Cholesterol intake. So, that's what we're cooking right now. Wild garlic, or onion or whatever you want to call it and cream. Lots of Sulphur compounds and lots of Cholesterol. So, unless you've got a stash of antibiotics—and this might be viral, in which case the antibiotics would have no benefit—this is the only thing I can think of at the moment. It might save their lives."

Miriam skinned her girls out of their clothes. They were listless, and it took all three women to best orient them on the blanket to the sun. Annie and Melissa brought the twins and Pilar the onion and cream broth a half hour later and spoon-fed the liquid to them and then instructed their charges to turn over to sun the other side of their bodies.

Roger and Roone brought a container of broth to Sandy, and Roger practically force-fed it to her while Roone held the horse and sat in the buggy. Then Roger and Florence dragged Sandy outside where they plopped her on a blanket. Roger left as Florence undressed Sandy to get maximum sun exposure on her bare skin.

Roger called back to Florence. "Keep her out in the sun for a half hour on each side. I will be back later with another batch of cream of onion, or whatever the hell that stuff is called, and to make sure you were able to get her back in bed."

By the time Roger and Roone got back to Roger's house, the girls were finished their sunbathing and dressed.

"Take Pilar and me home first and I will get-up a horse and my Dad's big wagon."

Pilar was weak, but she was able to climb into the buggy by herself. Roone noticed she had a little more color to her than she had before. Roger dropped Roone and Pilar and headed back to his house. Roone got Pilar into bed, and Jenny said she would keep an eye on her, as Danielle and the newborn had already moved to the main house with Manny to prevent the baby from catching the illness, and Walter and Jenny bunked in the other bedroom in the apartment. As promised, Roone hitched Thunder to the big buckboard wagon and headed back to Roger's house.

The Weiss twins were too weak to climb into the wagon, so Roger carried them and handed them up to Roone at the back of the carriage, and Miriam tried to hold it together. Martin was back home and waiting for them on the porch. Miriam was so distraught when they took the twins to Annie earlier that she forgot to write a note. Roone handed Aviva down to Martin and Hanna to Roger, and the men put the girls in their beds. Miriam took it from there and settled them under their blankets, and then she informed Martin of everything that happened since he left this morning. Jason appeared in the doorway after walking down from his house to check on the twins' condition.

"You guys go do what you have to do," Jason said. "I'll stay with Martin; I will walk home later."

Annie was waiting for Roger and Roone.

"Please go over to Roscoe's dairy and ask them for all the cream they've got. Take half of it to Emma Schwartz and bring the rest to me—as fast as you can. Go!"

That night, there was no improvement in the twins' condition, but they didn't appear to be getting worse. Their breathing was shallow and labored, their countenance apathetic, and their responses lethargic. Martin devoted the evening to prayer, and Miriam spent the evening in tears. At 9 pm, Roone stopped by to tell his father that Pilar was awake and lucid and did not appear to be getting worse. He also brought another batch of Annie's broth for the girls.

"Thanks for coming, Roone," Jason said to his son. "I'm just going to hang out here for moral support."

The girls sat up in bed and Miriam spoon-fed them, but even that minor exertion drained them of what little strength they had. Miriam slept on the floor of their room and checked on them every two hours. There was no change in their condition. Miriam didn't know if that was a good thing or not.

At daybreak, Emma Schwartz appeared at Weiss' front door with eggs, cream, butter, and more wild garlic and onion.

Emma didn't say "good morning" when Martin opened the door. She thrust an egg basket and a bag at Martin and said, "Annie said that eggs are high in sulfur, and to scramble them in gobs of butter with diced onion and feed it to the girls right away. She said she would come by soon, but that the girls must be out in the sun for an hour *at noon* with as much skin exposed as possible."

"Thank you, for coming and bringing this to us. How are your people?"

"Some of them are very sick." Emma's voice broke. She took a deep breath, and all she could get out was a whisper. "How are your twins?"

Martin could not maintain his composure and started to weep. And just above a whisper, he said, "They are very sick." He barely got those four words out.

Tears came to Emma as well.

The Amish Midwife and the orthodox Rabbi faced each other in the doorway and across the chasm of their beliefs and felt the agony—and saw the humanity—of the other. Neither had so much as touched a stranger of the opposite sex in nearly 40 years, but each reached for the other's shoulder and held on to it. Their eyes met. "We are in G-d's hands," Emma said. Martin, unable to speak, could only nod his head and squeeze her shoulder. Emma was able to add, "I shall pray for you and your children."

Martin was unable to respond with words. But he nodded his head, and she squeezed his shoulder back to communicate that she understood what he wanted to say, and then she turned and left. Emma cried so much on the way home that she couldn't see. Thankfully, the horse knew the way home and got them back safely.

Annie arrived at the Weiss home just after solar noon. Jason was no longer there, and Martin and Miriam were in the backyard with the twins as they sunbathed. More importantly, the twins were alive. They were not out of the woods, but they were alive.

"Hello, Annie," Martin said when she appeared beside them. "Miriam informed me of your theory regarding Sulphur, Cholesterol, and sunshine. I pray to G-d you are right."

"Well, it ain't my theory," Annie replied. "Back before antibiotics were developed, tuberculosis patients were sent to sanitoriums in the country to recuperate. The fresh air got the credit, but I bet it was the increased sun exposure. I took an interest in researching it after a friend of mine recovered from an antibiotic-resistant infection in his digestive tract. He was sick for two years and tried everything—nothing worked. Then he tried this therapy, and two months later he looked like King Kong. And he was in his 50's."

"Well, here we are," said Martin.

"Yea, here we are. Did it ever occur to you two that you could be next? How come you ain't out here catching some sun on your bare skin?"

This caught Martin and Miriam up short.

"Well, I… I…" Martin stumbled.

"Well, nothing. Take your shirt off, Martin. And you, roll your skirt and your sleeves up and put your face in the sun. And eat that stuff. We got enough sick people.   I gotta get going. Roger's waiting for me in the buggy. We gotta go check on Sandy. Do you have enough eggs and cream and onions and such?

"Yes, I think we do," Miriam replied. "And now that I know what to look for, there is plenty of wild garlic right here in our fields. By the way, why do you call it wild garlic? It tastes like onion."

"Some people say 'tomayto,' some people say 'tomahto.' The Sulphur is the key." Annie changed the subject. "This came up on us awful fast."

"Why do you think it struck far more women than men?"

"Well, we are going to find out soon enough."

"How is that?" asked Martin.

"Well, if everyone gets better, then we are on to something. But to answer your question: I bet that it's because the men work outside more often. And they ain't afraid to take their shirts off. Look at which women got taken hard with it. Amish women, your daughters, the pregnant Thomas girl, and Sandy. All women who wear too many clothes and don't get enough sun on their skin. But I have to go."

"Thank you," Martin said. "Goodbye."

Miriam and Martin watched her leave.

"Do you think she's crazy?" asked Miriam. "Or do you think she knows what she's talking about?"

Martin nodded towards the twins and started to take off his shirt.

"I think she knows what she's talking about."

When Roger and Annie arrived at Sandy and Florence's cabin, no one came out to greet them. Annie hopped out and went inside. She came right back out.

"Now they're both sick."

"Shit," Roger replied.

Roger hopped down from the buggy and tied the horse to the porch railing. Then he retrieved the soup and followed Annie inside.

Florence had not descended to the place where Sandy and the twins were, so they were able to get her outside easily enough, and she was able to feed herself. Sandy was as limp as a dead fish.

"Sandy, you have to sit up," Roger said. He helped her up and held her upright as Annie fed her. When she finished, he looped her arm over his shoulder and said, "I know you think I came here to see you sunbathe in the nude, but you're wrong. I came because I admire your mind."

"Fuck you," Sandy whispered, but she smiled a little.

"And your winning personality."

"Drop dead."

"See that? I've got her eating right out of my hand," Roger said to Annie. "Who says I don't have a way with women?" Then back to Sandy. "Alright. Enjoy your sun time. Annie here is going to help you expose your skin. I've had enough abuse for now. We'll be back in an hour or so to tuck you back in bed."

The ailment that afflicted the Sulphur Springs community burned out as quickly as it came. Within two weeks, everyone was back to work, and Annie's standing with the people rose to myth-like proportions.

"You are a hero," Melissa told Annie.

"The Romans told their victorious generals that 'glory fades,' and; to their emperors, they said, 'remember you are mortal.' Today, I am a hero. But tomorrow, a simple scratch could kill someone. We need to guard our health, but we also need modern medicines, especially antibiotics; and vaccines."

Chapter 32

The "Elders" of the Sulphur Springs community met at the old
Amish general store. All members of the community were
welcome, but most families sent the oldest husband and wife who
"headed" their household, hence "the Elders." The Amish sent
only one couple, Abraham and Ruth. The Elders resolved to
gather every other Wednesday to discuss community business.
With the growing season upon them, the elders tabled the issue of
medications for six weeks. They needed every able-bodied
person in the field, not gallivanting across the countryside. The
Elders nominated Jason, McCoy, and Ruth to visit the farms in
the community to determine the progress of the growing season
and to report back to them no later than the next meeting, and
earlier if they had concerns.

McCoy and Jason split the English farms between them, eight
for McCoy and seven for Jason. Ruth would report back on the
progress of the eleven Amish farms.

Rain gauges—pint-sized canning jars with inch markings to
measure rainfall—were installed in each garden. They would
examine these twice daily during the growing season and record
the data. If no rain fell for three days, the warm weather
vegetables would need water. There were significant logistical
challenges to water, but labor-intensive solutions were available.
The important thing was to never get behind on moisture. Of
course, the community did not have the infrastructure to irrigate
their corn and wheat crop. For that, they were at the mercy of the
weather. Some of the elders remembered a saying they heard
from their grandparents that summed up the situation perfectly.

Hoping for a miracle, praying for rain.

During the time between meetings, the weather and the
people cooperated. Jason, McCoy, and Ruth made their rounds
and compared notes. The bulk of the cold weather vegetable
harvest—broccoli, cabbage, spinach, kale, garlic, onion, brussels
sprouts, and lettuce—was nearly complete with the cabbage

preserved as Saur kraut in crocks, and onions and garlic hung to cure, and everything else consumed fresh or canned. The potato crop appeared healthy. The first round of sweet-corn—planted in four rotations every two weeks—was nearly a foot tall; that meant it was time to get the second round of seeds into the ground. And the tomato, squash, okra, and melon seedlings and sweet potato slips looked healthy and vibrant.

Today was the first of the field-corn plantings, and Jason, McCoy, and Ruth met at the field to watch two teams of horses pull the planters through the loose soil. Two Amish men walked behind the teams and driver to watch the seeds fall and get covered by dirt to make sure the spacing settings on the planters remained true. Every hundred yards or so they would recheck by brushing the soil away on a three-foot section of the row to expose the seeds, and then cover them again. With the critical business of the growing season done, for now, Ruth had personal business on her mind.

"Our grandson, Jacob, wants to get baptized and he wants to marry," Ruth said.

"Well, that's wonderful news!" Jason said. "Congratulations!"

"Yes, Ma'am!" McCoy said. "I do believe congrats are in order!"

"Yes, well, thank you," Ruth replied. Her response was somewhat understated. "You see, the thing is, what I want to talk to you about…" Ruth seemed to be having difficulty with what she wanted to say. "Oh, here it is. Jacob has not been living with us for several months now. He's been living-in-sin with one of your people. I mean, one of the girls from your side of the community. I mean, an English girl. What I am trying to say is…"

Jason took pity on her. "Easy, Mrs. Yoder," Jason said. "I understand you. It just occurred to me. You are talking about the Cutliff girl. I believe her name is Sally."

"Yes. My grandson is Jacob. Her name is Sally. They say they want to be baptized and then married in our church."

"Oh," Jason and McCoy said in unison.

Jacob Yoder and Sally Cutliff ran off together a week or two after the power went down. Her father, Roscoe, threw her mother, Belinda, out of their home a week later after a severe domestic dispute got ugly. And now Mindy, Sandy's former domestic partner, was playing house with Roscoe. To add another layer of complexity, what Ruth was diplomatically saying was that Sally would become a member of the Amish church group and a member of the Yoder clan.

"Well," Ruth said. "I wanted to bring this up with you gentlemen before the next meeting of the Elders. My husband is going to talk about this at the meeting. I wanted to give you a little warning to see if you might smooth the way on your side if that is possible."

"I don't recall Roscoe being all that upset when Sally ran off with Jacob," Jason said. "If he wasn't mad then, I can't imagine why he would be unhappy that Jacob and Sally are making it official."

"I didn't want this to come out of the blue," Ruth said. "I thought you should know."

"Yes, well, thank you for that," Jason said. "I will give it some thought and talk about it with some of the Elders before the meeting. That'll give everyone some time to get used to the idea."

"Then I will say good day to you gentlemen."

Ruth Yoder walked to her buggy, untied her horse, and departed for home.

"Well, you, Jason, and Martin are on the social committee," McCoy said. "I'll stick with farming. But if the shoe were on the other foot, the Amish would shun Jacob."

McCoy was being facetious. There was no "social committee."

"And we won't shun Sally," Jason said.

"Yep. That's a hell of a competitive advantage for them. Well, that and the simple fact that their women produce twelve children each and ours two or three."

"I think we are addressing that as best we can," Jason said. "I remember watching a video of a protest in the United Kingdom, maybe a year or two before the Famine. Britons of Anglo descent were walking through a London Muslim neighborhood to, in their words, 'raise awareness' that the Islamic culture was supplanting the Anglo culture. It didn't seem to occur to the Anglos that they were dying out—and that the Muslims were thriving—because of their respective cultural attitudes toward family and children. The Anglos were so thoroughly indoctrinated that they believed the thing to do was to march and chant slogans and carry protest signs. But the world belongs to the people who inhabit it."

"You know my line. 'Those who breed, succeed.' No group ever won a multigenerational cultural or political argument by refusing to put babies on the ground. It's a loser; every time."

"One of the leaders of the Anglo group was a young woman. She was strutting down a commercial boulevard shouting in anger at the top of her lungs. At one point, she was confronted by a Muslim woman—surrounded by her family—who chastened the Anglo to 'go home and mind her children.' The Anglo replied that she had no children; and it never occurred to her that that was problem—that the solution to the problem she perceived was staring her right in the face."

"Man, that protest culture and all that virtue signaling was fucking nuts. And now they are all dead. I mean, they were going to die sometime anyway, but what a waste of life."

"But back to the Yoder's and their grandson: why even bring it up?" Jason asked. "Sally and Jacob have been cohabitating for half a year."

"I'm sure Abraham has his reasons."

The meeting of the Elders got underway, and it seemed the entire community was there. Abraham's youngest son, Noah, and a couple of his friends were good enough to lend the meeting the portable benches they used for their church services and arranged the benches in two rows around the walls. A separate table and chairs stood in the center for the Elders.

"Thank you for coming!" Jason cried out to the throng. "There are a lot of people here tonight, so we are going to have to have someone chair the meeting. I nominate McCoy."

"I second that," Walter said.

McCoy looked at them with a "Gee, thanks for nothing" expression.

"No need to thank me," Jason said as he smiled and waved to McCoy.

"Okay!" McCoy's voice boomed. "If the meeting would come to order!"

Everyone noticed that the good-ol' boy McCoy was gone. U.S. Army Major McCoy was in the house—and he was a man to be reckoned with.

"Thank you. At our last meeting, Jason Thomas, Ruth Yoder, and myself were assigned the task of monitoring the progress of our garden produce. The cold weather vegetable harvest is pretty much over, and by all accounts we had a bumper crop. Is there a family here with a different experience?"

McCoy was silent and looked around. No one took exception to his analysis.

"We are going to run out of canning lids at some point," Audrey Harris said. Her husband, Sam, sat at her side holding her hand and nodding his head. Sam was a man of few words with the fortitude of a mule and the constitution of a billy-goat.

"I've made a note on that for the scavenging crew, and we are working on getting a metal stamping machine up to my workshop from Edinburgh. In the meantime, when lids are removed from canning jars we need to try not to bend or damage them. And keep them dry—once used they rust."

Audrey waved her hand to signal she had nothing else.

"Okay, other than canning lids: anyone here suffer a poor harvest from their cold weather garden?"

Everyone shook their head.

"Okay. Seed saving. Any problems there? Y'all saved your seeds for next year, right?"

Again, no negative response from the community.

"Alright! Moving right along," McCoy said. "The warm weather vegetables and grains are in good shape. It's only been a few weeks, and we've had plenty of rain. Wheat is best planted in fall, but we didn't have any seed then, so we sowed it in early March. It is my guess, and it is only a guess, that we will have enough of a harvest to seed all we could ever need for next fall's planting. But as far as wheat for bread? We should plan on another year of cornbread—and, of course, that depends on the field-corn crop."

"What's the difference between field-corn and the sweet-corn we grow in our gardens?" Florence asked. "I'm new to this."

"Sweet-corn has a lot more sugar and does not store well. It's a summer treat, and we could live without it. Field-corn has less sugar and stores well after it's dried and you can feed it to livestock and make bread and grits and such with it. We need field-corn; we don't need sweet-corn."

"And how's the field-corn lookin'?" Peter Westmoreland asked. The Westmoreland family had been here in the region for at least as long as the O'Neil's. Peter was long past his prime for work but had no problem bossing his clan around.

"We just got it in the ground," McCoy responded. "It hasn't even sprouted. Alright. Moving on to potatoes: We gave every family some seed potatoes. From what we can tell, that crop looks good, and the people have been diligent about removing potato beetles and their grubs and eggs. Listen up! Now is the critical time for potatoes. As soon as it gets hot, they will die. We need to keep every leaf on them that we can for as long as we can. For the next two weeks, we need to be very diligent. Don't even blink. That's how fast you can lose a potato crop. We are going to need all of the young men and every mower and team of horses we have to work hay starting tomorrow."

"How do you know when to cut hay if you don't know what the weather will be?" asked Peter Westmoreland.

"We don't. We plan to cut ten acres every day for the next twenty days and spread the risk. If we mow one day and ted the hay the next, we should be able to put it up the evening of the third day. So, every day from the fourth day on, we should be able to put up ten acres of hay per day. If it rains, we will ted the hay as soon as the rain stops. If it rains for days, we will lose the hay that's laying on the ground. That's just the way it is."

"I can tell you when it's going to rain," Annie cried out. "I can feel it in my joints."

The people laughed good naturedly at Annie's comment.

"Don't laugh!" Jason said. "She's more accurate than the Nashville weatherman was!"

"Alright! Listen up!" McCoy silenced the crowd. "We've posted lists for the young men for the hay harvest over by the door. Before we move on, does anyone have anything to say about the progress of the growing season? Anything at all?!"

No one answered McCoy, and a murmur rose from the crowd as the people talked among themselves.

"Okay! One more time!" McCall shouted. "We get only one growing season. If we blow it, we suffer next winter. Is there anything at all?!"

There was no response.

"Alright. Moving on; Abraham and Ruth Yoder have something to say."

Abraham stood and looked around the room. After a few moments, he called out, "Hello, to you, good people. I think everyone here knows me, and my wife, Ruth."

Abraham nodded to his wife; Ruth remained seated. The community waited patiently for Abraham to state his business.

"My grandson, Jacob Yoder is here with Sally Cutliff. They have been courting, and they have come to ask to be baptized in our church and then married."

Of course, everyone present knew that Jacob and Sally were not courting in the typical Amish fashion and were living together. During that time, Jacob no longer wore an Amish hat to signal his obedience, but since he was not baptized, he was not shunned.

All eyes turned to Roscoe and Mindy Cutliff. Roscoe stood up to address the community.

"My daughter Sally has my blessing," Roscoe said, and he sat back down.

The crowd seemed to murmur their ascent.

"Alright," McCoy called out. "There being no objections..."

"Hold on a second!" Sandy said as she rose from her chair. "What are we talking about here?"

"These two young people want to get married," Abraham replied.

"What does that mean, exactly?" Sandy asked.

Bewildered, Abraham replied, "Well, it means they will live together as man and wife."

"Sally, how old are you?" Sandy asked the girl.

"I will be 16 next week."

"Oh, my G-d!" Sandy cried out. "She's a child. Are you people nuts? She's too young for this. What if she gets pregnant?"

"What if she is already pregnant?" asked Peter Westmoreland. "They have been living together as man and wife since November!"

"You mean he's been raping her since November! They are not man and wife! She is a girl and can't give consent! She's not 18!"

The meeting erupted with shouting back and forth. It took McCoy, Jason, Walter, and Roger to shout over the crowd. Finally, McCoy's voice rose above the din.

"Sandy is a contributing member of the community! She is recognized by the chair and has a right to be heard. The Elders will hear her out. Please be quiet." Then McCoy addressed Sandy. "You have the floor. Say what's on your mind."

"Well, first off. She's too young; this is a major life decision."

"Are you asserting that she is too young to make any important decisions? Or too young to give consent?" McCoy asked.

"Both."

"Pick one. We do not conflate issues here. One at a time."

"She's too young to give consent."

"What about Jacob. Is he too young to give consent?"

"He's a boy."

"He's been working for a living since he was 14-years-old, as all Amish men do," Abraham said.

"Mr. Yoder," McCoy said. "Please address me as the chairman."

"I apologize."

"I'll get to you, sir," McCoy said to Mr. Yoder. Then to Sandy. "Please be more specific. The Elders are going to rule on this issue. Are you saying that boys can give consent, but girls cannot?"

"Yes."

"Even in the case of two men?"

Well, I… in that case, the boy cannot give consent."

"So, in that case, he is a victim."

"Of course!"

"But the boy is a perpetrator if his partner is a girl?"

"Yes."

"What age do you suggest a girl may give consent?" McCoy asked.

"Never. A woman must be eighteen to give consent," Sandy replied.

"And what should we do with people who engage in sex with women under the age of 18?"

"They are girls, not women. And the men should be punished."

"Even if the girl met the boy halfway?"

"Yes," replied Sandy.

"Fair enough. Let's take a procedural vote to see if this is something we want to pursue. All in favor of exploring options for having their sons punished for having sex with a willing girl, raise your hand."

No one raised their hand except Sandy and Florence.

"You people don't want to protect your daughters?!" Sandy shrieked at the crowd.

"Sandy, to me as chairman, please."

"Don't these people want to protect their daughters?!"

"Yes, of course, they do, Sandy," McCoy responded. "They also want to protect their sons."

The room murmured its ascent.

"Their sons don't need protection! Their daughter's do!"

"You don't have any sons!" Peter Westmoreland shouted to Sandy. "How would you know?"

"Mr. Westmoreland!" McCoy said. "Please sir! To me, as chairman. Or we will never get anything done." Then to Sandy. "I am trying to get to the other issue you raised. Would you please stop with the outbursts?"

"What other issue?" Sandy retorted.

"The people are not interested in punishing Jacob for his relationship with Sally, any more than they are willing to punish Sally. That is settled. The other issue you raised was, 'is Sally too young to marry?'" McCoy turned away from Sandy and looked around the hall. "Good people! The question is this: 'is Sally old enough to marry?'"

"That's only part of the issue!" Sandy shouted. "What does marriage mean here? Does she own property? Is she allowed to divorce? What are her protections?"

"Sally will have the protection of the Yoder family and our Amish church!" Abraham Yoder shouted back. "What more could she possibly need?!"

"So, she will be a slave to your church, and a sex slave for Jacob!" Sandy shouted back. Abraham collapsed back into his chair in shock. Half the community was engaged in a shouting match with Sandy and Florence.

McCoy leaned over to Jason, Roger, and Walter and said, "Feel free to step in any time here, fellas."

Jason stood up and screamed, "Order!" at the top of his lungs. "Okay, that's enough! That is *enough*!" When the hall went quiet, Jason addressed the gathering. "Any member can say whatever is on their mind. We believe in free speech, free expression, and the free exchange of ideas. Sandy is sharing her concerns with us; please, respect that!"

"Jason, she's the kind of person who would like to burn a scarlet letter on my sons' foreheads!" The speaker was Clinton Williams, a relative newcomer. Clinton moved to the area with his wife and three sons five years earlier.

"Calm down," Jason said. "No one is going to burn anybody."

"Hey, Jason!" a voice boomed. It was the taciturn Sam Harris. "Why don't we ask Sally and Jacob?!" The hall went silent. All eyes went to them.

"Thank you, Sam," Jason said. Then Jason spoke to the young couple. "I'm sorry about this. Is there something you two would like to say?"

The teenaged couple stood up and held hands. Sally spoke. "We've been living together for six months. I'm pregnant! My father has given us his blessing! What's the problem?" Her eyes bored into Sandy. "Why are you doing this to us?!"

"I didn't do anything to you!" said Sandy. "Your boyfriend did this to you!"

"Did what?! I love him. He loves me. And we are going to have a family!"

"You are 15-years-old!"

"I'll be 16 in a week! We're not bothering anyone! We made it through the winter without much help—but I need help when the baby comes!"

"Don't you want to know what options you have?!" Sandy shrieked back.

Silence: You could have heard a pin drop in the hall.

"Okay!" McCoy shouted as he stood out of his chair. "We can talk about marriage in general later this evening. Right now, I think the only thing before the Elders regarding Jacob and Sally is to congratulate them and wish them well. All in favor, raise your hands."

Thunderous applause erupted in the hall and most of the women went to Sally to congratulate her and wish her well and to offer their help and service. McCoy quietly suggested to Abraham that he might want to get his grandson and granddaughter-to-be home and he and Ruth nearly bolted for the door.

But Sandy wasn't finished. "That was a very touching scene, celebrating the rape of a child."

Audrey Harris stood up and said, "McCoy, I'd like to say something."

"Well, thank you for recognizing the chair, Mrs. Harris. I think you're the first! You have the floor."

"I was speaking to Annie and Melissa about just this subject over tea at their house not too long ago. My grandparents married at 16. My parents were 19 when they married. I don't think we want to encourage teenagers to marry, but we do want our children to form families and have children before they are too old. Look around this room. Notice anything? We don't have access to hair-dye anymore. And now all the mom's here— including me—look like grandmothers. Most of us started having children far too late in life. And some of us are going to die before we get all of our children raised. Is that fair to our children?"

"What are you talking about? The Amish women have children well into their 40's!" Sandy shouted.

McCoy started to rise from his seat, but Jason held his arm and pulled him back down.

"This is between the women," Jason whispered and motioned for McCoy to stay out of it.

"Yes!" Audrey answered Sandy directly. "And they have three and sometimes four generations living in the home! If tragedy strikes, they have aunts and grandmothers and older sisters. And a solid community that will support them in real and meaningful ways! They don't send 'thoughts and prayers' or 'hugs' over social media!" Audrey took her eyes off of Audrey and addressed the people present. "When the Hoover family's house burned down, and they lost one of their young children, their church-group took a collection, bought the materials, and forty of their men swarmed around them and cleaned it up, and had a new house built and ready to live in in three days while the women comforted the grieving mother! What do we have? My sister lives in Boston. I see her once every three years; my children have met her maybe a dozen times. And she doesn't have any children! What would happen to my youngest if I died?"

Now Audrey put Sandy back in her sights. "And you!" Audrey said. "You have no one! And you want to talk about 'options' with that young girl? You want her to know that she can just kill her baby and move on? So, she can grow old and alone like you? What happened to you? Why isn't life precious to you?"

"I think a young girl's innocence is precious," Sandy said.

"And you think a young girl can preserve her innocence by aborting her own child?"

Sandy was having none of it. "What are you going to say when a 40-year-old man gets a 14-year-old girl pregnant?"

"Do you always change the subject and argue from the margins?" Audrey asked Sandy. "We are talking about two 16-year-olds who fell in love, got pregnant and are getting married."

"No, we are not. We are talking about a young man who raped a young girl."

"Suddenly, he's a 'young man,' but she's a 'young girl.' They are the same age." Audrey turned to address the people in the hall. "Our women have an ethical responsibility to our men too."

"How is that?!" asked Sandy.

"We had a safe harbor for sexual relations between men and women. It was called marriage. The Feminists hated the idea of marriage! And they sabotaged it politically. Now there is no safe harbor. Some girl can lure my son into a hayloft with the promise of sex and then accuse him of assault in the form of the sex that she lured him there with the promise of in the first place? *That* is unethical. People—men *and* women—need to know what the rules are." Here, Audrey paused and looked around and made eye contact with the other mothers in attendance. "Our community must not permit women like Sandy to make the rules, or none of our men—our sons and brothers—will be safe."

No one in the hall moved a muscle or made a sound.

"And what does marriage mean here, anyway?" Sandy retorted. "What property is she going to own? What is she going to do when he cheats on her?"

"Machiavelli's political philosophy is not a good place to start for relationship and family advice, Sandy," Audrey replied. "We're out here trying to live together in a real community because all we have is each other. We are not living in a city and working for a corporation and fucking our co-workers after drinks on Thursday night and coming home to a cat! We are all families—just not you! Our men can't cheat unless one of the women cheats with him. And our women appreciate our men and all they do for us. We want to keep a happy home. And, by the way? Some people—man or woman—do not deserve a faithful spouse."

"What's that supposed to mean!? Are you giving cheating men a pass?!" Sandy was beside herself. She was red as a beet, and the veins stood out on her neck and forehead.

"No, of course not. But I am pointing out that a faithful husband is something you earn. And you have to earn it every single day. You can't take it for granted; a woman can't demand fidelity under threat of violence or coercion. We *earn* fidelity with passion, love, kindness, and warmth in the home. Some women just aren't any good at those things—and those women shouldn't be wives or parents. And there is nothing wrong with that—but such women should not be telling the rest of us how to live with our men. Because *we* are the women making the babies and paying the dues for civilization."

"Whatever," Sandy said dismissively.

"You know, you seem like a bright person. Can't you see the fatal flaw in your thinking? *You are* a *human being,* and as such you are the product of the human heterosexual experience. And I don't know if you have any personal knowledge of how things work between a man and a woman, but *the man initiates the chain of events* that lead to pregnancy and the birth of a child. You owe your very existence to the passions of your father.*"

"Is that so? You don't know a thing about my father," Sandy hissed. "But you keep working on that happy home—where you are nothing but a slave."

"And you are a hateful and lonely woman who wants all women to be as lonely and hate-filled as you are. But you are still the product of a man and a woman—not two women. And your father is not here to defend himself."

Audrey and Sandy stared each other down. McCoy looked from one woman to the other several times wondering if the fireworks were over. Finally, Jason hit him on the leg and motioned for him to move on with the meeting.

"Well, alrighty then," McCoy said. "I think we covered enough ground for tonight. I think the issue before the Elders is that the definition of marriage is between the parties and the families."

"I second that!" Roger said.

"All those in favor, raise your hands."

All but Sandy and Florence raised their hands.

McCoy and Roger sat around the Thomas' kitchen table after the Elders meeting with the brothers, Jason, and Walter Thomas. The women were out on the porch passing Manny and Danielle's daughter, Niki, around and loving on the infant.

"Good grief, I'm exhausted," McCoy said.

"Yea, but you were great!" Walter said.

"That Mr. Westmoreland," Roger said. "We want him at every Elders meeting."

"Yea, that old bastard knows how to move things along. How about when he asked, 'what if she's already pregnant?' I appreciate a man with a good sense of timing and delivery—and an uncanny grasp of the obvious."

"Well, he's a widower," McCoy said. "Maybe Sandy and Mr. Westmoreland are a match made in heaven!"

"I don't know about that," Jason laughed. "They might be a perfect duel—ten paces and two pistols. But not a match."

"And that Audrey!" Roger said. "Her comment on grey hair and the lack of hair-dye? I nearly fell off my chair."

"Why?" asked Walter. "I found the rest of her ideas far more interesting."

"Well, it was brutally honest. And she had the courage to point her high-powered abilities in observation at herself. Nature turns our hair grey for a reason."

"Oh, yea?" asked Walter. "Why is that?"

"I suspect that grey hair is a biological marker that warns potential mates that our age is problematic. The practice of hair dying might have fooled us: but it won't fool mother nature."

"Her comments on monogamy... I take it she is not from here?" Walter asked.

"Well, she's a country girl," McCoy said. "But she worked for a commodities broker in Chicago before she met Sam. And she is a ball of fire."

"Annie and Melissa think the world of her," Roger said. "I haven't gotten to know her, but she seems like a smart cookie. Her understanding of human nature impressed me. Anything we can do to put her in a position of leadership would help our cause."

"We don't have to do anything," McCoy said. "You couldn't stop Audrey from leading."

"Yes, that's my sense of Audrey too," said Jason.

"Why wasn't Martin there?" asked Roger.

"Martin has evolved into the spiritual leader and moral authority of the community," Jason said. "Objective truth and right and wrong doesn't mix well with the necessary compromises of politics. I think he is right to steer clear of the Elders meeting. There will be times when we will need his uncompromised moral authority."

"Well, I'll say this: when it comes to politics, that dang Sandy is a pain in the ass," McCoy said. "I wish she wouldn't come to the Elders meetings."

"Oh, I don't know about that," Roger said. "I thought she was perfect!"

"Yea! A complete pain in the ass."

"No, no, no, no, no, no... Sandy was *wonderful!*" Roger said. "She unites the community. It doesn't matter that the community is united against her. The important thing is unity—a common culture. And a sense of belonging to something. A heated argument like that is perfect! "

"And it lets everybody know that we will hear all sides," Jason said. "That we have complete freedom to share ideas without fear of being shamed. Did you notice that until the blow-off between Audrey and Sandy that there were no personal attacks? People were debating the merits of the ideas presented, not attacking the person. That's is a big deal."

"Sandy also divides the community," Roger added to his previous commentary. "And that might be just as important as uniting us. I've been struggling with how to reconcile the community into a common belief system. Perhaps that's the wrong approach. Voltaire said that if there are only two religions, they will cut each other's throats. But if there are a multitude, they all live happily, and in peace. Voltaire believed that religious differences were trivial, and that it was trade, or commerce, that was the critical thing that brought people together. I keep thinking about the fundamentalist Mormons I met shortly after the Famine began. I think they might be a good addition to the community for balance. And those atheist pot farmers too."

"I think we have done what we can to ensure that the community won't starve this winter," Jason said. "But for trade, we are going to have to come up with a medium of exchange—Money. Martin is a trained economist. I expect he will come in handy here."

"Yes, indeed," Roger said. "Barter won't cut it."

"Well, you keep on thinking on that, gents," McCoy said. "I think I've had enough for today. The light's fading. Thank goodness my buggy horse knows the way home. I'll be asleep before the end of the driveway."

"Hold on, McCoy," Roger said. "I think we need to invite ourselves to Jacob and Sally's wedding and participate in whatever festivities follows—house building, barn raising, whatever."

"Who said we weren't invited?" asked Walter.

"Well, maybe we are," Roger replied. "And maybe we are not. The Anabaptists are funny about such things. But Sally is from our side of the community. We can't let the opportunity pass. We need to show that we have value to them. We need to engage in trade, custom, barter, or whatever you want to call it as much as possible—inside and outside of the community. I am sure this is not the first wedding or funeral the Amish have had since the Famine began. I don't remember getting an invitation. But Sally changes the dynamic—and gives us an opportunity."

Chapter 33

The Elders choose Jason first to approach Roscoe, Sally's
father, and then Abraham. Roscoe was thrilled and humbled by
the expression of solidarity.

"You are a member of the community, Roscoe," Jason said.
"Of course, you can count on us to help your family find its way
to the future. And we are going to depend on you to do the same
for us. We must support every young couple in every way we
can."

Roscoe was moved to tears. Things didn't go quite so
smoothly with Abraham. Jason called on him at his home.
Abraham welcomed him as an equal.

"Come in, Jason," Abraham called to Jason from the great
room of his farmhouse after his daughter greeted Jason at the
front door. "I have been expecting you."

"Abraham, I am sorry about the way you were spoken to at
the Elders meeting."

"Oh, no need to apologize, Jason. Our way is not your way.
We understand that. I hope that I did not appear too proud. If I
did, I beg your forgiveness."

"That's not why I've come."

Jason explained the situation—that the English side of the
community wanted to come to the wedding and the house-raising
to show their support for Sally, and to be an asset to the Amish
church-group. Abraham listened patiently.

"Is that what you've come to talk to me about?" Abraham
asked.

"Yes. We have never received an invitation to any of your
weddings. We want to be invited to this one."

"I don't think we have ever been invited to any of your
weddings. I didn't know that this was important to you."

Jason was sure there were at least two meanings to what
Abraham just said, but he was sure that Abraham was trying to be
forthright. Manipulation was not part of Abraham's skillset.

"Abraham, about the other night…"

"Do you think that we don't produce homosexuals?" Abraham asked. Jason remembered that the Amish were not up to speed on the latest politically correct call signs for the various sexual identities. Part of him wanted to tell Abraham that most people preferred "LGBTQ." But then he remembered that Florence and Sandy often referred to themselves as "queer women." Jason decided that these social conventions were unimportant in the current circumstances.

"I am sure you do." Jason regretted his choice of words immediately.

"We lose our homosexual male children to the outside. They leave us. No one ever talks about it. I have eighty grandchildren, I think." Abraham paused to consider how many grandchildren he had. After a moment, he gave up. "Ah, it doesn't matter. I have at least eighty grandchildren. I lost three of my grandsons to society." Jason recalled that the Amish called the world outside of the Amish communities "society." Abraham continued. "Two I am sure are homosexuals. The other married an English girl and works as a state trooper in Iowa. I have at least five granddaughters that I am sure will never marry; or never should marry."

Jason's face must have betrayed his shock.

"You are surprised by this?"

"Well, I... I never thought about it."

"We don't baptize our children into the church as infants. Our church will only baptize adults, and we try to discourage those who have doubts. We advise them that it is far better not to take a vow than to make a vow and break it."

"So, your church encourages people who cannot live by the Ordnung to leave."

"Well, the 'church,' as you say is only the collection of families living in the community who are bound to each other by baptism. Yes, we have a bishop and several deacons, but there is no other central authority. It's just us. And while the bishop and the deacons *try* to convince our young people to think long and hard before committing to our church by baptism, their parents pressure them to conform. And that is understandable. But it has been my consistent observation that pressuring homosexuals to undergo baptism and marriage is that those poor people suffer. They have miserable marriages and difficult family lives, as you might imagine."

Jason was always impressed by the Amish success in getting all of their young people matched up. The downside of that success never occurred to him.

"I can tell by the look on your face that you understand," Abraham said. "Do you understand that I love *all* of my grandchildren?"

Jason could only nod his head. He was speechless.

"I have never spoken of this to anyone except a few of the Amish elders, deacons, and bishops. But I must show you something. Something I think you, above all, will appreciate."

Abraham rose from his chair and walked to his desk: a fine piece of furniture with a beautiful accordion roll-top cover; and there retrieved a large file of papers in a manila folder and laid it out on the desktop.

"Please come here, Jason." Abraham opened the folder and pushed the file toward Jason's side of the desk.

The first page held a title: "Quaker Marriage Patterns in a Colonial Perspective" by Michael V. Wells and Michael Zuckerman. William & Mary Quarterly 1972.

"Please turn to page 427."

Jason complied. He read the page twice, and then turned back to 415 and read the next 28 pages.

"Jason, your Quaker ancestors in colonial Pennsylvania, and the Congregationalists in colonial New England had almost the same percentage of women who declined to marry as my people have today—a little over 15%. That is one in six."

"I don't know what to say…"

"Do you know what the prospects were for an unmarried woman in colonial times?" Abraham asked. "There were no corporations or governments to work for—life was agrarian and artisan. People worked on their farms and in their workshops. An unmarried woman would live with her parents until her father died and they would get passed off to relatives to live as an impoverished domestic servant assisting her relatives with children and the chores until she died as a lonely old spinster. Can you imagine how miserable that must have been?"

"No, I can't..."

"That is how powerfully opposed those colonial women were to sharing a bed with a man."

Jason didn't bother to point out that some of the people who did not marry might have wanted to but had no offers. It didn't matter. Abraham's point was well made. Jason sat in stunned silence; this was not the conversation he expected to have.

"Jason, my people are confronted by the same issues that you are. In the past, the young people from our community who refused to marry left and were rarely heard from again. They went to the cities and made new friends and worked at jobs—and we pretended they didn't exist. What are we going to do now? Are we going to shun our young people who won't marry? They would starve: I am not willing to have any of my grandchildren starve.

"Jason, you've lived amongst us now for what? Four years? Five years? And before that, you spent ten years living in Shady Grove with the Mennonites. I remember when you came to the region. You were as helpless as a babe in the woods—you didn't know which end of the nail to hit with a hammer. You've learned much from us over past the fourteen or fifteen years. But I think the most important thing you've learned is that we cannot exist as we do without community. You seem to want what we have— and we were flattered by that! Well, to have a community, we must have the goodwill and fellowship of our neighbors, to live as we do, free of the burdens that drove you here from out there. There can be no goodwill and fellowship—and no community— if our women are at our men's throats, the way they are in your society.

"Jason, I love all of my grandchildren. But we cannot allow any of our people to sow discord amongst our families. I feel terrible about their suffering. But we cannot have our young women disrespect our bishops and deacons and their fathers and husbands the way your friend spoke to the Elders and me at the Elders meeting."

Jason's head swam.

"What I am trying to say, Jason is that I expect that some of our young people will leave us. Your people seem to accept such people. I hope your community will take them in."

"Holy smokes!" Roger said. "I bet you were not expecting that!"

"I am traumatized," Jason said and slumped in his chair.

Roger flipped through the pages of the "Wells Study" on marriage in colonial America.

"I have seen this same data point pop up in myriad ways and strange places, and I saw it in my days as a practicing clinician. Of course, no one in their right mind would study this. There was just no faster path to career destruction at the university than research on sexual deviancy and the associated personality disorders and attendant identity issues. You know how people come to study psychology? Because they were nuts, to begin with."

"Present company excluded?" Jason asked with a smile.

"No. I am at least as nutty as the next one." Roger sounded as serious as a heart attack. "But at least I admit how completely unscientific the study of psychology is. Using statistics is not science. If it were, then baseball is science—and not a sport. Economics? Not a science at all. Economists like to claim they practice the 'dark science,' I guess because they use a lot of fancy math like 'multiple regression analysis,' but it has no predictive value whatsoever—and that's why truck drivers are better stock pickers than economists. No, science has five basic requirements—and if any of these are absent, then the field of study is not hard science.

"First, clearly defined terminology; second, the object or experiment must be quantifiable; third, the experimental conditions must be highly controlled; fourth, you must be able to reproduce the same results consistently; and five, most of all, it must be testable. Well, the study of psychology cannot meet all of those requirements. That doesn't mean that the field is not useful. I think it is. But we are not anywhere near as valuable for many applications as the profession likes to pretend."

"You lost me. What does that have to do with anything?"

"You brought me this Wells study. I think it is very telling. I think Abraham is right—human sexuality is existential. That's what he must have concluded when he asked you to take in the people they are throwing out. Abraham doesn't think his people have any choice in the matter; he believes the issue existed 250 years ago, exists now, and will exist 250 years in the future, and; the Anabaptists are not going to make any changes to accommodate any form of deviancy. And that is their right! To freely associate with who they choose. Authoritarians use coercion or violence to control thoughts and feelings. Free people do not. Free people may accept others into their lives—or not—as they see fit.

"I think it also means that my theory—that men elicit a disgust response in women who suffer from heterosexual dysphoria—is existential; as are many other quirks regarding human sexuality.

"What we must concern ourselves with now is agriculture, commerce, trade, and stable families and happy children. Of course, our development must not end there—those are just first. We have so much to do; so much work ahead of us. Reestablishing civilization out of broadcloth will not happen in a single growing season—or even a single generation. What we can establish now is that Man is sovereign. That he has rights to the peaceful agency over his body, life, and efforts, and that no majority—be it the majority of a community, the Elders meeting, or a religious or political organization—can usurp those fundamental rights. Our responsibility to one another begins and ends in the voluntary exchanges of value and personal integrity—not at the point of a gun. When we show up with material, tools, and men to build Jacob and Sally a house, we are not doing it because altruism was jammed down our throats or to signal our virtue. We do so because Man is noble! We do so because we recognize the value of helping young families prosper and produce children to all of us! It was the same thing when the men on the construction crew appeared at Sandy and Florence's place and did all that work for them: We are a community! And all of us want the community to prosper because none of us can survive

261

without it. Left to their own devices, the men and Sandy and Florence worked it out. We have the foundation of something great here. An opportunity to get rid of all of the baggage mankind has been carrying around. To live as free people, and to prove that in the absence of oppression Man is noble."

"Well, I don't know exactly where we should start…" Jason began.

"Of course, we don't know! Isn't that what I just said? That the study of the human experience does not lend itself to the requirements of hard science for being sure of anything! Do you want to know what I think? I think you are still programmed; terrified that the Thought Police are going to get you and shame you into submission. But we don't have to be afraid anymore! They can't bully us, and they can't hurt us—they're finished. Finished! We can talk about *anything* without fear. We can think about anything. Examine anything. Challenge anything and make a counter-argument if we can support it! And change our minds whenever the evidence says we should—all without fear for the first time in years. Now *that's* freedom. We've got a lot of work ahead of us. But I am hopeful for the future."

Epilogue

The following spring, Florence left Sulphur Springs in the company of a young woman from the Amish settlement. The two women decided to move to a homestead twenty miles west to the edge of the Sulphur Springs community to get a fresh start. The men on Florence's work crew packed the women's belongings on horse-drawn wagons and helped them move. And when they arrived, the men built the women a cabin and a small livestock barn on their land and wished them well. Florence was moved to tears and hugged each of the men in turn before they left.

Several years later, Sandy's body was found in the converted Amish schoolhouse she had called home since she arrived at Sulphur Springs. Her body lay undiscovered for some time and was severely decomposed. Even Martin Weiss, who insisted on a proper burial for members of the community, understood that it was too much to ask the men to retrieve Sandy's body given its condition. "The Torah instructs us how to live. It does not ask us to risk death or illness in such circumstances." The community followed Martin in the Jewish funeral prayer, the Kaddish. After Martin departed, Jason and McCoy set fire to the structure. Sandy's remains would be cremated.

"Do you think she took her own life?" Jason asked Roger.

"It looks that way. Growing old is no picnic, especially when you don't have the major life milestones—the weddings of children and the birth of grandchildren—to look forward to; when the only thing you have to look forward to is lonely debility and suffering it is hard to want to go on."

"But we don't know that she took her own life," Jason said.

"No. We don't. Let's leave it at that," Roger said.

Many members of the community now practiced the Jewish tradition of unveiling a stone marker on the first anniversary of the passing of a loved one, and in keeping with Judeo-Christian tradition, a stone marker would be erected on the site of the burned schoolhouse. It was only then that the people realized that no one knew Sandy's last name. Several members of the community groused that because Sandy rejected the very idea of family, and since the family social unit was the foundation of the Sulphur Springs community, and because she left no issue, there was no need to expend the effort to cut and carve and transport a gravestone.

When Martin Weiss heard this, he paid a visit to the Elders meeting. It was his first.

"Sandy was a productive member of the Sulphur Springs community," Martin said. "She was a Human Being, may she rest in peace, and made in G-d's image. We don't need to know what her family name was, and it is not important that Sandy rejected our idea of family. She did not reject the idea of community. And the community owes her memory a gravestone."

Martin had evolved into the spiritual leader of many families in the community, and no one in the community challenged Rabbi Martin Weiss on matters of objective morality. Noah Yoder, Abraham's youngest son, was assigned the task of chiseling the stone, and the unveiling took place on the first anniversary of the burning of the schoolhouse. The grey granite stone stood in stark relief in the middle of a black ring of ash, the lone marking, "SANDY," carved in capital letters. Over the years, the grass grew around and over the stone, and then scrub, and finally trees. For all of her rage and anguish, Sandy didn't leave so much as a whispered echo behind with her passing.

Jacob and Sally were baptized into the Amish church in a small service and then married in the beautiful fertility ritual that is the Amish wedding ceremony. All of Sulphur Springs attended. The newlyweds spent their first few weeks in the cabin they had been living in. But when the first hay harvest was complete, the men—Amish and English—descended on an unworked piece of land on the edge of the Amish settlement closest to Roscoe and Mindy's homestead, and built Jacob and Sally a house and barn from materials reclaimed from the countryside. In the normal course of things, Sally gave birth to a healthy baby boy, the first of many children that would bless Jacob and Sally Yoder's home. The parents named him Abraham, after Jacob's grandfather.

Sally wore a blue dress on her wedding day, the customary color for Amish brides. Seventy years later to the day, Sally was buried in the same blue dress, as was their custom, next to her beloved husband, Jacob, who passed away just three months earlier. Her eldest son, Abraham, born when Sally was just sixteen-years-old, led the burial rights as the community's bishop. Also, in attendance were Sally's fifteen other offspring, many of her one-hundred and thirty grandchildren, and some of her four-hundred and five great-grandchildren.

The community departed the burial grounds and gathered at Abraham's farm, where he spoke to them.

"My parents were teenagers when the Famine came, and death and devastation consumed the land. They sought comfort in each other and survived that first winter by their wits. But it was their love that breathed life—our lives—back into a barren land. And today, we feel the warmth of the sun on our faces, and the joy of life, because of the love of Jacob and Sally Yoder. And we mourn her loss! But my mother taught us well, and now we are a thriving community, and her hopes and values live in all of us. My mother loved her husband, her children, and her community, and would often confess the sin of pride—the pride that she had for her family. But I don't think the pride she felt falls under the set of sin. What my mother felt was the joy and satisfaction that comes to those who work hard and achieve great things—for our community is great, and joy is no sin. There is nothing greater than family, for we are made in G-d's image, and we are formed by the G-d given passions that pass between man and woman. If my mother were here with us today, she would encourage us to live, to love, and to build our families. To lead by the example of our actions, not words, and to work hard and avoid the trappings of dependence on comfort and convenience that can lead to disaster. The Famine shaped my mother, and all of the people of her generation, as it continues to form all of us today. Let us heed her words. And let us celebrate Life, and all its seasons—even as we mourn her loss. So, when you return to your homes: Love your family, work your land, and pull the weeds and remove the *Stones in the Garden* of your heart and make it fertile ground. For as my mother, Sally Yoder, often said, 'on the day we die, meals must still be served, babies cared for, and cows milked; because Life—Precious Life! —must go on.'"

Abraham looked out to the somber faces of the adults, and then past them to the young children running barefoot and blissfully unaware—as it should be—through the yard of the farmhouse his great-grandfather lived in, and where he was born and recalled his happy childhood with his youthful parents.

50403728R00159

Made in the USA
Columbia, SC
06 February 2019